PRAISE FOR *NEW YORK TIMES* AND *USA TODAY* BESTSELLING AUTHOR ANNE FRASIER

"Frasier has perfected the art of making a reader's skin crawl."

—*Publishers Weekly*

"A master."

—*Minneapolis Star Tribune*

"Anne Frasier delivers thoroughly engrossing, completely riveting suspense."

—Lisa Gardner

"Frasier's writing is fast and furious."

—Jayne Ann Krentz

PRAISE FOR *HUSH*

"This is by far and away the best serial killer story I've read in a long time . . . strong characters, with a truly twisted bad guy."

—Jayne Ann Krentz

"I couldn't put it down. Engrossing . . . scary . . . I loved it."

—Linda Howard

"A deeply engrossing read, *Hush* delivers a creepy villain, a chilling plot, and two remarkable investigators whose personal struggles are only equaled by their compelling need to stop a madman before he kills again. Warning: don't read this book if you are home alone."

—Lisa Gardner

"A wealth of procedural detail, a heart-thumping finale, and two scarred but indelible protagonists make this a first-rate read."

—*Publishers Weekly*

"Anne Frasier has crafted a taut and suspenseful thriller."

—Kay Hooper

"Well-realized characters and taut, suspenseful plotting."

—*Minneapolis Star Tribune*

PRAISE FOR *SLEEP TIGHT*

"Guaranteed to keep you awake at night."

—Lisa Jackson

"They'll be no sleeping after reading this one. Laced with forensic detail and psychological twists."

—Andrea Kane

"Gripping and intense . . . Along with a fine plot, Frasier delivers her characters as whole people, each trying to cope in the face of violence and jealousies."

—*Minneapolis Star Tribune*

"Enthralling. There's a lot more to this clever intrigue than graphic police procedures. Indeed, one of Frasier's many strengths is her ability to create characters and relationships that are as compelling as the mystery itself. Will linger with the reader after the killer is caught."

—*Publishers Weekly*

PRAISE FOR *PLAY DEAD*

"A nicely constructed combination of mystery and thriller. Frasier is a talented writer whose forte is probing into the psyches of her characters, and she produces a fast-paced novel with a finale containing many surprises."

—*I Love a Mystery*

"Has all the essentials of an edge-of-your-seat story. There is suspense, believable characters, an interesting setting, and just the right amount of details to keep the reader's eyes always moving forward . . . I recommend *Play Dead* as a great addition to any mystery library."

—*Roundtable Reviews*

PRAISE FOR *BEFORE I WAKE*

"Anne Frasier's latest novel once again demonstrates her mastery of atmospheric suspense."

—*Crimespree Magazine*

"An original, highly suspenseful, ingeniously crafted tale that dares to question reality . . . Frasier has filled this clever plot with daring twists, realistic characters, and a chilling narrative that thrills with each page."

—*New Mystery Reader Magazine*

"Words like 'thrilling' 'riveting' and 'intense' are often bandied about when describing Anne Frasier's writing, and for good reason. That is exactly what she delivers."

—*Romance Reviews Today*

PRAISE FOR *PALE IMMORTAL*

"Frasier's latest rivets as she masterfully creates a perfect atmosphere for suspicious death and compelling mystery in this nail-biting thrill ride."

—*Romantic Times*

"Frasier delivers twist upon twist. The characters are rich, complex. The story is masterfully spun."

—*Spinetingler Magazine*

"Easily the best work I've read this year."

—*Maximum Horrors*

"Magnificently written story and characters."

—*MyShelf.com*

PRAISE FOR *THE ORCHARD*

"*The Orchard* is a lovely book in all the ways that really matter, one of those rare and wonderful memoirs in which people you've never met become your friends."

—Nicholas Sparks

"A hypnotic tale of place, people, and of midwestern family roots that run deep, stubbornly hidden, and equally menacing."

—Jamie Ford, *New York Times* bestselling author of *Hotel on the Corner of Bitter and Sweet*

THE
BODY READER

ALSO BY ANNE FRASIER

Hush
Sleep Tight
Before I Wake
Pale Immortal
Garden of Darkness

The Elise Sandburg Series

Play Dead
Stay Dead
Pretty Dead

Short Stories

"Made of Stars"
"Max Under the Stars"

Anthologies

Deadly Treats
Once upon a Crime
From the Indie Side
Discount Noir
Writes of Spring
The Lineup: Poems on Crime 3

Nonfiction (as Theresa Weir)

The Orchard: A Memoir
The Man Who Left

THE
BODY READER

ANNE FRASIER

THOMAS & MERCER

Published by Thomas & Mercer, Seattle

www.apub.com

Amazon, the Amazon logo, and Thomas & Mercer are trademarks of Amazon.com, Inc., or its affiliates.

ISBN-13: 9781503935204
ISBN-10: 1503935205

Cover design by Damon Freeman

Printed in the United States of America

Stories linger in the faces of the dead.

CHAPTER 1

One day she stopped screaming.

It was the same day she quit thinking about the world beyond the windowless cell. That world no longer existed. Not for her. Now there were just the plates of food that came at uneven intervals, eaten in darkness, without visual cues, her taste buds unable to discern what went into her mouth.

Her life was listening for his footsteps on the stairs. Her life was listening to the shuffle of his feet across the cement floor and waiting to hear his voice when he spoke. God help her, she'd come to look forward to his voice, his visits. Anything was better than the quiet in her head.

Then there were the times he pulled her from the room within a room, pulled her from the darkness. She would blink at the blinding brightness of the single bulb hanging from the basement ceiling. When she tried to speak, her voice scratchy and unfamiliar and hollow, he'd smack her across the face.

And that was okay.

Today he led her to a drain in the corner of the basement, cranked open a faucet, and aimed the nozzle at her naked body, blasting her with ice-cold water.

Even then she didn't scream. She had no scream left in her.

"You're disgusting."

She supposed she was. Maybe that's why he'd quit touching her. Disgusting was good.

Done giving her a dousing, he turned off the hose while she trembled violently from the cold—her shivering, *a curious thing*, she thought with detachment.

"Go on. Back in the cell."

At first she'd tried to retain her sense of self. For a while she'd tried to remind herself of who she was. She'd tried to recall the color of her hair and the shape of her face. But eventually she let go of all that. This was her life now, and her hair and face made no difference here. Once you no longer desired anything, surviving became easier. Once you gave up and accepted your fate, existence became tolerable because every day wasn't a reset of a nightmare that wouldn't end.

In the cell, she curled into a ball on the floor, knees drawn up to her chest as she continued to shake.

Now he would lock the door.

"Can you stay awhile?" she asked, her voice thin as a thread. "Talk to me?"

He stared. Untrimmed beard. Cruel yet distracted eyes. Tangle of brown hair. He wasn't thinking about her. She'd become an unpleasant chore—the dog he wished he'd never gotten but now had to feed. When he remembered to feed her.

Behind him, the lightbulb flickered, then went out, the entire house falling silent. He mumbled a curse in the darkness.

Blackest of black, but black was her friend. In a world of no sight, her hearing had become acute. She was used to looking beyond the darkness to mentally visualize her surrounds, imagining the distance to the walls and the height of the ceiling.

Moments after the light went out, she felt something strange, something she hadn't felt in a long time.

Hope.

She knew how much space he took up, knew how tall he was and how much he weighed. She knew about the calluses on his hands, and the long, wide scar on his belly. She knew the circumference of his biceps and how his breath smelled of cigarettes and beer.

Odd that she was thinking of escape when she'd given up so long ago. But maybe she'd been hibernating, unconsciously waiting for just the right moment, for the time when the universe tipped the scales in her favor. For the second when she had the advantage.

She could see in the dark.

Not in a mysterious way, but more like a naked mole rat that spent its life living in total darkness. After a while the darkness was no longer a barrier.

The man wore a Taser on his left hip. An unfamiliar model, but the numerous times he'd used it on her had taught her everything she needed to know. In the darkness, in the darkest of darks, her mind calculated the distance and she shot to her feet and lunged. Her hand unsnapped the holster and pulled the Taser free.

She hit the "On" button. The weapon powered up, making a whirring sound. She felt a rush of air against her face as the man made a grab for her.

Like someone thrusting a sword, she aimed for what she hoped was his chest. The Taser connected, and the man's throat emitted an involuntary gargling noise as he dropped to the floor and convulsed at her feet.

She slipped past him, moving awkwardly forward until she made contact with the railing and the wooden stairs that led to ground level.

She'd spent days and months listening—to the way he walked across the floor above her head as he removed his holster, to the sound of the gun hitting the table.

Arms outstretched, she stumbled blindly up the stairs. In the kitchen, her fingers sought the table and found what she was looking for.

Abandoning the Taser, she unsnapped the holster and pulled out the weapon. From the weight and shape, it felt like a .40-caliber Smith & Wesson—standard police issue.

Behind her, footfalls pounded up the steps.

No time to check the magazine. She steadied the gun with two hands, listened for the sound of movement coming from below, heard his crablike scuffling and his ragged breathing, sensed his rage drawing nearer.

She fired. Three times, each pull of the trigger creating a spark in the darkness as hot, empty cartridges bounced over her bare feet and the smell of gunpowder filled her nostrils.

The man let out a grunt, and his body crashed down the stairs.

Now I can go home.

She turned, felt her way to the back door, and opened it.

Winter.

She hadn't expected winter. The cold took her breath away.

Her mind screamed, *Run.* Instead, she forced herself to go back to the kitchen. A search of the coatrack next to the door turned up a heavy canvas jacket. She slipped it over her naked body, zipping it knee to throat, then tugged a stocking cap from one of the deep pockets and pulled it down over her wet hair.

Everything smelled like the man, and an unexpected wave of sorrow washed over her. Had she done the right thing? Killing him?

She shoved her feet into a pair of boots that were too big, stuffed the gun into her pocket, and ran from the building, never looking back.

Home.

To a different man. One whose name she couldn't recall. But his face. She remembered his face and his touch and his smile.

The houses she passed were dark, and even the streetlights were out. No stars. No moon. *Blackout*—an explanation from her old life.

She dragged her feet so the boots would stay on, not caring that her legs were numb from the cold. It felt good.

Headlights illuminated the snowbanked street as a car approached from behind. She hugged the coat tighter and kept walking.

The car stopped at the intersection, and she saw it was a taxi.

She ran, caught up, opened the back door, and slipped inside.

And then her mind stumbled. There were things she still understood from the old life. She knew she should somehow contact the police. She thought about telling the man behind the wheel about her escape, and yet she felt reluctant to engage, to share any of herself. All she could think about was getting home.

The driver let out a choked sound of disgust, looked over his shoulder at her, and said, "Oh, hell no. Out. Get out. I don't give rides to homeless people."

The last thing she planned to do was get out of the cab. No way in hell was she getting out.

"I have a home. That's where I'm going."

Her voice sounded weird inside the cab. So much different than it had in the basement, in her cell when she'd talked to herself. That voice had been hollow. Here, she could almost see the sound waves bouncing off the interior of the cab, and she could detect an echo that gave her voice, scratchy and hoarse though it was, resonance. The cell had been soundproof, and now, in the cab, it was like there was nothing dampening any of her senses. It was unbearable, really, when she thought about it. How did people stand it? The vibrations of the world. The odors. The way the seat felt on the back of her legs. Clammy, touched by too many people. The deodorizer hanging from the rearview mirror that made her lungs burn and her eyes water.

She pulled the gun from her jacket and pointed it at the man. "Drive." She gave him the address. It just came to her. Just popped into her head like she'd used it yesterday.

He drove.

When she saw the duplex, her eyes stung and her throat burned all over again, this time from happiness, from relief. He would be there, and he would wrap his arms around her and hold her close. Maybe he would cry, and she would tell him she was okay. And they would just hold each other for a long time. And then he would cook something for her to eat, all the while looking at her with happiness and love.

She could pull up this dream because she'd had it so many times. Almost every day she'd played it like a movie in her head, often with slight variations, but basically the same.

The driver stopped in the middle of the street. There had never been a cab in her mind movie, so she wasn't sure what should happen next. She got out, thinking to suggest he send her a bill, but he squealed away. The second he was gone he no longer existed.

She stood in the street, taking in the duplex that loomed in front of her—a dark shape among a row of houses.

Home.

So odd to walk up such a familiar sidewalk, such familiar steps to a familiar porch. She tested the knob, then knocked. The door opened, candle flames illuminating the faces of a man and woman.

Now she remembered his name.

Eric.

She waited for him to recognize her, waited for the scene to play out the way it had always played out in her head. But he didn't say anything, just stood there with a question on his face.

"It's me," she finally said, as if that would explain everything. And it *should* explain everything.

Her voice sounded even stranger out in the open. Like her words might just drift away on the cold air. This must be what an alien would feel experiencing Earth for the first time.

He stared for what seemed like minutes; then his expression gradually changed, morphing from one emotion to another, finally settling on shock.

In a self-conscious gesture, she touched a long strand of wet hair, wondering for the first time in months what she looked like.

"Jude?" The tone of his voice held disbelief.

Jude, that was what people had called her. She'd forgotten. How silly. To forget.

The letters of her name hung in the air and brought with them a whisper of days she'd clung to, days that had kept her going. Days of sunlight and cafés and lattes shared on Sunday mornings after a tangle of sheets and lovemaking.

"I'm home," she said by way of explaining something that shouldn't need explaining. She was gone, and now she was back.

He glanced at the woman standing next to him.

Over the weeks and months, she'd learned to read the man in the basement. When his visits were the only stimulation in her life, it became easy to pick up signals from every blink, every breath, every turn of his head. And now, in this instant, she read the man in front of her—not just his expression, but something more, something in his cells. And she understood that the movie she'd played in her head for so long was not going to happen.

They're a couple.

This woman was probably sleeping in Jude's bed and maybe even wearing her clothes.

"It didn't take you long to find someone new." That's what Jude said. If she'd been prepared, she might have come up with better dialogue.

His mouth opened and closed, and he finally choked out the words: "It's been three years."

She blinked, and in her mind she traveled back to the cell. She would have said she'd been there months, not years. He was lying. He had a new girlfriend, so he was trying to cover up his betrayal. "No." She shook her head, the movement broken, the single word trembling in denial, and she knew in her heart of hearts that he was right and she was wrong.

His eyes were sad as they glistened in the candlelight. *Tears.* "Yes."

He'd been a good man, a sensitive man. She remembered that about him. "How long did you wait for me?"

Now he looked ashamed. He looked like he might break down into full-blown sobs. She didn't want to see that.

"A year," he said.

Because she couldn't handle his sadness, she tried to find words to comfort him. "That's okay." Then she added bluntly, "I never want a man to touch me again anyway."

The meaning behind her words shook him even more. "I'm sorry, Jude."

Now she saw something more than sadness in his face. A man who'd once looked upon her with love was now looking at her with pity and revulsion.

The pity she might have been able to take, but not the revulsion.

"I killed somebody tonight," she said. "I killed somebody to get back to you." Then she turned and ran.

The boyfriend with the name she'd only just remembered called after her, but she kept going. Back into the darkness. And God help her, for a few brief moments she thought about returning to the basement, to the cell, to the dead man she almost wished she hadn't shot.

There was only one other place to go, only one other place that felt like home. Locking into a pre-established pattern, she turned the corner and headed in the direction of downtown and the Minneapolis Police Department.

CHAPTER 2

G ot a woman who insists she works here." Officer Myra Nettles stood in the doorway of the Minneapolis Police Department, homicide division. "She was trying to get past the front desk." Detective Uriah Ashby didn't have time to deal with a crazy person. It was like a damn apocalypse out there. Not Uriah's job to delegate tasks, but Chief Vivian Ortega had left him in charge while every available cop hit the streets. "I think you can handle it," he told Nettles.

Emergency lighting had kicked in, the way it had kicked in previous times the city experienced a blackout—blackouts that had begun a year earlier when a major substation exploded and caught fire, leaving them with one less source of power. The ramifications were deep and widespread, the blackouts recurring due to the overtaxed remaining stations, each outage an open invitation to loot and burn. Similar behavior had been seen across the country over the years, the worst being the New York City blackouts of 1977. More recently, New Orleans after Katrina. Darkness brought out the criminal opportunists. For Minneapolis, it wasn't over yet. The new substation wasn't expected to be up and running for another six months.

"Says her name is Jude Fontaine."

That got his attention. "Fontaine? You sure?"

Shrug. "I'm just the messenger."

"Escort her to my desk."

Returning with the woman trailing behind her, Myra said, "She was armed with a Smith & Wesson."

Uriah had never met Fontaine, but he'd seen photos and enough media coverage to know the person standing in front of him wasn't the missing detective who was presumed dead. "This is not Detective Fontaine," Uriah said.

Fontaine would have been close to his age, around thirty-five or so by now. This woman had to be much older, and her hair was white, not brown.

A homeless person, then. Someone who was mentally unstable, and since this particular unstable person had tried to enter the building armed . . . "Put her in Holding," he said. "Get her food and a blanket. I'll deal with her later." It would take further questioning to determine whether she should be booked, and the Hennepin County Jail was at capacity—a new situation for the city, a by-product of the power outages. And God knew that over half the people in custody really needed to be under psychiatric care and not in jail, but thanks to the closing of state mental institutions years ago, that wasn't going to happen.

Myra pulled the woman's arms behind her back, slapped handcuffs around her wrists. The woman seemed oblivious as she stared at Uriah. "Did you replace me?" she asked.

With one twirling finger, Uriah motioned for Myra to take her away. Enough raving lunatics outside to deal with. Reports were coming in of neighborhoods being torched, far more than their fire department could handle. It was now a question of which houses should be allowed to burn to the ground. A story that had become too familiar.

"Wait." It was common knowledge that kidnapping victims, hostages, could change drastically. When they returned to civilization, they no longer looked like themselves and sometimes even family couldn't ID them. "Bring her back."

Myra turned the woman around and pushed her forward.

"Where was your desk?" Uriah asked. "Show me."

She strode past him in boots that thumped and dragged.

The chief's office was private, as private as an office of glass could be. The rest of the department amounted to a scattering of desks throughout the room. Open, no cubicles. On a sunny day, light poured in from the row of windows that overlooked the city street below, and if a person had a green thumb, plants could do well. A couple of officers even grew herbs alongside the typical array of framed photos.

Nodding to a tidy desk that held no pictures and no framed photos, she said, "Grant Vang, my partner." Nodding the other direction, "Jenny Carlisle." Kept going, stopped. "Right there."

The desk belonged to Detective Caroline McIntosh. She was fairly new, a single mom, someone they probably wouldn't have hired if they hadn't been desperate. After Uriah's partner had retired, the chief suggested Caroline step in, but Uriah had declined. Caroline's head wasn't in the game. She was actively dating, often late for work. He couldn't deal with her undependability. Sometimes he suspected she was flirting with him. He couldn't deal with that either.

"Have you met anybody new yet?" his mother was always asking whenever they spoke on the phone. A relationship was the last thing on his mind.

A homeless person off the street wouldn't have been able to point out Fontaine's desk. Uriah stared at the woman in front of him, looking closer, his mind putting together another scenario as he took in her ill-fitting coat and boots, along with her filth and smell. God, did she smell. Like that sour-sweet stench of a person who hadn't bathed . . . *in years*.

The eyes. Hollow and defeated. *Shut off. Dead inside.*

"Remove the handcuffs."

The woman glanced at him in surprise, and he got the sense she'd picked up on the hint of emotion in his voice, but that was ridiculous. He was good at keeping it together. He'd been keeping it together a long time.

Once the cuffs were removed, Uriah pulled out his phone, opened an app. "Hold out your hand."

Her nails were broken, every crevice of her palm lined with grime. The bones of her wrist were covered in a thin layer of transparent skin, and what flesh remained bore evidence of abuse—deep red lines, swelling, and signs of infection. When he looked back up, he found himself staring into the face of starvation.

He pressed her finger against the screen, capturing the print, hit a few buttons, and within a minute he had a match. In horror and fascination, he stared at the photo of a dark-haired, attractive woman. Not your standard department headshot—the person on the screen looked vibrant and mischievous. Detective Jude Fontaine.

He knew her story. One evening she'd left her house to go for a jog and never returned. A team of detectives, many no longer with the force, had failed to solve the case.

He glanced back at the sunken cheeks, cracked lips, skin the color of paste.

Squinting as if the weak emergency lighting hurt her eyes, she asked, "What did that tell you?" Her words were thick and breathless, as if it hurt to breathe, hurt to speak. He took note of her swollen jaw, and looking back down at her hand he saw that some of her fingers were slightly crooked, possibly from old breaks. Evidence of torture. He swallowed.

"Don't," she whispered.

She'd read him again. Of course, this time his reaction would have been apparent to a blind person. *Don't feel sorry for me.*

He'd witnessed unspeakable brutality in his line of work, and this woman in front of him was nothing new when it came to victims. In fact, she was doing better than many. *She was alive.*

Maybe it was because she was one of them. A cop. Maybe that's why seeing her this way bothered him so much. Maybe that's why he felt something even though he hadn't allowed himself to feel anything for a long time.

She'd asked if he'd replaced her. It was close to the truth. He'd been brought in a few months after she'd gone missing. Grant Vang had been in charge of her case, but Uriah had been briefed on it, enough to know there were few clues left behind other than a witness claiming to have seen a woman fitting Fontaine's description being pulled into a van. Nothing ever came of that story. Tip lines were half bullshit, but abduction had always been the most likely scenario. Uriah had figured her for dead. They'd all figured her for dead. It had the hallmarks of a pro job, the conclusion being that she'd been murdered the night of her abduction, her body disposed of. Probably a revenge killing. Unfortunately not unheard of when it came to cops.

"How'd you get here?"

"The power went out. I escaped. I walked."

He had a million other questions. The who, the how, the why. But this wasn't the time. Right now she needed medical help, not an interrogation. "I'm going to have Officer Nettles escort you to the Hennepin County Medical Center. Later I'll stop by to talk to you. How does that sound?"

"Will I be able to lie down in a bed?"

A hospital, the thing most people dreaded, sounded appealing to her because it would have a bed. He felt that tightness in his throat again. "Yes," he said quietly.

CHAPTER 3

W hat are her injuries?" Uriah asked. "Other than the obvious."

In the hospital hallway, the doctor stuck her hands deep in the pockets of her lab coat. "I don't even know where to begin."

Six hours had passed since Jude Fontaine's appearance at the police station. Power was back, and streets were calm. She'd been examined, cleaned up, and given a private room. Uriah had made it home long enough to grab a few hours of sleep and a shower. He'd also contacted Chief Ortega, who'd put him in charge of Jude's case, her reason being that it might be easier for Fontaine to deal with someone she didn't know. Uriah agreed.

The news of the escape had hit Ortega hard, and guilt was going to weigh heavy on the entire department. Yes, years had passed since Jude Fontaine's disappearance, but that didn't change the fact that they'd given up on one of their own.

"She's had broken bones that were probably never set," the doctor said. "Concussions. Scars over much of her back and chest. Less serious, but needing immediate attention—some questionable teeth. A dentist will address those issues once we get her stabilized. Everything about her blood is off, and she's deficient in almost everything—understandable in someone who's been starved. You say she escaped by herself? And walked to the police station?"

"That seems to be the case."

"Honestly, I don't know how she did it." A pause. "Look, you can go into the room, but try not to upset her."

He nodded. "I need to find out where she was being held. I need to find out what went down. Her life could still be in danger, for all we know."

"I'm just saying handle her gently, and don't push if she's unwilling to talk to you right now. She might break, and then you'll end up with nothing."

"I understand."

The doctor left, and Uriah tapped at the open hospital-room door before entering.

Now that she'd been cleaned up and dressed in a hospital gown rather than a heavy coat, she looked worse—if that was possible. He could see the bruises, old and new, on her bare arms, scars and lesions on her thin wrists. It appeared someone had made an attempt to wash her hair, then given up. He had the urge to grab a pair of scissors and cut out the mats.

"Hi." He dragged a chair next to the bed. "Remember me?"

She pushed a button on the lift control to raise the head of the bed several inches. "My replacement."

"I wouldn't say that."

"Detective Ashby, right?"

"Yeah, right." He was surprised she remembered. "I need to ask you some questions."

The brittle morning light fell across her face, revealing eyes that were an intense blue and a gaze so direct it made him uncomfortable. In stark contrast to her hair, her brows were so dark they looked almost black. He crossed the room and reached for the curtains.

"Don't."

He paused, arm in the air.

"Leave them open."

"The sun's in your eyes."

"I want it in my eyes."

He let the full meaning of that sink in. *Of course.* Judging by her pallor, she probably hadn't seen natural light in a long time.

He took a seat beside her, thrown off by her unexpected composure and alertness. But then he wasn't dealing with somebody who'd been held captive for a short time. She'd had years to shut down her emotions, years to rewire her brain to accept whatever presented itself. Even freedom.

"Don't feel bad," she said.

Was he that obvious? Uriah prided himself on remaining at least outwardly unaffected. Not in a cold kind of way, but a controlled way. It had gotten him through a lot of tough situations, including the last year. His personal ordeal was different from the horror Fontaine had suffered, but maybe not so different when it came to coping.

"Don't feel bad about the questions you have to ask me," she said. "Don't feel bad about what I've been through. Talking about it isn't going to make things worse. It's not like I've *forgotten* and discussing it will bring it all back."

"Yeah, well . . . that's exactly what I was thinking," he confessed.

"I'll make it easier. I can tell you that I don't know where the house is."

"But it was a house." Statement. "Not an abandoned building or storage facility. Anything like that?"

"A house. In a neighborhood."

And then they got down to her escape. The how of it. She told him about killing the man who'd held her for three years.

"With the gun you had when you showed up at the station."

"Yes."

The weapon's serial number had been filed off. The gun, along with the coat, hat, and boots she'd arrived in, had been sent to the crime lab.

Uriah was hoping for a print or DNA match. "The man—are you sure you killed him?"

"I'm sure." But her eyes clouded in doubt. "It was dark."

Uriah once again had the urge to close the curtain. The sun was too bright. It revealed too much, from her sharp chest bones to her transparent skin to the bald spot on one side of her head—either she'd pulled out her own hair or someone else had done it.

She could be wrong about her captor being dead. The moment would have been highly charged and had probably felt unreal. She would have been terrified and in flight mode.

"Would you recognize the house if you saw it?" he asked.

She didn't look at him but instead concentrated on something in her mind. Digging. Trying to remember. "No. I never saw the outside of the house. I have no idea what it looked like."

"And you walked straight to the police station."

She faltered. They always faltered somewhere in the story. Here it came. The lie. He'd been interrogating people long enough to see it forming. But to her credit, he saw her toss the lie aside to settle for what he hoped was somewhat the truth.

"I went home."

"Home." He frowned, trying to understand, filling in the blanks with what he knew of her personal history. Single, but she'd had a boyfriend when she'd vanished. "What happened when you went home?"

She swallowed. "I'd rather not talk about that right now."

"Okay, we'll save it for later." He recalled the doctor's warning about pushing her too hard too soon. "How about we start at the beginning? The day you vanished?"

That seemed to be something she was willing to discuss.

"I don't remember the abduction," she said.

Understandable. Emotional trauma aside, she might have suffered one of the concussions that day.

"The first thing I was aware of was coming to on a basement floor, in a room with no windows. Not big enough to lie down in. I had to curl up to sleep. I never saw anybody but the man I killed last night. And I'd never seen him before that moment when he opened the cell door three years ago." She paused, and he could see they'd reached another place she didn't want to go. But he'd eventually have to get a full statement of what happened in that basement so the man who'd held her against her will could be prosecuted if still alive.

"I'm going to send a sketch artist to see you today. Are you okay with that?"

"Yes."

She was tough, but his short visit had worn her out. He'd get more when she was fresh. "Let's finish this tomorrow." In the meantime, he'd talk to her ex-boyfriend and get cops on door-to-door canvassing of areas she might have walked through, even though the chance of any-one having seen her seemed remote considering the blackout. Relevant case information would be pushed to the entire Minneapolis Police Department. Maybe a neighbor heard shots fired. Maybe the sketch artist would be able to give them something to go on.

Now that the questioning was over, at least temporarily, her body relaxed.

"If you'd rather talk to a female detective about the details of your ordeal, I can arrange that."

"You'll see my official statement anyway, right?"

"Correct."

"And you'll be handling the case?"

"Yes."

"Then I'd rather talk to you."

He put the chair back and was turning to leave when someone rapped at the door.

Uriah was surprised to see a man he recognized from local media stories. Adam Schilling. Expensive leather jacket. Slacks that cost a month's salary, glowing skin, and a deliberate five-o'clock shadow, along with plucked and sculpted brows. He was a playboy and one of the city's most eligible bachelors. Then Uriah remembered what he'd somehow forgotten in all this. Jude Fontaine was Governor Phillip Schilling's daughter, and this guy was her brother.

Uriah wasn't from the Twin Cities, and he didn't follow celebrity gossip, yet he recalled something about Fontaine emancipating herself when she was sixteen. Apparently she had nothing to do with the Schillings anymore and had even taken a new name. Judging by the horrified expression on her face, it looked like her feelings toward her kin hadn't changed all that much over the years.

"What the hell are you doing here?" she asked.

Schilling frowned. "I wanted to see you. Chief Ortega contacted us about your escape, and Dad wanted me to make sure you were okay." He swallowed, his eyes glistening as he continued to stare. "My God. You look like hell."

"Get out," she whispered.

Upsetting her would not be helpful to the investigation. "You'd better leave," Uriah told him.

Schilling raised his hands, giving up. "Okay, okay." He backed away, turned, and vanished out the door.

Jude fumbled for the bed's lift control, gave up, closed her eyes, arms limp at her sides, face ashen.

Afraid she was going to black out, Uriah grabbed the control, hit the button, and lowered the bed.

"Curtain," she whispered breathlessly.

He pulled the fabric across the window, darkening the room. "You okay?" he asked. What a question.

Like someone afraid to move for fear of throwing up, she gave him an almost-imperceptible nod.

"Need a drink of water?"

"No."

The subscript being that she wanted him to go away. He'd stayed too long. "I'll be back tomorrow."

In the hallway, he found Schilling leaning against a wall. Upon hearing Uriah's footsteps, he straightened.

Uriah introduced himself and flashed his badge.

"She looks like a different person," Schilling said, openly disturbed by what he'd just seen. "I mean, I knew she'd probably look rough, but . . ." He shook his head. "Wow."

"Can I buy you a cup of coffee?" Uriah asked. It was a polite gesture, meant to open up communication.

Five minutes later, they were situated at a corner table in the cafeteria, white diner mugs in front of them.

"I really can't tell you much of anything." Schilling measured out two teaspoons of sugar, then stirred noisily, stainless steel against ceramic. "I've had no contact with Jude since she was sixteen. None. I guess it was stupid of me to come. I thought maybe she'd be happy to see family, you know? I thought she might need somebody with her."

"Obviously not you."

Schilling flashed him a look of irritation, then launched into an explanation of their situation. "She was diagnosed with mental problems back when she was a kid. Honestly, if she hadn't looked so bad today, I would have said the last three years were fake. Something she concocted. Her disappearance." He shrugged. "Just to get back at us for whatever she thinks we did to her. But seeing her like that . . . I guess it was real. And I feel bad that we didn't try harder to find her."

This was the first Uriah had heard of Fontaine's mental instability. She would have had to pass a psych evaluation to join the department, but Schilling had known the child, the teen, not the adult. And teenagers were volatile. "Does she have any family she associates with? Somebody who can help her through this?"

Schilling shook his head. "Not that I know of. She was living with a guy when she was abducted, but I'm pretty sure he's moved on. I've seen him with somebody. And who can blame him?"

Uriah had an uncomfortable thought. "The guy she was with before? Does he still live in the house they shared?"

"No idea."

How messed up would that be, to get out of the place you'd been held captive for three years, go home, only to find another woman in your house?

"Just remember," Schilling said. "She was unstable before any of this happened, and you just saw her in there. That wasn't the reaction of a rational person."

Any decent detective knew better than to trust one person's version of any story. "Are you younger? Older? Any other siblings?"

"Just the two of us. I'm four years older. Our mother died in a gun accident when Jude was eight and I was twelve. Jude didn't see it happen, but she was on site, staying in the family cabin up north. She saw the aftermath. Everybody freaking. My dad out of his mind. I'm sure seeing adults lose it like that, seeing her own father fall apart, had to be tough on a kid. I think that's when she started getting weird. Understandable, right? Shortly after that, she became paranoid. Delusional. She started saying our father killed our mother. She just wouldn't let it go."

Adam Schilling's mention of the tragic loss of their mother recalled something else: he was the one who'd accidently shot her. That omission to his story said something about his character, and yet it was probably a dark event he didn't like to talk about, especially with a stranger.

"I feel like a gossip," Schilling said, his eyes somber with what seemed like sincerity, "but this is personal history I think you should be aware of so you know what you're dealing with."

"The more information I have, the better."

"Could she tell you anything?" Schilling asked. "About the day she was abducted? Or where she's been? Who kidnapped her? How she escaped?"

"So far, we know nothing. And if I did know more than nothing, I wouldn't be able to discuss it with you." Uriah pulled out his card and slid it across the table. "If you think of anything you might have forgotten, no matter how slight, give me a call."

Schilling read the card, then pocketed it. "Keep an eye on her, will you? Regardless of what she might think about me, I believe in watching out for family. If I can help, even under the radar, let me know." He gestured vaguely. "Money, whatever she needs."

Jude Fontaine didn't seem the type to welcome help from anybody, let alone an estranged family member. The one thing Uriah could do was make sure they found the bastard—dead or alive—who'd done this to her. He could make sure they didn't fail her again.

CHAPTER 4

The detective returned to her hospital room the next day, and this time he brought clothes.

"I heard they're releasing you tomorrow," he said. "Figured you'd need something to wear. I just guessed the size."

As Jude looked up from the hospital bed, Detective Ashby placed a white plastic shopping bag on one of the chairs that lined the wall, then sat down next to her and pulled out pen and paper, along with a digital recorder.

He was dressed in a suit and tie, his dark, curly hair messy and on the long side. Jude figured him for late thirties, but it was hard to tell in this business. Crime aged a person, that she knew full well. Maybe he was twelve.

Three years in solitary might have chewed up her brain, but she still had a sense of humor.

"Odors are so strong," she said.

He frowned, attempting to understand. Thick brows over deep-brown eyes.

"I can smell everything," she explained. "The fabric of your jacket. The coffee you've been drinking. The plastic bags. Food down the hall. It's like I've never smelled anything before. Isn't that weird?" She didn't add that he was giving off a faint scent of the alcohol he'd consumed last night or even this morning, along with something else—maybe soap—she couldn't identify.

He rubbed the back of his hand across his mouth. "Isolation will do that."

And not only odors. She couldn't stare hard enough, and she made no apology for visually examining every pore on his face and every hair on his head, every curve of every eyelash, even when he shifted uncomfortably.

The interview took maybe an hour. Not that long considering she was relating the past three years of her life, but she could have been reciting a grocery list, for all the impact the sharing of events had on her. At some point in the past three years, something inside her had shut down, shut off. If that hadn't happened, she probably would have lost her mind, but now she was left with a person who could relate atrocities without emotion. Finished, she looked up and saw that his face was pale. And that wasn't all . . .

"Your hand," she said.

He glanced down, made some small sound of dismay, and clicked the pen, the motion effectively stopping his shaking.

She didn't like witnessing his reaction. She didn't know what to do with it, and in some odd way, seeing his shock made her feel dirty. It occurred to her that what she'd been through had somehow robbed her of her humanity, made her feel subhuman. Maybe that's why women often didn't report abuse. Forget about their fear of retaliation or their fear of tomorrow or their fear of being alone or their love of their abuser. Once it was out there, once the facts were hung on the line for the world to see, that abuse robbed the victim of dignity and the victim suffered twice. Once at the hands of the abuser, and once at the hands of the world.

Ashby shut off his recorder. "What about tomorrow?" he asked, closing his notebook.

He'd listen to her statement again once he left. She was sure of it. For a moment she thought about grabbing the recorder and smashing it.

"What *about* tomorrow?" she asked.

"Do you have anywhere to go?"

"I'll find a place."

"How about money? Do you have money?"

"Chief Ortega was here earlier and brought a check. She claimed it was backpay." Jude suspected the check had been pushed through by Ortega in order to make sure she had enough to live on, at least temporarily. Ortega had come on board six months before Jude's kidnapping, hardly enough time to have established much of a working relationship, but long enough for Jude to get a solid sense of her caring nature.

"And I called my bank. Apparently I still have an active account. I had a little saved up"—*before I died.* Wait. That wasn't right. Not died. But it had been like a death, the past three years, and now she was a ghost, moving through the familiar and unfamiliar terrain of a new life, complete with a new cast of characters. No home, no boyfriend, no job. "Not much, but it will get me by for a while."

Ashby seemed pleased to hear that she wasn't broke. "I can pick you up, and if you feel strong enough, we can drive around and see if anything looks or feels familiar to you. See if you can spot the house where you were held captive."

She nodded. "Okay." A lie.

"And I can help you find a place to stay. Get you set up with a phone. Whatever you need."

"That isn't necessary."

"Ortega's orders."

"Thanks."

The afternoon was exhausting. The sketch artist arrived with her charcoal and her tablet. Once she was done, Jude lay back against the pillows in relief. She'd spoken more in the past two days than she'd spoken in three years. For so long she'd wanted to see another face other than the face of the man the artist had drawn, but now she wanted everybody to leave her alone. Just for a while. So she could adjust. So she could enjoy her freedom.

Even though she was tired, it was hard to rest with the bright lights and the strange odors and all the noise. The building itself had a heartbeat of motors and blowers and gears and pulleys, and she swore it almost seemed to breathe. When someone knocked on the open door, she kept her eyes closed. No more talking. No more questions. But then she smelled coffee and had to look.

Detective Grant Vang stood in the doorway, a white paper bag in one hand, carryout coffee container in the other. "Vanilla latte and a cranberry scone," he announced, holding the bag high.

Grant was a few inches under six feet, slim, muscular, dressed in a dark suit, his straight black hair swept across his forehead. More alarming than his unannounced visit was how little he'd changed. His lack of change seemed unfair, and yet what had she expected?

Maybe an older version of Grant. Maybe a few gray hairs and stress lines. He was proof that three years was forever when you were being tortured but not long when you were just living your life.

She wondered if he was seeing anyone, wondered if he was still single. Wondered if he still liked her like that. Hoped he didn't. It hadn't been easy working side by side after he'd confessed his feelings for her and she'd rejected him.

"You should see the circus outside," he said, entering the room. "There must be a hundred newspeople near the front doors hoping to get a scoop on you."

Too soon.

Seeing someone from her old life, especially someone she'd worked with so closely at one time, threatened to shut down her brain. She struggled to stay in the scene as he placed the coffee and bag on the patient table, rolling it close. Then he looked at her for too long, and she knew he was trying to match the hideous person in the bed with the somewhat-attractive woman he used to know.

"I looked for you." His eyes were pleading. "I want you to know that. For months."

Everybody wanted forgiveness. Once again she found herself in the role of making someone else feel okay about her capture. Once again she was the one doing the comforting, the reassuring. "It's okay," she told him.

"I asked to be put on your case." He pulled a chair close and sat down, a potpourri of scents mingling with cotton fabric and hospital food. "But Ortega seems to think you'll be more comfortable talking to Ashby."

"That's true" was all she said. All she needed to say.

He nodded, looked down at his hands. "Do you remember anything? About the day you were abducted?"

She felt trapped, smothered by the room and his presence and all the things he wanted from her, ranging from simple conversation to an emotional connection. She didn't even know how to tell him she needed to be alone.

Too soon.

"No. Nothing." She turned her face toward the wall, and feigned sleep until he left.

The next morning Jude got dressed. The clothes Detective Ashby had brought the day before fit fairly well, mainly because they were sweatpants, black, along with a hooded sweatshirt and a puffy blue coat that smelled like Target, a scent so established she could recall it three years later. She pressed the coat to her nose, closed her eyes, and inhaled deeply. She tried to imagine the detective shopping for her—someone he didn't even know.

She slipped into the coat, stuck her hands in the pockets, and found gloves and a stocking cap, also a nice shade of blue, everything clean and new. Her luck ran out with the shoes. Serviceable brown ankle boots that were a little too tight, but they would do for now.

"Ready to go?" asked a nurse holding a clipboard.

"Yes."

"Is someone picking you up?"

"I'll catch a cab."

"Just sign this release form." The nurse passed the clipboard, and Jude signed her name.

She tried not to appear in too much of a hurry even though she was anxious to get away before Detective Ashby showed up. She didn't want to see the pity in his eyes, and she especially didn't want to read the expression on his face and know he'd listened to her statement again.

The elevator took her to street level and the Eighth Street entrance, and then she was out the automatic doors and standing on the wide walkway in the patient drop-off area. The cold stung her eyes, and the sky—it was *so blue*.

Cabs were lined up and waiting. A WCCO van was parked in a prime metered spot, and people who were obviously part of news crews stood in hunched clusters, clutching their Caribou coffee and waiting to broadcast any bit of information that might come their way. She'd seen them from her hospital window, but now that she was yards away, no one even recognized her. How could they? She didn't even recognize herself.

The television in her private room had been full of her story, running on local stations along with national outlets, but her photo had been pulled from the police-department profile. Along with her old picture, they were blasting the image drawn by the sketch artist.

Did it look like him? Maybe. On the surface. Eyes and nose and mouth. The hair, the beard. But no drawing could capture him, not the real him, the him he'd shown her every day. That him looked nothing like the sketch. That him would have been too frightening for anyone to gaze upon, let alone see from the safety of a living room.

But that was over now.

She took a deep breath of fresh winter air, tucked her hands in the pockets of her puffy Target jacket, turned in the opposite direction, and began walking.

Nobody tried to stop her. By simply doing nothing, she was incognito.

Jude didn't give the newspeople another thought. She didn't think about where she was heading, or where she was going to live, or how she would survive, or if the man she shot was dead, or if she'd ever find the house where she'd spent the past three years. Right now she just wanted to walk in the cold, under a blue, blue sky.

CHAPTER 5

Two blocks into her freedom walk, Jude spotted the logo for her bank, along with the digitally displayed time and a temperature of thirty degrees. Balmy for winter in Minnesota. This particular branch wasn't one she'd ever visited, but she figured they'd have her thumbprint ID on file.

In the end, it didn't really matter. The personal banker recognized her name due to the media coverage. She seemed both uncomfortable and starstruck. Weird to think that being abducted turned a person into a celebrity.

Jude deposited the check from Ortega and withdrew several hundred in cash, stuffed the envelope in her jacket pocket, and began walking again, stopping at a café on South Tenth Street, one she'd visited many times. Inside, her plan to order a latte was derailed by the dessert display.

She felt more human than she had a couple of days ago. A fluid IV and nutritious food could do wonders, but her senses were still in overdrive, at times feeling so finely tuned that it seemed she could almost hear the melody of the blood moving through her veins. Was this the way the world was for animals, especially dogs? She noticed everything around her, from the dark cracks in the polished cement floor to the ornate ceiling. Beneath the hiss of the espresso machine and a Dylan song, she heard the ticking of a wall clock and individual sentences buried in a blanket of conversation.

The warm café smelled of coffee and chocolate, of the cold that people carried on their clothes, of fabric and winter and skin both young and old.

"What's that?" She pointed.

The kid behind the counter peered into the case. "Caramel cheese-cake brownie." He straightened, looking faintly curious about the over-stuffed white plastic hospital bag in her hand. Her tangle of matted hair was covered with the stocking cap, but there was nothing she could do about her face. She'd seen herself in the mirror and knew she could still easily pass for a street person. But her sunken cheeks and the dark circles under her eyes hadn't been the biggest shock. She'd never been especially vain, but her hair was something people had always complimented her on—the thickness and shine and richness of the color. There would be no compliments now.

She shifted her finger. "And that?"

"Rum and coconut."

"That?"

Seeing she might never be able to decide, the kid said, "You wanna know what I like? The raspberry dark-chocolate brownie. It has a little bit of cayenne pepper in it."

"That sounds unbelievable." She ordered his suggestion, along with a latte. While waiting, she grabbed a copy of *City Pages*, the Twin Cities' free weekly paper. Before she reached the want ads, her order was announced at the end of the counter.

"How's your day going?" the barista asked. "Got any big plans?"

The question had no doubt been part of her training, so it wasn't the girl's fault. But the delivery came with the prepackaged assumption that there was no suffering in the world. Maybe that's what coffee shops sold. The idea that everything was okay, at least here, in this moment. It kinda worked.

Jude picked up her cup in its paper sleeve. "My big plan is to drink this latte and eat this brownie."

For some reason, her response evoked a flicker of interest before the girl moved on to prepare the next drink and ask the next person about plans.

Jude found an empty table near a plant-filled window and opened the paper to the back pages.

Bringing the forkful of brownie to her mouth held all the majesty of a spiritual awakening, and when the dessert made contact with her tongue, she felt the release of endorphins.

How could certain foods make a person feel better? Instantly better?

While savoring the brownie, she perused apartment rentals. Borrowing a pen from the cash-register counter, she circled a few prospects.

Like a regular person. Was it that easy? To return to real life?

One of the ads stuck out. *No background check. No references.* Located on Chicago Avenue South, two blocks from Powderhorn Park.

She returned the pen and asked about a pay phone.

The kid at the register stared at her. "I think I saw one in a movie once."

That got a slow smile out of Jude. It might have been her first smile since her escape, maybe her first smile in years, and she wasn't sure how she felt about it.

He noticed the *City Pages* in her hand, folded to the circled ads. "Here." He pulled out his cell phone. "You can borrow this."

She put the paper down on the counter, made the call, set up a time, handed the phone back. "Thanks."

"Have I seen you somewhere?"

It would be like this for a while. Her face must have been plastered everywhere at one time, and with her recent escape making local and national news . . . "It's possible" was all she said.

He pushed the paper toward her. "Powderhorn? You don't wanna go there."

"Why not?" She'd always liked the Powderhorn area. It was one of those neighborhoods that had spent years fighting a bad reputation, deserving and undeserving.

"That place was rough before the increase in crime, but now? Businesses have folded, and a lot of the houses are empty. Vandals cleaned everything out. Like gutted the homes, stripped them to the studs to get the copper wire. You should be looking in Tangletown. Or maybe around Lake Harriet. Uptown is still okay too."

Both Tangletown and Lake Harriet would most likely be out of her price range, and Uptown was too hip, too noisy, too claustrophobic. "Thanks for the warning. And thanks for the phone."

A few blocks away, she caught a city bus to Powderhorn and the apartment where she'd arranged to meet the building manager.

The kid at the coffee shop had been right. As the bus chugged down familiar streets, past record stores and cafés and vintage shops, evidence of neglect was everywhere. Some of the windows were covered in plywood, graffiti, and band posters, and many of the spaces looked empty. Even the four-story brick apartment building, when Jude found it, gave off a deserted vibe.

"Washer and dryer in the basement." The building manager, a guy named Will Sebastian, stood with muscular arms crossed, watching her examine the advertised space. He had long hair tied back in a ponytail, a leather vest, a beard, and tinted aviator glasses. He was big and burly, with tattoos on his neck and fingers that looked prison grade. He smelled like old sweat and cigarettes, his body odor having taken on that heavy stench that came with winter.

As advertised, the apartment was on the top floor. Nobody would be dancing above her head. One bedroom, the living room and kitchen combination separated by a breakfast counter and three stools. A lot of sunshine pouring in, and shades that could be pulled down at night.

Radiator heat, hardwood floors, crown molding. Bathroom with a claw-foot tub and subway tile that had probably been there from day one. It was easy to feel the hundred years of living that had occurred there, ranging from bright and promising when the place was new to hard and downtrodden in recent decades.

"Previous occupants moved without taking their stuff," Will said. "Three months behind on rent and they skipped town. Just left it. Even the dishes, but I can haul anything out you don't want."

"I could use all of it." Vintage orange couch and an oval coffee table. Braid rug. On the wall was a poster of the Grain Belt beer sign done by a local artist whose name escaped her.

"Now for the best part." He led her from the apartment, down a dark hallway, and up a narrow flight of metal stairs.

Jude would be lying if she didn't admit to feeling uneasy. The tightness of the space, the darkness, even the smell of old building and damp brick. For a moment she considered turning and running, even calculating how far she'd get if he came after her and brought her down like a lion bringing down a gazelle.

In her condition, she wouldn't make it far. She could already feel weakness invading the legs that had gotten little use over the past three years.

At the top of the stairs, the manager threw open a door.

The transition from darkness to brilliant sunlight almost blinded her, but she had no trouble following him through the door to the roof.

Flat, covered in tar paper and gravel and surrounded by a two-foot brick wall typical of a lot of old apartment buildings. The black tar paper had soaked up heat from the sun, making the day feel a lot warmer than the thirty degrees posted earlier on the bank sign. But it wasn't just a tar-paper roof. There was a small area where a raised wooden deck had been added, along with cheap plastic lawn chairs and a small glass-topped outdoor table. In the center of the table was an ashtray overflowing with butts. When Jude stepped close enough, she recognized the odor of the cigarettes as the same odor that was embedded in the manager's clothing, an odor she associated with gas stations and greasy food. Then she realized why the smell was so familiar. Her captor had smoked the same brand.

"What kind of cigarettes do you smoke?" she asked.

"What's that?"

"Cigarettes."

Confused, he fumbled inside his leather vest and pulled out a crushed white pack of smokes, holding them up for her to see. "Whatever's on sale. These are the ones I get the most."

Brand X. That's what they were actually called. Brand X.

He gave the pack a shake; a few staggered butts shot out for the picking as he offered her one.

She shook her head. "No thanks."

"Too cheap?"

"I don't smoke."

Puzzled, he grabbed a protruding cigarette with his lips, lit it with a plastic giveaway lighter. Then, with a smooth motion that came from years of practice, he returned the pack and lighter to his shirt pocket. "We're running a special deal," he told her, cigarette bobbing. "No deposit. Two hundred bucks off your first month's rent."

So obviously desperate.

She'd seen the rooftop—he no longer had to sell her on anything, but he continued his pitch. "Building was built in 1930, if you're into that kind of stuff. They don't make them like this anymore. Parking garage below for an extra hundred. Secure. That's the big plus in this neighborhood. You don't have to leave your car on the street. And a room on the fourth floor is as safe as anywhere in the city."

"I don't have a car. At least not yet."

"Recently get out of prison? You kinda have that look about you."

"Something like that."

"Hey, I get it. I did time too. Drugs, but I've been clean for five years. I like to be up front with people about my prison days. Don't want you to find out later and freak."

This would have been the time to share her recent history, but she suddenly felt too tired to get into it, and she figured he'd find out soon enough. "Do you know anybody with a car to sell? I can't afford much."

"I got a motorcycle I'm trying to unload, but it's a bad time for that. Winter and all. Who the hell buys a motorcycle this time of the year in Minnesota?"

She'd never ridden a motorcycle. Well, she'd ridden *on* one, but she'd never been the one in control. "I might be interested, but I don't know how to ride."

"It's not that hard. I could teach you, or you could take a motor-cycle-safety course. That's what I'd recommend." He sucked on the cigarette, then blew out a cloud of smoke. "Here's a deal. Buy the motorcycle, move in here, and I'll keep the bike running for you."

Three years ago, she would never have considered a motorcycle. How odd that she was thinking about it now.

Downstairs, in a garage that was dark and damp, the cement floor caked with white road salt brought in by car tires, she met the bike. It was pretty. Yellow, with shiny chrome.

"It's a '76 Honda 550," Will said. "You don't see many around here in this shape."

"How much?"

He shot her a price. They haggled a little. He gave up some ground.

"I'll take it," she said.

CHAPTER 6

Y ou no longer work for the department," Uriah said, stating the obvious.

A few days had passed since Jude Fontaine stood him up at the hospital. Today she'd just appeared out of the blue, demanding to see him, with no apology, no explanation of her hospital disappearance. Given her situation, he cut her a lot of slack, didn't blame her, wasn't even angry. Annoyed, yes. But she'd walked out of the hospital on her own, apparently without fear. That took guts.

The two of them had spent the afternoon in a futile attempt to locate the house where she'd been held captive. An hour into the search Uriah realized cruising up and down streets in hopes of spotting something that looked familiar was a waste of time. She didn't have a clue. And how could she? The darkness, combined with her physical and mental state . . . He wasn't sure he would have taken note of his surroundings under those circumstances. Now she sat across from his desk expecting him to turn over the files on every case she'd been working at the time of her abduction.

Since he'd last seen her, the tangle of long white hair had been chopped off. That was the best way to describe it. As if she'd taken a pair of scissors and started cutting a few inches away from her scalp, just like Uriah had wanted to do that first day he'd visited her in the hospital. Now that he thought about it, that's probably exactly what she'd done, but it looked like something someone else might have paid a lot of money for. Funny how that worked. She could almost pass for heroin chic.

"I want to see my old files," she said. "I don't know if my abduction had anything to do with a case, but going over the files is the obvious place to begin."

"We've already done it. When you were abducted. Again yesterday. It's ground that's been covered numerous times. And," he repeated, "you no longer work here."

"I want to see them." Her face was almost expressionless—except for her blue eyes, which were watching him with that unnerving intensity he was afraid might be permanent.

He stared back, but she won.

He supposed her single-minded focus had made her a good detective back in the day, but he was finding it a pain in the ass right now. It was apparent she wasn't leaving until he either caved or was forced to toss her out. Maybe something in between would satisfy her.

"When you were abducted, you were working three major cases." He opened a drawer, pulled out a stack of folders, and dropped them on his desk. "All of them are right here. At my fingertips. A high-profile case you were working with Detective Vang was solved." With a flick of his wrist, he tossed that file aside.

"Solved doesn't necessarily rule out a connection."

"I understand, but you're going to have to trust me when I say we've gone over everything thoroughly."

He stared at her and she stared back. Calm, defiant, waiting. She wasn't leaving unless he produced something to assure her of his diligence.

He and the department had not only failed her; he'd basically taken her job and now he was telling her she couldn't see her own files. All

things considered, she was handling it pretty well. Coming to a decision, he pushed his chair away from the desk and stood up. "Let's go
downstairs."

Together they walked to the elevator. Once inside, he punched "B."

"Everything in your desk ended up in the evidence room," he said
as their car descended and the numbers above the door decreased until
the elevator came to a shuddering stop.

In the basement, they walked to the evidence room. She practically
led the way, making it obvious she remembered the layout of the building and had made this trip many times before.

"I'm going to need to see the Fontaine evidence," Uriah told the
armed guard behind the counter.

Spotting Jude, the officer lit up. Over the years, he'd never so much
as smiled at Uriah. "Hey, Detective Fontaine. Glad to see you're back."

"Thanks, Harold." She gave him something that almost passed as
a smile, but didn't correct him about being back. Back could mean different things, like back in the world, but Harold obviously thought she
was back at Homicide.

"We need to see the evidence pertaining to her abduction," Uriah
told him.

Eyes on the computer monitor, Harold clicked keys. "I see desk
contents, computer and hard drive, clothing, and DNA."

"Let's go with the desk," Uriah said.

While he and Jude waited on the other side of the counter, Harold
vanished into the evidence shelves, returning a couple of minutes later
holding a large brown box with cutout cardboard handles. Uriah signed
the evidence out and carried the box to a private room. Under long
tubes of fluorescent light, he and Jude sat across from each other at what
was the equivalent of a lunchroom table.

"Everything taken from your desk after your abduction," he said,
removing the lid and setting it aside.

"How long was I gone before this was filed?"

It was a question he'd also asked. "Almost immediately, thanks to Chief Ortega."

Jude looked at the chain-of-evidence tag attached to the box. "It's been signed out several times over the years."

"You can see that your case hasn't been neglected."

It had been strange going through the belongings of a missing officer, but it was doubly strange now with her sitting right across from him.

He removed the typical items found in a desk. Pens, pencils, notepads, notebooks. And more-personal things, like photos. A lot of photos. Some were of her, back when her hair was brown, back when her expression wasn't intense and her smile was easy. Pictures of her and her boyfriend, someone Uriah had spoken with two days earlier, confirming what he'd suspected: the guy *and his girlfriend* had been home when Jude showed up expecting a warm welcome. But other than adding to the timeline, the boyfriend had no information to help piece together the puzzle of what had transpired the night of her escape.

Along with the boyfriend, there were photos of Jude with department officers—some he recognized, others he didn't. Most were taken at those common after-duty wind-downs where they'd all leave work and head to a nearby bar. He'd done it a few times, but not often. Not his thing, plus he'd usually been anxious to get home.

Not anymore.

Uriah spread the photos on the table, turning them so they faced her. He was curious about the ones of her and Vang. In some they looked like a couple. But maybe the clinging was just the result of alcohol. Some people got affectionate when they drank.

"Anything in there you think merits a comment?" he asked.

She scanned the photos and shook her head.

"What about this one?" Not his business, nothing to do with anything, but he asked anyway, pointing to a snapshot in which Vang's arm was around her waist. "Were you two dating? I never heard anything about that."

She frowned, then shook her head. "We went out a few times."

"Sleeping together?"

She looked up at him. "That has nothing to do with anything."

"It might. I always thought it curious that Vang never mentioned having a relationship with you."

"That's because we didn't *have* a relationship. It's none of your business."

Yep. Slept together. Never a good idea in any work situation, but cops . . . Bad.

He continued pulling out items until the box was empty and everything was on the table. "The only thing that seemed a little odd was this." He slid another photo across the table. "Remember anything about this girl?"

She picked up the small, square photo, examined it, and shook her head.

"Her name is Octavia Germaine. Not a homicide, a missing person. Not your case."

"Sometimes a Missing Persons case can be a suspected homicide. I'm guessing someone asked me to look into it. Sorry." She slid the photo back. "I don't remember her. Was she ever found?"

"No."

"What about the notebooks?"

"Nothing jumped out at me." He passed the spirals to her. They were the kind kids used in school. Multicolored, wide ruled, almost every page filled with notes and scribbles. It would take hours for someone to read them word for word—maybe days if you really wanted to do a decent job. He'd read them. Not thoroughly, but he'd read them.

She riffled through the pages of one notebook, then another, apparently coming to the same conclusion about the time involved. "If I could take these with me . . ."

"Out of the question. You know that."

"But if I were back in Homicide?"

"Nothing to even consider, because it's not gonna happen."

"Really? And why not? Because of what I've gone through? Because I wasn't smart enough to keep from getting captured?"

"None of those things."

"Because I'm too damaged?"

She watched him in that unnerving way of hers, and he knew the moment her conclusions settled into place. "That's it, isn't it?" she said. "I can see it in your face."

He stacked the notebooks and put them back in the box, then gathered up the photos, all the while feeling her eyes on him. "Homicide probably isn't the place for you," he said.

Don't look, he told himself.

"What *is* the place for me? Where do you see me in a month, Detective Ashby? In six months? Two years? Working at Starbucks? Or behind the counter at a Kwik Trip?"

A new tone in her voice broke his resolve. He looked. She was mad. Maybe that was good, because it replaced her spooky lack of emotion. "Not here," he said quietly and firmly.

"Really? Because I don't see myself anywhere but here." She leaned back in her chair, arms crossed. "Where do you see me? I want to know."

"Enjoying life. Going to movies. Reading. Take up a hobby. If that stuff seems too self-indulgent, then help out at a women's shelter or a food bank. An animal shelter. I dunno." He sorted through the photos, finally finding the image he was looking for—one of her with a teasing smile on her face. Holding the image with two fingers, he turned it around so she could see it. "While you're at it, why not try to find this girl?"

She barely gave the photo a glance. "That girl no longer exists."

"She might."

"She doesn't."

"Sounds like you hate her."

"Maybe I do." She raised her eyebrows, seeming surprised by her own words. "And you're right to call her girl and not woman."

"You need to give yourself a break."

"I resent her for leaving me there for three years." She nodded her chin at the photo he still held. "You know, I used to be funny," she said. "Really funny. I was always making people laugh."

"I've heard that about you." He paused, considering his next words. "You can be funny again."

"I don't think so. I don't think I can be the old me again."

"She might come back. Maybe a little, anyway." He looked her in the eye—something he was getting better at. "Do you want her to?" he asked. "Come back?"

"Kind of. Maybe. I don't know." She hesitated. "The old Jude was weak."

"She couldn't have been that weak. She survived."

"That's true."

"I wonder why we always feel disdain for our old selves," Uriah said. "We should feel thankful. We should appreciate the people we used to be rather than being ashamed of them."

After he returned everything to the box, he replaced the lid and got to his feet, chair scraping the cement floor. "I'll sign this back in, then escort you upstairs." Not his intention, but the word *escort* seemed to drive home the reminder that she was a guest and he'd done her a favor by allowing her to look at the box of evidence.

She let out a sound of disgust and stood up. "You're wrong about me."

"I don't know about that, but I do think you're kind of scary."
He'd question the appropriateness of the word *scary* a little later. "Look,
Jude." He rested the box against his stomach. "You need time to read-
just. It probably feels like weeks to you, but you've only been outside
for a few days. *A few days.* That's nothing. You're a soldier who's come
home from war. You're in transition. You need counseling. You need
to learn how to reenter society. That's the kind of stuff you should be
concentrating on right now. I brought you down here because I wanted
you to see that I've got this." He hoped his words brought her some
small bit of reassurance. "Go home and take care of yourself."

He waited.

And, Jesus. She was staring at him again.

"What kind of soap do you use?" she finally asked.

"What's that?" At first he thought he'd misunderstood. "I don't
know. I just grab something off the shelf and hope it doesn't stink." He
frowned. "Have you been listening to anything I've said?"

"I'm detecting a bit of something sweet, maybe almond."

It took him a few more beats to get it. "Ah, your senses are still in
overdrive."

She nodded. "It's so strange."

"If you don't like any of my other suggestions, maybe you should
consider going into the perfume business. A finely tuned sense of smell
would be a big plus." A joke, but he wasn't sure she'd respond to his
attempt at humor. After all, the reason for her sensitive nose was nothing to laugh about.

She shook her head—and she might have almost smiled. Hard to
tell. But then, delivered in her deadpan way, she said something that
killed him. *Killed* him.

"I've been in a box. Don't put me back in one."

He made a small strangling sound that might or might not have
been a whimper.

"I'm not going to go home and take up knitting," she told him. "I'm going to go to the firing range and work on my shooting skills. I'm going to take a refresher in self-defense. And"—pause—"I'm going to learn to drive a motorcycle."

He was far from being sexist, but he realized that's how he'd come across. Telling her to take up a *hobby*. "I didn't mean to imply that you should go home and keep your mouth shut."

"Really?" she asked. "Because that's exactly what it seems like to me. But don't worry. In a few months I'll return. Not to bug you about the cases you might or might not be looking into, but to get my job back."

CHAPTER 7

His girl.

He called her his girl.

On the second day of her captivity, he found out she journaled, so he brought her a stack of blank books. The cheap kind you could get at the Dollar Store. The pens were shitty too, not the gel ones she liked. The glide of a good gel pen across paper was part of the whole thing.

But what difference did ink make when she was being held in some windowless prison where nobody could hear her screaming for help?

The number of blank journals had been alarming. It meant he planned to keep her a long time. But the number was also a good sign, because she took it to mean he might not kill her, not as long as he kept bringing her journals and she kept filling them.

At first she wrote constantly, keeping track of the passage of days, faithfully winding the clock that had been ticking away in the corner that first day when she'd come to on the mattress. When the month of her seventeenth birthday rolled around, she wrote about how she would have celebrated if she'd been home.

Later she even wrote about the miscarriage, and about how he began supplying her with birth-control pills so it wouldn't happen again. She wondered what he'd done with the fetus. Had he buried it? She obsessed about it, playing out different scenarios in her head.

She wrote about all of that.

Back there in the world, she'd been a bit of a geek. She'd liked poetry and politics and animals. Her senior year of high school she'd raised $1,000 for Walk for the Animals, and she'd marched for marriage equality. She wrote about that too.

One day she realized one of her journals was gone.

He was taking them. He was reading them.

Her deepest thoughts.

For a while she quit writing completely, but pouring out her feelings was the only thing that kept her from losing her mind, so she began writing again—with the knowledge of her audience of one.

She would play with him.

That had been her plan, her objective. To mess with his head, to make him feel remorse for what he'd done and what he was doing, to maybe make him feel guilty enough to let her go.

That was the dream, her fantasy . . .

He had a nice voice. Weird to think that, but it was true. And his body, while it didn't belong to a teenager, wasn't gross. He always smelled clean. But she had no way of knowing what he really looked like. When he brought her food, when he came to retrieve the piss bucket, he wore a black ski mask.

Even though she'd never seen him, she began to imagine a handsome face. And she began to obsess about his visits and about how she could please him and how she would make him fall in love with her.

She wrote about her adoration, and how much he meant to her, and how she lived for the sound of the key in the lock and the sound of his voice and the feel of his hands on her body. But the trick was on her, because she began to believe the words she wrote. Pretty soon, *she* was the one falling in love.

She wrote about that too.

She also wrote about how much *he* loved *her*, and how sad he was about the miscarriage. She wrote poems about him and drew pictures of two people together. She drew pages of hearts.

One day she got up enough nerve to ask him his name.

"What would you like it to be?" he asked.

"Harrison." She thought a moment. "No, Colin."

"That's my name, then."

When they made love—made love was what she'd begun calling it—he'd douse the battery light and remove the mask.

She touched him then, because he let her. Fingers across the whiskered skin of his face. The hair on his head wasn't very long, his lips were soft, his body firm and hard. He had a scar on his right biceps.

"How did you get this?" she asked him one day, her fingers tracing the raised flesh.

"How would you like me to have gotten it?"

"In a shoot-out. In a bank robbery. In a car wreck where you were the only survivor."

"How about a plane crash?"

"That works."

She wrote about that too. The plane crash and how he'd landed the Cessna in the mountains and walked out. It took days, barefoot, in snow, without food, but his arrival in a small village made him a local legend.

These were the stories she created for them, for her, in order to survive.

He was her hero, and she loved him.

He took the journals, but he also brought them back. And pretty soon they were her best record of the passage of time, because she'd lost track of individual days long ago.

The journals grew. They lined the floor and crept up the walls of her windowless room. The stacks became so tall they sometimes tumbled to the floor and she had to restack them, with care, by number, because they were all numbered. Instead of being inside the room for a month or a year, she'd been there for ten journals or twenty journals. And finally two hundred journals.

CHAPTER 8

What do you have against working with Fontaine?"
The question from Chief of Police Vivian Ortega brought
Uriah back around, and he reeled in his mind drift—
something he found himself doing a lot lately. He turned away from the
office window and his contemplation of the streets below. Behind him,
the desks were empty, the other detectives having already hit the streets
for the day, Ortega's plan being for Fontaine to arrive late in order to
ease her in gradually. She'd also nixed the idea of the "welcome back"
cake suggested by Vang.

Just a regular day.

"I've accepted the idea of her working here," Uriah said, "but
why not give her a desk job? I wouldn't trust her to not crack in a
highly stressful situation. Or even a not-so-stressful one. And I sure
as hell don't want her as a partner." He didn't know why the chief
kept trying to pair him up with unlikely people. Maybe Ortega saw
this as a way for Uriah to keep an eye on Fontaine—the last thing
he wanted to do.

"Fontaine's been cleared for duty," Ortega said. "And we need the
manpower. She's been recertified for everything. Taken extra firearms
training. Self-defense. Four months has given the media a chance to

die down and move on to the next big story." She braced her hands against her hips.

Some thought Ortega dressed too sexy for Homicide, with her loose dark hair, long nails, tight skirts, and cleavage-exposing tops, but Uriah gave her credit for doing what she wanted. And Ortega was a role model when it came to balancing life and a job that could be unrelentingly dark.

In the face of everything, she was the epitome of normal. House in a nice neighborhood, two smart kids, two goofy yellow Labs, and a husband who adored her. There was even a push for her to run for mayor. Not a bad idea, Uriah thought.

"Also, let me point out that I keep suggesting partners and you keep turning them down," Ortega said. "I'm not asking anymore. It's our policy that detectives work in pairs."

"What about Vang? Didn't his partner just quit? And he and Fontaine used to work together. Seems the obvious choice."

"I'm not going to defend my decision."

"I just want you to know where I'm coming from. I think it's a bad idea. I've been dealing with her off and on, and she still has that thousand-yard stare." Not to mention the way she continued to examine him whenever they had a conversation. Like she was sniffing out the scent of his soap and counting every hair on his head.

Even though they hadn't had a blackout in months, it was still a war zone out there. People kept comparing the recent increase in crime to the eighties, when Minneapolis was dubbed Murderapolis. Back then, crime had been rampant, and hardly a day had passed without a few shootings. Now, in this throwback world, Uriah needed someone he could trust, someone who'd have his back.

That person wasn't Fontaine.

He regretted that his investigation had been unsuccessful. No DNA match from her abductor's clothing, no full, usable fingerprint, no gun trace, no flagged reports of shots fired, no hospital reporting

a gunshot victim on the night of her escape. The cab driver who'd
given her a ride never came forward, even though the department
had asked for the public's help. After months of investigation, Uriah
had been forced to move on, and Jude Fontaine was once again a cold
case. Failed her again.

Ortega eyed him thoughtfully. "Thousand-yard stare? You could be
describing yourself."

"I'm fine."

Ortega shrugged in disagreement and returned to the bigger issue.
"We might be a city in crisis," she said, "but we owe it to the residents
to do our best. If we all do our parts, we can get back on our feet."

The chief thought they'd recover. Thought they could hit the
"Reset" button. Uriah was beginning to think otherwise. People
had reached a tipping point, and the city no longer felt safe. How
did you recover from that? People, even good cops, were moving
away from the area, and Uriah couldn't blame them. What Ortega
hadn't said, and something that was probably closer to the truth,
was that they had to take help where they could get it, even if it
meant Fontaine.

Ortega glanced across the open floor plan that was Homicide.
"Here she is." A warning. *Act normal. Act like we haven't been talking
about her.*

Fontaine's height always surprised him. She was tall, lean, wearing clothing more appropriate for undercover work—jeans, an ancient
leather motorcycle jacket—and carrying a black helmet. Apparently
she'd checked the motorcycle off her to-do list.

"I like to be out in the open," she explained.

Had she read his mind, or was he getting too damn transparent?

She tucked the helmet under her arm and offered more information. "I like to feel the sun and the wind."

Three years was a lot of sun and wind to catch up on.

He'd heard she was living in what some dramatically referred to as the crime zone—an area southeast of downtown in a neighborhood that had once been on the rebound but now, thanks to the blackouts and an increase in crime, was in need of new blood and revival. Something the mayor was working on, but his promises were beginning to sound more hollow all the time. Decent citizens were leaving. Criminals were staying. And then there were the people like him and Fontaine, the ones who probably had nowhere else to go.

But she wouldn't be around long. He'd give her a week, tops.

CHAPTER 9

While the disapproving shadow that was Uriah Ashby loomed nearby, Jude shook hands with Chief Ortega and thanked the woman for letting her return on a trial basis.

"Good luck on your first day back," Chief Ortega said. "Take it slow. Communicate with me. Keep me in the loop." Pausing on the way to her office, she said, "And remember. Even though you two are partners, Detective Ashby is in charge."

Having her assigned as his partner had to be his worst nightmare. The old Jude would have thought the whole thing funny since no one had been more adamantly against her return than Ashby. In the past, she would have immediately set about proving him wrong. Today's Jude accepted the pairing without feeling the need to prove anything to anybody.

"You can have that spot." Ashby pointed to a gray metal desk tucked away in a corner. The location was probably meant to be some form of punishment or an insult, but she wouldn't have wanted her old desk in the middle of a sea of people.

As she moved toward the corner, he continued: "Just got a report of a female body found floating in Lake of the Isles."

So much for taking it slow. He was testing her. A body before she'd as much as put a notebook or paper clip away.

"It's in a high-crime zone," he added.

"I'm not afraid of high-crime zones." Something told her this wasn't news to him. She settled the helmet on her desk and attached her badge to her belt. Turning back to him, she said, "I *live* in a high-crime zone."

"Is that wise?"

"I need space. Skyway living isn't for me." She couldn't imagine herself in some glass-enclosed human Habitrail even if the elevated walkways did connect most of the downtown buildings. "Suburban living isn't for me either."

"So you'd rather be out there, with the criminals?" he asked.

She nodded. "Yep." She watched him, unblinking.

"I don't live *in* the skyway," he said. "My apartment complex is attached to the skyway. It's easy. Convenient. And I don't like cold weather."

"Minnesota isn't an ideal place to live if you don't like brutal temps."

"I transferred here."

"From where?"

"Southern Minnesota."

"Farm boy?"

"Farm country."

"Cold in southern Minnesota too."

"Not as bad as Minneapolis."

They left the office and walked side by side down the hall toward the elevators. They made an odd pair with him in his suit, her in jeans and leather jacket. "Truth?" Uriah asked. "I don't like breaking in new partners, which means I'm looking for a long-term relationship. That ain't gonna happen if you live in a high-crime zone. Why invite trouble?"

She got the feeling that where she chose to live wasn't his biggest gripe. He expected her to fail. He expected her to be out of there in a few days, and he thought the harder he pushed, the more quickly it would happen. "I have no plans to die soon, and I don't have to prove anything to you. As you pointed out, after being held prisoner for three years I still had the resourcefulness to escape. I'd say that's all the résumé you need from me. And it's not as bad out there as you think."

"I know how bad it is. And four months isn't enough time to recover," he added. "I'd still have my doubts after a year."

She had her own doubts, if she was honest. If people could see inside her head, some might consider her unsound. Maybe that's what he was getting at. A sound person wouldn't be living where she was living. "I passed my mental-health evaluation."

He smiled slightly. "Not that hard to do."

Jude wasn't like Ashby. She understood that. Not only because of who she was and what had happened to her and what those events had done to her core being, which was to muffle her and dilute her and forever change her, but also because the damaged substation that had led to the blackouts and the destruction of parts of the city was the very thing that had set her free.

Ashby had mentioned her safety, but the thing was, most people tended to leave her alone. Like the crazy person wearing headphones to block out the voices, she gave off something that bothered people, something that told them she was different. And when everything was boiled down, maybe she had nothing left to fear. Maybe that's what really set her apart from everyone else. Her fearlessness born of ambivalence, not bravery, because she'd lived through some of the darkest stuff a person could live through.

Been there, done that.

Three Years of Torture and All I Got Was This Lousy T-Shirt.

From the corner of her eye, she caught a blur of movement as a body hurled itself at her, arms wrapping around, holding tight. Her mind recoiled, threatened to shut down. She reached for the gun at her waist, then stopped, realizing the arms belonged to someone she knew.

"Jude. My God, it's good to see you back," Grant Vang said. "I tried to call you. I left messages."

"I got them." She didn't explain that she'd been avoiding him since his hospital visit. That she'd lost the skill of casual conversation and speaking to Grant on the phone would have been uncomfortable. She might find herself pretending for him, trying to channel the person she once was. For him. She couldn't allow that.

Grant set her away from him, hands still on her arms while Ashby stood to the side, watching the exchange.

Ashby had been right about her and Vang sleeping together. A mistake, something that had happened before she and Eric got serious. "I'm glad you're still in Homicide. Ashby tells me a lot of people are leaving."

He smiled. "Where'm I gonna go? I grew up in Saint Paul—city dude through and through." He linked his thumbs in his belt. "I tried to talk Chief Ortega into pairing us up," he said. "Figured since we were partners before, but she wouldn't budge."

That had been Jude's doing. She'd asked to work with someone who didn't know her, someone who wouldn't compare her to the Jude Fontaine she used to be. She just hadn't expected that person to be Uriah Ashby.

The elevator dinged and the doors separated. Jude recalled past social skills and managed to tell Grant good-bye as she and her new partner stepped inside the elevator to take it to the parking garage.

CHAPTER 10

They exited the parking ramp in an unmarked vehicle. It was nice to see residents walking and riding bikes, and yet the city felt darker and sadder than Jude remembered. It was hard to believe that a series of blackouts had brought about such change. And yet she shouldn't have been surprised. Not after what she'd been through. *People do awful things to one another.* The question was, had she lost faith in humanity?

It didn't take long to arrive at their destination.

Lake of the Isles was located in Minneapolis, northwest of Uptown. Once an area of wealth, it now ranked up there with neighborhoods hit hardest by fires and vandalism, with blocks of mansions reduced to crumbling, burnt-out shells. Before the blackouts, people strolled around the oddly shaped lake in envy of the mansions that overlooked the water. There was no envy now.

"I used to walk around this lake," Jude said. In that other life. With Eric. Like a couple in a magazine. Like a dream she could only half recall.

Uriah pulled to a stop behind the coroner's van, cutting the engine. Yellow crime-scene tape had been strung, and a crowd of observers had gathered.

Seat belts unlatched. Doors slammed.

One of the first things Jude noticed was a difference in tone from crime scenes of the past. Where was the hushed reverence? The respect and sorrow? This felt . . . salacious, with people shoving one another, jockeying for a good viewing position while a few cops stood nervously at the perimeter, trying to contain the crowd.

She recognized the coroner—a young woman with black hair that stopped at her chin. Seeing another familiar face gave Jude a jolt. She didn't like the reminders of her old life.

One of the first officers on the scene—male, about forty—met them. "Kids were walking around the lake and spotted the body. Female, young, probably happened last night. Bystanders fished her out before we could get her in a bag, so the body has been compromised. Crime-scene team is gathering evidence on the shore."

"Likely cause of death?" Uriah asked.

"Suicide is my uneducated guess."

Uriah made a faint sound of distress that Jude failed to understand. The officer pointed with his thumb. "Take a gander."

The deceased was young, probably not over seventeen. Dressed in a white nightgown, wet and clinging to the nude body beneath. Blue lips, long hair the color of dandelions.

Upon seeing the detectives, the two crime-scene officers backed off to give them full access to the body, one of the team passing out black latex gloves.

Jude tugged on the gloves and crouched next to the dead girl, the world fading as she focused on the body. The officer was right. She hadn't been in the water long, and she hadn't been dead long. Except for the blue lips and a hint of creamy eye, she could be sleeping.

Around the girl's neck was a cheap necklace. Jude turned the pendant over. A heart, engraved with the name Delilah.

"Is that the kind you can get from a machine at a carnival?" Uriah asked.

"I think so." She remembered using the very type of machine at a tourist stop in northern Minnesota. You put money in the slot and spelled out your name on a keypad. Then, through a glass window, you could watch the engraving. Once done, the necklace dropped into a receptacle to be scooped up.

Jude did a quick visual exam, her gaze moving from the top of the girl's head to her feet. Acting on impulse, she gently touched the back of the hand nearest her. She had the overwhelming desire to pull the girl into her arms and hug her close. Instead, she grasped her hand very gently.

"What are you doing?" Ashby whispered loudly as he leaned over her shoulder. Gone was all evidence of the panic he'd displayed earlier.

"Holding her hand," Jude said.

"Why?"

She shrugged. "I want to."

"Bloody hell." Words delivered in an exhale as he straightened away from her. "That's enough." He gave her a *come here* wave. "Up."

Jude didn't move. "We should cover her with a blanket."

"She's dead. She can't feel anything. She can't feel cold, and she can't feel sad, and she can't feel lonely."

Jude looked up at him. "I know she's dead, but she's telling me something."

Uriah squeezed his eyes shut. Seconds passed. Once he got himself under control, he zeroed back in on her. Behind him, the sky was blue as only a Minnesota sky could be, and off in the distance birds sang so cheerfully Jude could almost see the notes floating in the air.

"You'd better be glad I'm the only one hearing what's coming out of your mouth right now," Uriah said.

Their first hour of partnership was getting off to a rocky start. "I don't think this is a suicide," Jude said.

"Look." Uriah crouched next to her. With impatience masked as patience, he pulled a fold of wet fabric aside, revealing a pocket in the nightgown tangled around the body. The girl could have been one of those beautiful marble statues at the Minneapolis Institute of Art. "Rocks," he said. "Her pockets are full of rocks."

Jude focused on the girl, experiencing the crime scene from the viewpoint of the person she was now, and not the cop she used to be. In the months since her escape, she'd struggled to ignore the heightened awareness, that bombardment of sight and sounds and odors, because those revved-up senses got in the way of everyday life. Now, though, she realized she was picking up information much in the same way she'd picked up information from Uriah, much in the same way she'd picked up information from her captor. The dead girl had a story to tell, and she was telling it to Jude.

"Not a homicide," Uriah said. "Not our case." He stood and circled away from her, then returned. "Not every death is a murder. She filled her pockets with rocks and walked into the lake. Rocks. Lake."

"I think it was meant to look like a suicide." Now Jude looked at him, gauging his reaction.

"And how, after a two-minute cursory exam, did you arrive at this theory?"

"She's telling me things."

"My God." He glanced over his shoulder. "Don't say that kind of nonsense out loud. She's dead," he said. *"Dead."*

"Yes, but what she was feeling before she died is written on her face and in her muscles. It's still here. *I* see it. I can *read* her."

He let out a snort. "Anything else she's saying?"

Jude wanted to stroke the girl's hair in a comforting gesture but restrained herself so as not to disturb evidence. "Fear. She was terrified before she died." Jude knew and understood that kind of fear. That kind of fear was caused by someone else.

"If she's telling you so damn much, maybe she'll give you a full name and address."

Jude ignored his sarcasm. It didn't matter. The body was all that mattered. She gently placed the girl's hand back at her side, then stood up and looked into the distance, to a curve in the lake where the sunshine made a repeated pattern on the surface of the water, to the white sails moving in a skilled dance. The day was beautiful, and that made the death even sadder.

"Your name means *light*," she told Uriah. An odd and misplaced comment, yet the words were her attempt at momentarily shifting his attention to something else, away from his annoyance, offering a new place for his thoughts to land. She turned. "Do you ever think about that?"

His expression went through several transformations until his shoulders sagged. "Damn it, Jude." He spoke quietly and calmly. "I can't begin to grasp what you've been through, but you aren't ready for this. You might never be ready for this. You should go home. The department offered you a severance package. Take it. Why do this when you don't need to?"

"Why are *you* doing it?"

The wind kicked up, bringing with it the scent of charred wood. He stared at her for a long moment. "It's all I know how to do."

"Me too."

A moment passed as they sized each other up.

"It's not as crazy as it sounds," she finally explained, deciding she would share a little bit with him, but only a little. "I didn't read her dead mind. It's not anything psychic. I spent three years in solitary confinement. I had no books, no music, no movies, no color. The only thing I had was one evil man's face and body, and reading him became my entire existence. I lived for his visits, for the stimulation. Every line, every nuance, every muscle contraction, every flicker of thought—I read him. And I can read this girl even though she's dead. I know that sounds weird, but echoes of her experience are frozen in her face and in her muscles."

The explanation placated him, and she could see she was making more sense. "Can you read living people?" he asked, searching for confirmation of thoughts formed and unformed. "Can you read me?"

She didn't think it wise to mention that she'd read him moments earlier when the first responder had spoken the word *suicide*. Jude had seen the quake that Uriah quickly hid. She didn't tell him she'd read him every time she'd met with him at the police station. She didn't tell him she knew he was feeling sorry for her all over again right this minute because the full impact of what she'd been through was slowly and continuously sinking in. And maybe that was part of his reluctance to have her around. She was a constant reminder of unspeakable acts and unspeakable pain, all wrapped up in his failure to find her or close the case. "Kindness," she said. "That's what I see."

"Really? Kindness?" The annoyance was back. "That's a pretty worthless trait."

"Would you say it's inaccurate? I'd like to know. While I was in that basement, my brain was rewired, and what I see as one thing might be something else entirely."

"Kindness is a weakness, especially today, especially for a cop," he said, not answering her question.

He was right. If she'd only been tougher, stronger . . . "But kindness is a trait we can't lose." She frowned, concentrating. "It might be one of the most important parts of being human. Maybe even more important than love."

He was staring at her again, long and hard, harsh lines between his eyes, almost as if he were trying to read her right back. "I can't believe we're standing here having this conversation. You really are certifiable, aren't you?"

CHAPTER 11

That evening, like so many evenings, Jude rode her motorcycle over streets she'd been up and down a hundred times in her search for the house where she'd been held captive. Not that she wanted to visit the place she'd rather forget, but because she needed to walk through that door and see the man's rotting corpse on the basement floor.

Confirmation of death.

Five male bodies wound up in the morgue the night of the blackout. None was her guy. So she kept trying to find the house, constantly broadening her search zone. Nothing. Which led her to believe the body was still at the bottom of the stairs, or it had been disposed of in secret.

Or the man was still alive.

She wanted a name. She wanted a rap sheet. Only then would she begin to piece together why he'd abducted her in the first place, because deep down she'd felt that it hadn't been some obsession or some random act.

In her need for proof of death, she imagined putting up flyers that said, *Have you noticed an ungodly stench coming from your neighbor's house?* Below that would be tear-off phone numbers. How long would it take for the numbers to be gone? Days? Hours? Because who didn't have a suspicious neighbor?

She searched for a certain building style because over the years she'd constructed a layout and design in her mind, but the house could have been made of wood or brick or stucco or straw. It could have been one story or two stories. She had no memory of her arrival, and she'd escaped in darkness, not a star in the sky, her mind a tangle, her body so weak she could barely put one foot in front of the other. Taking note of any small landmark hadn't seemed a priority. Escape, getting home, had been a priority. But now . . .

She didn't know what the house looked like, but that didn't stop her. Almost every evening she rode the streets, coming home to mark off sections of the detailed city map she'd taped to the wall of her apartment as she methodically took her search into new, unexplored areas. And every evening she failed to find anything that felt right.

Despite the grimness of her quest, she was encouraged by what she saw riding through neighborhoods touched by the blackouts, and she took a vicarious pride in the signs of returning culture: the street vendors and food trucks, the bohemian cafés, the diners and bars and sidewalk gardens.

Back home for the night, she ran into Will in the hallway.

"How's the bike running?" he asked.

"No problems." After selling her the motorcycle, Will had helped her find a class and get a license. He'd also taught her several things about maintenance, but she understood he was using the bike as a way to interact with her. She made a point of being polite, but not overly friendly.

In her apartment, without removing her gun from her belt, she ate a solitary meal of grocery-store sushi. When she was done and her plate rinsed, she washed her face and brushed her teeth. Upon returning to the kitchen, she grabbed a can of cat food from the cupboard for the feral she'd been feeding, tucked a pillow under her arm, and looped a finger under the nylon strap of her rolled sleeping bag. She left her apartment, locking it behind her and pocketing the keys, to head up the narrow stairway to the roof.

Outside, she unrolled the sleeping bag, dropped the pillow, and settled under the night sky.

From the street below came sounds of traffic. In the distance, shouts. A restaurant had opened down the block, and she could smell the grill exhaust.

It was never dark on the roof, and there was rarely a night when she could see many stars. Too many city lights, their number increasing in the fight to stop vandalism, but tonight the moon was visible. Half of it, anyway.

She slipped her gun from the holster and placed it next to her sleeping bag. Then she peeled off the metal top from the can of cat food. Stretching, she placed the can a few feet away, rolled to her back, stared up at the moon, and thought about the girl in the lake.

CHAPTER 12

Dressed in protective gowns, face shields in place, Uriah and his new partner followed the Hennepin County medical examiner into the autopsy suite, where the body of the young girl waited under a white sheet.

They now had a full ID. Delilah Masters. From a wealthy family, attended a private school.

Uriah made a choking sound behind his plastic face shield. The ME, a big blond woman of about fifty, named Ingrid Stevenson, didn't bat an eye at the overwhelming stench. Jude didn't seem to notice either, but then again he couldn't recall her physically reacting to anything other than the visit from her brother. Her current lack of response to the odor told a darker story of abuse conditioning. Captives learned the art of no reaction in order to remove the cause and effect of torture, the joy experienced by the torturer.

"I have to apologize for the air quality," Ingrid said. "Our air system is acting up. My husband had me take off my clothes before I stepped from the garage into the house last night. Even after I showered, he still complained."

Uriah tried to breathe shallowly through his mouth. That made him feel light-headed.

"I know it's unpleasant, but this won't take long," Ingrid said. "I have a few things I thought you should see."

She moved deeper into the room, motioning for them to follow. "What I wanted to show you . . ." She pulled back the sheet, uncovering the girl with the dandelion hair. "Cutting." She pointed. "Self-mutilation." The girl's stomach was a crisscross of scars.

"Recent?" Uriah asked.

"Some fairly new, but some older."

"How much older?"

"Years. On top of the cutting, I found signs of sexual abuse. Bruising and tissue damage. Some old scarring, but some recent. Maybe less than twenty-four hours old."

Uriah looked at Jude. He could see she was thinking her theory had merit. In reality, it meant suicide was all the more likely. The poor girl had been in mental distress for a long time. Add sexual abuse to that . . .

"Also, her lungs were filled with water."

"Drowning," Uriah said. No surprise there.

"Lake water?" Jude asked.

"I'm glad you brought that up." Ingrid pushed the overhead lamp aside. "The water we found in her lungs had a high level of chlorine in it."

That was unexpected. "Interesting." Uriah might have to toss everything he'd been thinking about suicide. Also? No sign of gloat on Jude's face. He had to give her credit for that. And no mention of body reading. He'd give her credit for that too. Right now it seemed to be their little secret. He hoped to keep it that way—something that surprised him, given his feelings about Jude coming on board in the first place. One whisper of her "gift" and she'd be out of there. Ortega would see it as proof of Jude's instability.

"So she drowned, or was drowned, most likely in a swimming pool," he said.

"That's correct. There's no freshwater in her lungs. She was dead before she was put in the lake."

"Anything else? Signs of struggle?"

"Nothing under the nails, but there's bruising on the arms that might or might not be significant."

"Drugs?"

"No signs of needle usage, but we're running toxicology labs." Ingrid covered the body. "Should have the results in a couple of days."

"Thanks."

Uriah bailed from the room, ripped off his mask, and gulped air—immediately regretting it, since the prep room smelled almost as bad as the autopsy suite. Jude followed at a leisurely pace.

"You were right," Uriah said once they were outside, in the unmarked car, heading to the girl's house to interview the parents. A cold call—nobody would be expecting them.

"What do you think? A relative? Boyfriend?" Jude asked. "Assaults her, then, fearing she'll tell someone, drowns her, fills her pockets with rocks, and tosses her in the lake to make it look like suicide?"

"A valid theory."

The GPS told him to turn. He turned.

"So you approve of my outfit?" Jude asked.

Like most things about her, the unexpected question was unnerving. When she'd arrived at the department that morning, he'd been surprised to see her wearing something almost stylish: black pants, a white shirt, and a black fitted jacket. Uriah wasn't into clothes, but in their job it was important to have the right threads. A suit generated a certain amount of respect for the position.

"I never said anything about how you were dressed yesterday."

"You didn't have to."

"Of course not."

"I'd planned on seeing what my boyfriend had done with my clothes, but I kept putting it off. And then I realized none of it would fit me anymore anyway."

"You could get them altered. I know a guy in Uptown. Believe it or not, I got this suit at a vintage shop. He modernized it."

"I think it's better if I start fresh. New person, new clothes."

He wanted to say that starting over wasn't always the answer, or starting over was hard, or starting over didn't really fix anything, or starting over was just a delusion, but he kept his mouth shut.

"You okay?" Jude asked.

Reading him. The suicide stuff had thrown him, and it was obvious she could tell something was off. He didn't know if he should lie when she'd know he was lying, or tell the truth—which was just too personal. And anyway, she'd find out about him soon enough.

"I'm not okay," he said, settling on the truth. "But I can't discuss it."

What he didn't say was that he couldn't talk about it because of what she'd been through. He deserved none of her sympathy. None. He knew that, but damn.

Now she was frowning, watching him, picking up on something in his face. "Did I say something? Do something?" she asked.

"No."

"I'm sensing you're holding back."

"Just because we're partners doesn't mean we have to share everything." Harsh. As soon as the words were spoken, he regretted them.

The victim was from the Tangletown area of Minneapolis. Upper-middle class, nice lawns, most of the houses Tudor-style or what Ellen had called witch houses. The brass frog knocker made a dull thud when it hit the burgundy door. Genevieve Masters, Delilah's mother, answered. Her hair wasn't the color of dandelions but had instead been lightened and expensively processed, her roots a darker blond.

Uriah pulled out his badge and made introductions while Jude offered condolences. He was surprised by her genuine effort to reach out to the woman. And she didn't stop there. "Mind if we come in?" Jude asked.

They got a death stare until the request finally sank in and the woman took a step back, opening the door wider. "I don't understand,"

Mrs. Masters said. "Delilah committed suicide. Why would homicide detectives be here?"

A young boy appeared from around the corner. "Aren't we leaving?" he asked, skateboard under his arm, hair on the long side.

"In a little bit, honey," his mother said. "The police just want to talk to me."

"They already did."

"It's okay. Go on outside. We'll leave in a few minutes."

Once he was gone, she turned to them and said, "He's not taking this very well. I thought going to a friend's might be a good idea." Her voice faded as she questioned her decision. "Get him out of the house."

"That's okay," Uriah said.

The woman wandered to the couch and sat down. Uriah and Jude followed, taking a seat in the two overstuffed chairs. Between them was an oval table.

Mrs. Masters seemed to pull up a memory of what a hostess should do and say. "Would you like something to drink?" When Jude and Uriah shook their heads, her shoulders sagged in relief.

"First of all," Jude said, "we're terribly sorry for your loss." She glanced at Uriah, and he gave her a slow blink. Better for her to break the news, and she'd done a good job so far. He had the feeling Mrs. Masters would be more receptive hearing it from a woman.

"You asked why we're here." Jude leaned forward, elbows on her knees, eyes locked with the mother who'd just lost a child. "We have reason to believe your daughter's death wasn't suicide."

A sluggish move toward understanding as Genevieve Masters's thoughts sifted through everything she'd dealt with in the past twenty-four hours and struggled to make sense of this new information. "I don't understand. Yesterday I was told it was a suicide."

"We just came from the autopsy," Jude said. "And preliminary evidence indicates she might not have died by her own hand."

The air left the room. Mrs. Masters clutched her throat and stared at Jude in horror.

It was weird how suicide had most likely seemed unbearable just moments ago. Now the death had gone from being something Delilah's mother felt she should have seen coming—something a mother should have been able to stop—to this new thing, this even more unbearable thing.

"What . . . ? How . . . ?"

But she didn't really want to know. They never wanted to know.

Jude glanced at Uriah, and he saw a brief flash of self-doubt in her eyes before she looked down at her clasped hands, pulling herself together. Because it wasn't about them. Their job was to deliver the information in the most compassionate way possible while maintaining the stability of the room. He wished the husband had been home. They should have waited. Come back. Let her take the kid to his friend's. What would a few hours matter? And yet Jude was doing a good job. If they'd waited, someone else might have delivered the news. Someone who wasn't as good at it, like a reporter.

"She didn't drown in the lake," Jude said. "Which leads us to believe someone might have killed her." She didn't mention the sexual assault. That was good. Let it come later, once Mrs. Masters processed this new information.

"Do you know of anyone who might want to harm your daughter?" Uriah asked. Too abrupt, but sometimes a direct question actually helped. It gave the shocked survivor something to think about.

"No." She frowned and shook her head in protest. "People loved her. My daughter was an angel."

Something that might or might not be true.

"Did she have any enemies?" Jude asked. "Maybe at school?"

"I'm sure she didn't get along with everybody, but Delilah was popular. Friendly. Well liked." She looked from Jude to Uriah, and he could see her thoughts clarifying. "She had rocks in her pockets." Suicide.

"We know," Uriah said evenly. "We think someone else put them there."

"Do you have a child, Detective? No? Do either of you have a child? I didn't think so."

This is how it often played out. The attack. And that was okay. That was fine, although Uriah was now feeling a little guilty for allowing Jude to take the brunt of it. The person delivering the news never left unscathed.

They asked Mrs. Masters the standard questions, along with a request for names and addresses of people her daughter had been in close contact with.

"Did Delilah have a job?" Jude asked as she folded a piece of paper containing the list of classmates.

"No, but she volunteered."

"Where?"

"A nursing home."

They learned the husband had moved out recently and was living in a condo in Edina. Then they asked to search Delilah's room. Mrs. Masters led them upstairs and down a hallway with a long oriental rug, stopping in front of a white door. She pushed it open to reveal a typical teenager's room.

Transfixed, she stared into the space, then finally whispered, "I can't bear to be in here." Her voice trembled. "I have to leave. Try not to disturb anything." She backed out of the room. "I want it left just the way it is."

Mothers of dead children were the most likely to shrine, although Uriah had witnessed the behavior among the relatives of adult victims too. The opposite of shrining was packing every memory out of sight and either remodeling the house or moving. "We'll be careful," he said.

They searched the dresser and bed; then Uriah moved to Delilah's laptop while Jude read her diary.

Everything seemed almost boringly commonplace. Jude reported that the diary was filled with the expected entries: writing about friends and writing about boys and writing about classes and movies and music and bands.

Fifteen minutes later, Uriah was about to declare the search a bust when Jude spoke his name in a way that got his attention. He glanced up from the computer as she tapped the diary, head bowed.

"She keeps referring to a nameless person." Jude read passages aloud. "'We finally did it.' Then later, she says, 'He wants to see me again. I snuck out last night. Lola likes him too, but I think it's because he's old enough to buy her beer, not to mention other stuff.' Frowny face."

"Beer?" Uriah said. "So not a classmate."

They bagged and tagged the laptop and diary. Downstairs, they asked about Delilah's cell phone.

"I haven't seen it," Genevieve said. "I didn't even think about it." She gave Uriah her daughter's number, then promised to look for the phone.

They asked about the beer-buying man. Mrs. Masters was surprised by the question and obviously knew nothing. Outside, as the detectives walked toward the car, Uriah called downtown and told their private-data specialist to obtain cell records for Delilah Masters and also see if her current phone location could be pinpointed.

With the list of names given to them by Mrs. Masters, they drove to the high school, where they met with the principal. The girls on the list were brought into a private room one at a time to talk to the detectives. All but the girl named Lola Holt.

"She's absent today," the principal explained.

"We really need to talk to her," Jude said.

The school secretary gave them the address of an impressive colonial located in the affluent Bryn Mawr neighborhood, just a few minutes from downtown Minneapolis. At first no one answered the door. Finally

a woman opened it a crack—enough for them to display their badges
and introduce themselves. The air smelled like freshly mowed grass,
wood chips, and fertilizer.

"I know who you are, and I want you to stay away from my daughter," the woman said. "She doesn't want to talk to you. She doesn't know
anything."

"It's our understanding that she was a friend of Delilah Masters."

"They weren't friends. Lola was forbidden to go anywhere with
Delilah. Delilah was a bad influence, and they hadn't associated in
months."

"Why exactly was she a bad influence?" Jude asked.

"She drank and smoked and did drugs. And that's just the stuff I
know about. You're the detectives. Figure it out." The door slammed.

As they walked back down the sidewalk, Jude glanced at the house.
"Lola is in there. I just saw a curtain move upstairs."

"She's scared," Uriah said. "Let's give her time; then we'll try again.
I'd rather not have to bring her in for questioning. We'll get better
information from her if she gives it willingly."

Back in the office, they spent the rest of the day following up on
leads, finally calling it quits long after everyone else had gone home.

Home.

Not a place Uriah looked forward to going, because could an apartment ever really feel like home? He hadn't been living downtown long,
and for all his defense of it, he wondered what he'd been thinking. In
retrospect, he could see he'd done the opposite of shrining. He'd boxed
up everything, sold the house, and moved, hoping to leave his pain
behind. But that decision now felt like a mistake that only amplified
his grief and sense of loss.

CHAPTER 13

Uriah had always been fond of Emerson Tower—a downtown building that had once been one of the tallest in Minneapolis—but he'd never imagined living in it. Art deco, ornate trim, Italian marble, African mahogany, wrought iron, gold doorknobs, the structure itself patterned after the Washington Monument, with rooms that got smaller with each floor.

After the substation was hit and crime went rampant, the hotel rooms in the Emerson had been converted into apartments. The downtown conversion of hotels to living spaces was part of the mayor's "Stay in the City" campaign, his theory being it was safer in the heart of the city, where police patrols were dense. Uriah agreed, but so far the plan didn't seem to be working all that well. Even though the units were affordable, half the apartments in the Emerson were empty.

He remembered coming to this area of Minneapolis when he was a kid. His parents had warned him to stick close as they gripped his hand tightly. Their nervousness had transmitted to him, but he'd never been scared. What he'd felt was excitement. It didn't matter where it came from, whether it was the guy on the corner talking to himself, the dude crawling along the road growling and barking, the hookers, or the street people. The whole foreign world excited him. It was so different from his hometown—a place that on the surface appeared

boringly conservative and safe. Of course he now knew no place was
safe, but as a kid, his hometown had seemed the old-school version of
middle-class America.

When relatives visited, his parents had felt compelled to take them
on a trip to the big city, the dark city, full of crime and filth and sex
and drugs. And Prince.

And then Block E came along. Sort of an eradication. The homeless, the street people, the druggies, the whores, the panhandlers, the
street musicians, the hippies, the crust punks—they were all chased
away, to be replaced by Target, a movie theater nobody went to, and a
parking ramp nobody parked in. And so this . . . this new Minneapolis
was actually a throwback and maybe even a correction. Uriah would
never voice those thoughts aloud, but there was a part of him that
took pleasure in the return of the true character of the city. Reverse
gentrification.

And now the city was his home. And a giant building that had
loomed over his young self was where he lived. It was both odd and
comforting to wonder if he'd felt his own future presence on those family trips to Minneapolis all those years ago.

Ten hours after he and Jude visited Delilah Masters in the autopsy
suite, Uriah entered his apartment building through a skyway revolving
door that spit him onto the mezzanine. One floor down, the street-level
lobby was deserted. No surprise. It was late; the hucksters and vendors
had packed up their carts and gone home.

The day had been crazy and long, and reentering the building
gave him a sense of skewed time. It seemed like he'd been gone a
week.

Uriah ignored the elevator and instead hiked the stairs to the seventeenth floor. He was getting faster.

The scent of curry and garlic permeated the hallway—a sign of
life behind closed doors. In his cramped apartment, he hung up his
suit and pulled on a pair of ragged jeans and a well-worn T-shirt. He

grabbed a beer from the refrigerator, along with a take-out container of sweet-potato fries. He settled on the couch, hunched over the laptop on the coffee table, and ate the cold fries and drank the beer. Opening Facebook, he typed Delilah Masters's name in the search box, clicking through to the dead girl's profile.

Like a lot of teens' pages, hers was filled with selfies and girlfriend photos. He was especially interested in the group photos. Most of the people were tagged, so he pulled a pad of paper close.

She had just under three hundred friends. He began by visiting their pages one at a time, jotting down the names of people who might merit a visit from the police.

Some kids in her class had profiles that embraced violence. He wrote down those names. Under "Family," he found Delilah's parents and younger brother, along with other relatives. Movie and music choices weren't unusual for a seventeen-year-old girl. A lot of photos of animals, mostly cats but also dogs. And, as to be expected, people leaving either condolences for her family or comments that spoke directly to Delilah.

Uriah went through those too, especially names that recurred several times in a thread. The face that came up the most belonged to the girl they'd been unable to interview earlier that day, Lola Holt. And, despite Mrs. Holt's insistence that the two were no longer friends, it appeared they'd hung out not long before Delilah's death.

He made a note to contact Genevieve Masters about getting the log-in to her daughter's Facebook page in order to read her private messages. If she couldn't provide it ASAP, they'd have to issue a warrant.

Done with the Masters girl, he started to close the laptop, his hand on the lid.

He wasn't a fan of Facebook. Too busy, and he had no interest in sharing himself with old friends or new friends or people he didn't know or barely knew. And being a cop, he had to be careful.

But years ago Ellen had set up a page against his protests. Wasn't anybody's business what he was doing—that's what he'd said at the time.

"Everybody should be on Facebook," she'd told him.

Now he logged in. Below a photo of him, shirtless, on a dock, holding a catfish, were the words *In a relationship*.

His profile looked empty in comparison to most Facebook pages. No movies. No music. Very few friends. On the left, he clicked the "Family" tab to find the usual suspects: his parents, his brother.

Ellen.

He clicked her name. That click took him to her page, and there she was, smiling at him.

He swallowed, stared. Took a drink of beer. And another drink of beer, finishing off the bottle, staring at the screen, finally clicking the "Photo" tab to scroll through images, most of Ellen, but many of the two of them together. Vacations. Family events. Just hanging out. One had been taken at his parents' house, Ellen sprawled across his lap, laughing up at him.

They'd made love shortly after that, in the bedroom he'd slept in as a kid, laughing as they tried to be quiet.

Seeing the photos, remembering, hurt in kind of a good way, and he suddenly understood how Delilah Masters might have felt when she'd dragged a razor blade across her stomach.

It took a while, but he went through every picture. Once the pain began to subside, once the numbness fell over his heart once again, he read the comments people had left. It was like the Delilah Masters page, with words written directly to Ellen most of the time:

I miss you.

Gone too soon.

I miss your sweet, smiling face.

Most from people he didn't even know.

Nobody mentioned suicide. Nobody ever mentioned suicide. And maybe it didn't matter. Maybe it mattered only to him. The *why*.

She'd seemed so happy. That's what got him.

The department psychologist tried to tell him it wasn't his fault. That Ellen was ultimately responsible for the choice she'd made.

What really drove him crazy was that he'd never seen it coming. Not a hint. Not a *fucking* hint. What kind of husband didn't know his wife was in pain?

A shitty husband. A husband who was wrapped up in his job.

He'd been relieved to hear the Masters girl hadn't been a suicide. A stupid reaction, because a homicide was every bit as horrifying as suicide, but the people left behind had to cope in a different way. He'd been relieved because it meant he wouldn't have to deal with that reminder of Ellen. And when they were talking to Mrs. Masters, he caught himself almost saying, *At least it wasn't suicide*, because she'd be able to turn her pain outward rather than inward. The blame wouldn't be her blame, but instead maybe the fault of a society that couldn't get its act together. In truth, the loss of a loved one was a pain that never stopped, no matter how it happened. No matter the hand behind the deed.

He read everything on Ellen's page, starting long before her death a year ago, before they'd moved from southern Minnesota to Minneapolis, before she'd started taking classes at the U, everything written as if it were happening now. And the photos. The goddamn photos . . .

Uriah and me skating at the Depot.

First day of classes at the University of Minnesota, Folwell Hall.

When he got to the day she started Facebook, he wasn't ready for his visit to end. He didn't want to leave or get sucked back out into the world where Ellen no longer existed. Maybe there was more. Maybe there was stuff he couldn't see since he wasn't logged into her account.

He logged out, then attempted to log in as Ellen. She'd had a favorite password. It didn't work. He tried three more possibilities before giving up.

Never saw it coming.

He grabbed a bottle of vodka and headed upstairs to the observation deck—another great thing about his building. Through the curved glass, he looked into the distance, at the sky and the stars.

He put a quarter in the binoculars.

Never saw it coming.

He scanned the sky through the glass barrier. As the meter ticked away, he watched chains of car lights snaking through the city. Turning the binoculars 180 degrees, he spotted the moon reflecting off Lake Harriet. Jude lived down there somewhere south of Lake Street, from what he gathered.

He swung back the opposite direction, to the area where houses were no longer laid out in a grid, but rather wound around streams and lakes, and streets were called things like Pleasant Valley Circle and Maple Drive and Park Place.

He located the area where he and Ellen used to live and stared a long time, until the binoculars stopped ticking and the lens went dark. Then, the way he'd done so many nights since moving into the Emerson, he sat down on a reclining chair and proceeded to get wasted.

The department psychologist said drinking didn't help. She was wrong. It was the *only* thing that helped.

CHAPTER 14

Jude's phone rang. She groped around on the roof where she'd spread her sleeping bag, found the phone, checked the screen, saw Uriah's name, hit "Answer," and croaked out a yes.

"Is this Detective Fontaine?"

Not Uriah. The voice belonged to a young woman. Jude propped herself up on her elbow, alert. "Yes."

"My name is Leona Franklin. I wasn't sure who to call, but we have a situation here." Pause. Breath. "About a year ago my husband and I bought a house on Juniper Street."

Jude rechecked the screen: *Uriah*. Had someone borrowed his phone? Hitting "Speaker," she said, "I think you have the wrong number."

"Hear me out. We bought the house from Detective Ashby. Do you know him? We found his phone and saw *detective* in front of your name, so we thought you might know him."

"He's my partner."

"Well, he's here right now. *In our house.* In the wine cellar. Because he was a cop, we never got the locks changed. Apparently he just let himself in."

Wide awake now, Jude got to her feet and grabbed her sleeping bag and gun. "What's the address?" she asked, heading for the rooftop stairs.

The woman gave her the house number.

"I'll be there as soon as I can."

Inside her apartment, Jude dropped the sleeping bag, tugged on jeans and boots, strapped her holster and gun around her waist, slipped her iPhone into her back pocket, and tossed on a jacket. Helmet under her arm, she hurried out, locking the door behind her, then pounded down the stairs to the parking garage, where she straddled the bike, fastened her helmet, started the engine, and hit the remote on the key chain. The electronic garage door cranked open.

On the street, passing under traffic lights and rolling past dark shops with neon signs, she squeezed the clutch and foot-shifted through the gears to race toward the address the woman on the phone had given her.

The area where Uriah once lived turned out to be quintessential Minneapolis, from the tree-lined streets to the stucco houses. When she spotted a building blazing with lights, she figured she'd located the house, quickly confirming it as she pulled into the driveway, her headlight bouncing across the number above the front door.

She shut off the bike and secured it on the stand. After removing her helmet and hanging it over the handlebar, she approached the house and knocked. It was answered by a young couple: a very pregnant woman wearing a floral nightgown, a man wearing a T-shirt and pajama pants.

The house . . . the pregnant woman . . . Symbols of normality. It was hard and even impossible to imagine Uriah puttering around this place on a Saturday, doing mundane chores like painting and repair, lawn mowing.

"His wife committed suicide, you know," the woman whispered.

Jude felt a thud deep in her belly as everything fell into place. The drinking, his reaction to the body in the lake . . .

"He couldn't bear to live here anymore, so he sold the house. You should have seen him the day we signed the papers. He was gutted. I had to leave the room because I started crying."

It came to her that she and Uriah had both lost their identities in slightly different ways. He was now a grief-stricken widower who'd once lived a fairly charmed life. This was where that charmed life had taken place.

The woman led Jude through the living room and kitchen to a gray basement door.

A basement.

At the top of the stairs, Jude's heart beat in her ears. Was this a trick? Had she been lured into a trap? The couple felt genuine to her, but could she trust her read of the situation? Really?

Hand to the gun at her waist, she spoke Uriah's name, her voice carrying down the steps.

He responded from the depths of the basement. "Jude? That you?"

Relieved yet still reluctant to join him, she asked, "What are you doing down there?"

"Checking out the wine selection."

She took a deep breath and descended to find him in a corner, sitting on the floor, back against the wall, one knee bent, a bottle beside him and a wineglass in his hand. He was wearing jeans and a T-shirt. She'd never seen him in anything other than his suit.

"Apparently 2005 was a good year," he said.

He didn't seem that drunk, not nearly as drunk as he needed to be to have gotten himself into this situation. The professional drinkers were the ones who often seemed more sober than anybody else in the room.

Jude lowered herself beside him on the floor. Uriah offered her his glass. She accepted and took a sip. "Not half-bad."

"Right?"

They drank in silence for a while, continuing to share the glass; then she said, "It's time to go."

"I feel pretty comfortable here."

"This isn't your house."

"It sure as hell is." He put out his hand for the glass. She passed it to him.

"Not anymore. You sold it."

"Really? That explains the people upstairs."

"Let's get out of here and let this lovely couple with a baby on the way get back to sleep."

That seemed to get through, because the one thing she knew about Uriah was that he had compassion in him.

She put the glass and bottle aside and helped him to his feet. Once upright, he swayed, caught himself, then pointed to the stairs. "After you."

"You might want to get the locks changed," Jude told the couple as she and Uriah passed them in the hallway.

"Calling first thing in the morning," the husband muttered with relief.

Outside, Jude and Uriah paused on the sidewalk. Behind them, the porch light went out. "How did you get here?" she asked.

Uriah looked up and down the street. "I dunno." He gave it some thought. "I think I took the light-rail. Or maybe a cab."

Jude straddled the bike and maneuvered it around to face the street, ready for launch. "Hop on."

Uriah swung his leg over and settled himself behind her, hands at her waist, his touch impersonal.

Fuel, choke, ignition. She kick-started the bike and gave it gas as she shifted into first and took off, heading in the direction of downtown. Ten minutes later she slowed for a right turn on Marquette, the heavy machine feeling awkward and unsteady with the addition of Uriah's weight. At Emerson Tower, she found a parking spot in front of the building and cut the engine.

Both of them off the bike, she removed her helmet.

Uriah spun around and launched himself at the double doors. "Thanks for the ride!" he shouted over his shoulder.

She followed in order to make sure he made it safely to his apartment. In the lobby, she watched as he owlishly managed to punch the elevator's "Up" button. A green arrow dinged, a pair of doors separated, and Uriah tumbled inside to lean heavily against the wall. "I usually take the stairs," he confided, carefully choosing a number on the control panel and pressing it with the intensity of a baby. The door shuddered closed, and the elevator began to move. "My record is two minutes, twenty-three seconds." He gave her a long look. "We should race sometime."

"I'm not very athletic. I'm more of a croquet type of person, but sure. I'll race you." Come morning, he'd never remember.

He nodded. Then, more to himself than her, he mumbled, "Deal."

At floor 17, the car stopped and the doors opened. Uriah walked carefully down the hall, stopping abruptly to prop himself against the wall, eyes closed. The night and the booze had caught up with him.

Jude searched his pockets, found a set of keys, one with a number on it. She located his apartment and unlocked the door while Uriah shouldered himself away from the wall to follow her inside.

Up until now, if Jude had bothered to wonder about him, she would have mentally constructed one of two environments, the first and foremost being a kind of ultramodern bachelor pad. Second choice would have been a space with just the essentials. Bed unmade, possibly just a mattress, shower, hot plate. Basically a place to sleep between the long hours of work. Yes, that would have been more likely than the bachelor pad. Scratch the bachelor pad.

Scratch the bare space too.

She closed the door and hit the wall switch. The ornate glass fixture above her head did little to illuminate the space.

The dark apartment smelled like an antique shop—that mixture of ancient paper and ancient wood and stories about people who'd lived a long time ago. Underfoot was an oriental rug in shades of burgundy and forest green. Windows were covered with thick red drapes. But the biggest surprise? Floor-to-ceiling books, many with leather spines, most protected by clear covers.

Everything was old. Vintage lamps with dark shades. In the corner, near a sixties-style green couch, were shelves of vinyl records and a turntable.

The apartment wasn't very big, or maybe it just didn't seem big because of all the belongings packed into it. From where she stood, she could see an adjoining kitchen and a hallway that led to what must have been the bedroom and bathroom.

The clutter was overwhelming and comforting at the same time. A world within a world. She was surprised to find that it felt like a safe cocoon rather than a trap, a cell.

Uriah walked with drunken deliberation, taking a straight shot down the hall. She followed to find him sitting on the bed, staring blankly into space before he tumbled backward, eyes closed, arms spread.

An ordinary person might have tugged off his sneakers for him and rolled him to the side in case he threw up. Jude was no longer an ordinary person, and the limits of what she felt comfortable doing had been exceeded, yet she found herself unwilling to leave him alone in his present condition.

She grabbed a spare pillow from the bed, returned to the living room, tossed it on the couch, but didn't lie down. Instead, she pulled a book from one of the shelves and opened it to the copyright page. A first edition of *Fight Club*. She put it away and pulled out another book. First edition of *Silent Spring*.

She remembered how it felt to be that passionate about something. She mourned the loss of that feeling and marveled that a cop who dealt with death on a daily basis could still be engaged in life on such a level.

She put the book away and picked up a framed photo. It was a typical couple's snapshot, taken in a typical couple's spot in front of the *Spoonbridge and Cherry* at the Walker Art Museum. Hadn't she and

Eric stood in that very place? Didn't they have just such a photo? What had happened to it? That physical proof of a life that no longer existed but had once been real?

She thought she wanted nothing to do with anything in the house she'd shared with Eric, but that was a lie, a way of protecting herself, and now she began to wonder what else had been left behind, if anything. Or had he thrown all reminders of her away when the new girl moved in?

What if things had been different? What if no new girlfriend had been standing beside him on that cold night last winter? What if he'd welcomed her in the way she'd always imagined? What would her life be like now? Because the truth was, she was having a hard time reentering, and most of the time it felt as if she were standing behind a thick glass that separated her from the rest of the world.

She put the photo back on the shelf. Ten minutes later she returned to the bedroom long enough to roll Uriah onto his side and prop a pillow behind his back.

CHAPTER 15

J ude woke to the smell of food cooking. She unfolded herself from the couch and wandered stiffly to the kitchen. Uriah stood at the counter in front of a small apartment stove, a spatula in his hand as he stirred a skillet of scrambled eggs. "This is nice," he said without looking at her, a towel tossed casually over his shoulder. "Waking up, cooking eggs for more than one person."

She crossed her arms and leaned against the doorframe. "I'm amazed you're standing. Your head must be killing you."

"It's not too bad, but then, I think there's a really good chance I'm still drunk."

She pulled out a vintage chair—metal with red cushions—and sat down, hugging a knee to her chest. "Do you remember what happened?"

"Unfortunately, yes." She heard the wince in his voice.

"They're getting new locks installed."

"Good idea." He continued to focus his attention on the pan in front of him. Embarrassed? Maybe. Probably.

"Plates." He pointed to the cupboard above the sink.

She got up, pulled out two blue plates, put them on the narrow table, sat back down. With a spatula, he scraped the scrambled eggs from the pan, creating a small mountain on each plate. Then he produced two mugs and filled them with coffee from a french press and sat down across from her.

Uriah had inadvertently created a moment. One of those inexplicable things in life, *real* life, that made everything better. It made her wonder if maybe real life could exist for her in this new world.

They picked up forks and began eating.

A few bites in, Uriah broke the silence: "I don't remember the couple that well, but I remember riding on your motorcycle; then I woke up here."

"That's pretty much what happened." The cooked meal, simple though it was, tasted surprisingly good, and it was hard for Jude to make herself stop eating long enough to expand on her reply. "I stayed the night because I thought it was a bad idea to leave you alone."

Uriah finally looked at her, *really* looked at her. Then, without warning, he reached across the table and grabbed her free hand. Just a human response, meant to be a gesture of thanks, but when his fingers made contact with hers, she jerked away—a simple reminder of what had passed when she was in captivity and what wasn't right about her.

His gaze quickly fell away to focus hard on the food on his plate.

Feeling as if she owed him an explanation, she said, "I don't like anybody to touch me."

"I'll remember that." Still, he didn't look at her. They continued with the motions of the meal, living through the awkwardness that had descended.

"My mother collected books too," she finally said.

"It's kind of an obsession of mine," he confessed. "Mostly first editions." Eye contact. "Why are you looking at me like that? Is it so strange?"

"Yeah, it is."

"Why?"

"I don't know. It's just unexpected, that's all."

A shift of eyebrows. "You should see my Beanie Baby collection." When she didn't respond, he continued: "I'm kidding about the Beanie Babies."

"Oh."

"For somebody who claims to be able to read dead bodies, you sure seem off sometimes when it comes to living, breathing people."

He was right. Her mistake had come from making assumptions about him. "I wonder how much of a person is simply fabricated by others," she said. "And think about this: None of us see the same person in the exact same way. We bring ourselves into the equation. So an individual is never *really* an individual."

"This might be a little too deep for a hangover. Are you saying we're not only a product of our environment; we're also informed by accurate and inaccurate observations by others? That makes my head hurt even more."

"One thing I know, before my capture I saw myself through everybody else's eyes, if that makes any sense. Every single person I engaged with throughout the day. I read their reaction to me and saw what they saw, accurate or inaccurate. That hasn't happened since my escape. I don't know if this new me is normal or abnormal, but that skewed reflection no longer exists. It should feel good, but it's like something is gone."

You become the person he sees.

At that moment she realized that was what had happened to her. For three years. With nothing and no one to bounce herself off of but a sadistic man, she'd had no choice. Not really. She'd become the person he saw.

How long had it taken for him to break her? Days? Weeks? Months? How long before she'd given up and become the docile and complacent person who'd done whatever he said? And not only done it, but had looked forward to his visits?

Maybe the length of time it had taken to break her didn't matter. What mattered was that she'd succumbed. She'd quit fighting, quit planning escapes, quit trying to overtake him. That's where her shame came from. And she wasn't sure she'd ever be able to forgive herself for that.

Done eating, she took her plate to the sink and rinsed it under the faucet. "I saw a list of names on the coffee table," she said over her shoulder. "Classmates of Delilah Masters?"

"I got them off Facebook last night. I say we visit Delilah's school again today. Interview more kids, along with some teachers. And maybe Lola Holt will be there."

He'd gotten drunk after spending time on Facebook. Seemed an unusual sequence of events until she decided he'd probably also visited his wife's page. She shut off the water and turned around. "I used to collect Beanie Babies," she confessed.

"That's embarrassing." He got up, chair scraping the wooden floor. "I had a Teddy Ruxpin talking bear, but that information better never leave this room."

CHAPTER 16

The walking funeral procession for Delilah Masters made its way up Hennepin Avenue, moving in the direction of Lakewood Cemetery. Beginning at the mortuary, a scattering of people lined both sides of the street, some silent, some sobbing, some just there because the murder had been the lead story for the past few days. That kind of media attention drew a crowd. And activists. Just the night before, a group of concerned parents had organized a vigil, launching hundreds of paper boats containing small candles across the still surface of Lake of the Isles.

Visually powerful and newsworthy, especially when combined with parents concerned for their own children's safety.

Death was always sad, but it was achingly tragic when that death involved a beautiful girl on the cusp of adulthood. The fact that it was a murder disguised as a suicide made it the biggest story in town. Add Jude Fontaine to the mix, and it meant national outlets had picked it up, the feeding frenzy over her name renewed.

Jude and Uriah followed on foot, keeping a respectful distance at the back of the crowd. As they walked, Jude spotted a group of girls watching from the curb. Girls they'd interviewed, but still no sign of Lola Holt. She continued to elude them, but Jude hoped the funeral would flush her out.

Both detectives wore black, Uriah in the suit that seemed a part of him, and Jude in a sleeveless dress she'd picked up at a department store. Dress shoes seemed part of her old life, so she'd decided her black leather boots were a practical choice, while not an aesthetically good one.

Minneapolis was tough to navigate because of the lakes. Major streets ended abruptly, and Hennepin Avenue stopped where the gates to Lakewood Cemetery began. Once inside those gates, the terrain shifted from flat to hilly, with dark valleys and trees so big they cast moving shadows over everything and everyone.

Jude and Uriah weren't the only cops on site. Several officers, Grant Vang and Caroline McIntosh included, were in the moving crowd, all of them keeping their eyes open for anything out of the ordinary. Killers often attended their victim's funeral, savoring the sense of anonymous notoriety the event presented. After the burial took place, the grave would be watched for suspicious visitors. But today, unfortunately, the killer could easily blend in.

The procession stopped in a deep valley, giving people a moment to look skyward. Lakewood was located in the Minneapolis–Saint Paul Airport flight path, and planes traveling at various altitudes could be seen leaving white trails across a cloudless sky.

Jude guessed maybe two hundred people were now gathered inside the cemetery gates—scattered on the hillside and clustered around stone monuments of sorrowful angels. The officiating minister opened his Bible. From somewhere in the distance, a flute began to play. The sound of those sweet and haunting notes triggered an unexpected response in Jude. Her eyes welled with tears, and her throat tightened. For a moment, she forgot about her purpose at the funeral. In a cemetery surrounded by death, Jude felt a small spark of life. She didn't like it. It made her sad and made her feel emotions she didn't want to feel.

Snapshots of an existence lived and unlived flashed through her brain, clips of days spent in a basement, of a voice and hands and the longing for human contact. And the big question: Could a new life be built now, after everything she'd been through?

At the same time these thoughts rushed through her, Jude was acutely aware of how static her world felt. She no longer sensed that sweet delusional promise of something good, something better, around the corner. Could a person exist without it? Was she forever condemned to the scent of other people's fires?

The service ended, and funeral attendees wandered toward their homes and cars. The detectives stood at the base of a towering oak tree and watched as the crowd dissipated and gravediggers waited in the shade to cover the coffin.

Jude was thinking about her reaction to the flute, when Uriah whispered, "Look."

He stood with hands clasped, head bowed, furtively watching the crowd through the curly hair that hung over his forehead. She followed the direction of his gaze, stopping on a young woman with dark, smooth hair wearing a blue dress.

Lola Holt.

The elusive girl moved toward the lane that led to the main gate. In unison, Uriah and Jude fell into step, walking just a notch above normal pace. Maybe it was still too fast, or maybe their urgency somehow broadcast itself to the girl, because she glanced over her shoulder, spotted them, turned, and dove into the mob filing through the gate.

Jude and Uriah ran after her, apologizing to funeral goers as they wove in and out of the crowd.

They raced up the street, legs a blur, arms pumping, after the girl with dark hair.

Lola Holt took an abrupt detour, cutting down an alley. They cut after her.

Another turn and there she was.

"Homicide!" Uriah shouted. "Hold it right there."

The girl could have squeezed between two brick buildings, but she must have realized the futility of continuing to flee.

She turned and faced them, hands at her side as she gulped in air. "What do you want? Leave me alone!"

Uriah pulled out his badge, introduced himself and Jude, then tucked the badge back in his jacket. "We just want to ask you a few questions."

"I don't want to talk to you. I didn't do anything. I don't know anything."

"Then you have nothing to worry about, do you?" From Uriah.

"You were her friend," Jude said.

"We used to be friends."

Lola was an attractive girl. Not beautiful, but she had an interesting face. Dark eyes heavily enhanced with thick black liner, high cheekbones, slashing eyebrows.

"When did you stop being friends?" Jude asked.

Lola shook her head. "I don't know. Six months ago, maybe."

"What happened? We've seen Delilah's room. There were pictures of you there. Looks like you were friends for a long time."

"We grew apart." She shrugged.

"Could you elaborate on that?" Uriah asked. "How did you grow apart?"

"It wasn't one thing. Just a lot of little things. You know. It happens. I don't still run around with my grade-school friends either."

Uriah pulled out his iPhone, scrolled, stopped, and turned the device toward the girl. "We haven't found Delilah's phone, but we were able to access her old texts. Because, well, we're cops."

Lola looked at the screen and paled.

"According to this," Uriah said, "you were in contact with Delilah a week ago."

"My uncle is a lawyer, and he says I don't have to talk to you."

"That's right, to a point," Uriah told her. "But we can bring you downtown for questioning."

"I don't know anything!"

She might have come across as tough and independent, but it didn't take advanced perception skills to see that the girl was terrified. "We're trying to find out the truth," Jude said calmly. "And if you're in any danger, we want to protect you. We can't protect you if we don't know what's going on."

"Aren't you the cop who was abducted? I saw it on the news. I mean, how can you protect anybody when you can't even protect yourself?"

Attempting to ignore the sting of those truthful words, Jude pulled out a business card and presented it to the girl, who didn't budge as she eyeballed the card suspiciously.

"Go on." Jude held the card closer. "We're on your side. We're here to help you. If you're afraid, if you need to talk to someone, if you feel you're in danger, call me. Day or night."

The girl reluctantly took the card. She'd probably throw it away as soon as they were out of sight.

"At least let us walk you to your car," Uriah said. "We're not going to leave you alone in an alley."

Lola muttered something about their being the ones who'd chased her into that alley in the first place. All the same, she grudgingly fell into step beside them as they headed back to civilization.

"You don't need to walk me to my car," Lola said once they were on Hennepin Avenue and a sidewalk full of people. Before either detective could comment, she slipped between two parked cars, watched for an opening in traffic, and dashed across the street, neatly ditching them.

"She's afraid," Uriah said as he and Jude headed back to their vehicle, parked a few blocks away.

"Afraid would be putting it mildly." Jude spotted their car and pointed at it. "She's terrified."

"I'd like to put a protective watch on her," Uriah said, "but without any justification, the request would never get approved, especially with our manpower shortage."

"We made contact," Jude said. "That's something."

At the car, Uriah hit the "Unlock" button on the fob while watching for traffic before circling to the driver's side.

Jude opened the passenger door. "And maybe we planted a seed of trust," she added as she slipped inside. "She has my card if she hasn't already thrown it away. Hopefully she'll call me."

CHAPTER 17

*H*is girl.

In the beginning, her journals contained stories of rescue. German shepherds on black leashes leading policemen through the woods to her hiding place. They would break open the door, and she would shield her eyes from the unaccustomed light. Hands would pull her outside, where she would breathe deeply. A female officer would appear and tell her everything was going to be okay. Someone would hand her a phone, and she would hear her mother's voice.

And they would both cry.

But she didn't have those dreams anymore.

She now understood how easy it was for a person to adapt. Whatever was thrown at her, she made a mental adjustment. No matter how unbearable and how impossible a situation, her brain learned to accept it as normal.

She'd heard of Stockholm syndrome. She'd heard of beaten and humiliated women who didn't leave their husbands. People talked about how they had no place to go, but she wondered if anybody ever talked about how the brain made staying okay. How the brain accepted the abuse and made it okay.

Turn the darkness into light.

So in her head and in her dreams, the cops with dogs no longer came. Instead, she waited for him. For the man who brought her food and made love to her in the dark.

And while she waited, she spent her time creating a world beyond the walls of her room. Sometimes she imagined herself deep in the heart of Minneapolis, maybe in some massive, abandoned warehouse. Other times, she was on the tallest floor of a skyscraper, her room surrounded by clouds. Other times she was deep in the woods.

Her mind kept her company because she'd long ago decided nobody was coming for her. She no longer remembered what her parents looked like, and she no longer remembered what the sun felt like or what snow felt like. All she knew was one man. He was her world.

CHAPTER 18

Emotionally wiped after the funeral and a day of dodging the media, Jude shot out of the police-department parking garage. Darkness came late in Minnesota this time of the year. It was after eight, and dusk hadn't yet hit as the mood on the street continued its transition from work to play. She liked this time of day, the golden hour, when she and Eric used to stroll around the lakes.

Weaving up and down residential neighborhoods in her habitual search, she added a new section of streets to her grid as she moved methodically west.

Today felt different. Today she found herself slowing down, found her eyes drawn to a one-and-a-half-story stucco house on a tree-lined street that looked like it had gone to hell long before the blackouts.

She pulled to a stop and straddled the bike.

The house had a broken window in the attic and a yard that had been neglected, complete with a plastic trash bag stuck to a tall weed, but the property didn't stand out as being much worse than any other on the block. And yet . . .

Her heart slammed in her chest and her senses shot into overdrive as she took in details: cracks in the sidewalk, limbs cut by the power company, rust on the chain-link fence, street trash blown and trapped in corners against the crumbling foundation, plus the sweet scent of a neighbor's flower garden.

It was said that those bad places, places where you'd been the most miserable—those places called to you. Maybe it was curiosity. Maybe it was simply that the bad memories were covered in a protective layer and tucked away so deep that they no longer seemed your own life but something you might have read or a movie you might have seen. So you found yourself needing to go back there to touch the place, see the place. Not to reassure yourself that it was real and that it had occurred, but to observe it from the distance of a safe mind, to marvel that this thing happened to you and you survived.

Her memory of her time in the basement had changed over the past few months, morphing into a combination of real and unreal, but that protective mental distance didn't keep her from wanting to revisit her past long enough to find a dead body on the floor. Or, at the very least, a grease spot where a dead body had been.

She shut off the bike, secured it on the stand, and swung her leg over the seat to walk across the lawn and stand in front of the house. She checked to make sure her belt was around her waist and her weapon in place.

With a pounding heart, she approached the front door and knocked. When no one answered, she circled to the side of the house, where three cement steps led to a back door. She remembered just such steps covered in packed snow. She knocked before peering through the murky glass, hand shading her eyes in an attempt to see inside.

Then she tested the knob.

It turned.

Holding her breath, she pushed open the door with her shoulder and entered the kitchen. The basement steps were directly in front of her. "Hello?"

Her gaze tracked nervously until she spotted the Taser on the table where she'd left it. On the floor were the spent shell casings that had bounced around her bare feet. And the smell . . . Death, yes, certainly death, but the other odors were still there, embedded in the walls, ceiling, and floor. Nicotine and fried food, mildew and urine. She'd never forget the smell. If she didn't smell it again for thirty years, she'd recognize it.

Home sweet home.

Robotically, she pulled out her phone and called Uriah.

He answered after two rings.

She might have said something. She must have said something, because he responded with "What's going on?" There was no missing the concern in his voice.

"I found the house," she told him with no further betrayal of emotion. No need to explain *what* house.

"Don't go inside. Give me the address."

"I'm *already* inside."

"Then get the hell out of there."

"Everything's covered in dust. Nobody's been in or out for a long time."

"Damn it, Jude. Where are you? What's the address?"

She'd been unprofessional and unaware. "I don't even know the street."

He made an exasperated sound. "If you aren't going to leave, at least stay on the line."

She knew she shouldn't have come here by herself, and yet she couldn't imagine coming here with another person. She had to see it alone, with no one watching, no one listening.

"Jude?"

The basement door was open, just like she'd left it. "I'm going downstairs."

"Listen. Get out of there. Go outside, go to the front of the house, figure out the address, give it to me."

"It'll be fine."

"Jude!"

"I have to go." She disconnected.

The light switch at the top of the stairs did nothing even though she flipped it twice. She resorted to using the flashlight app on her phone. Hand on the railing, she descended. Each step seemed to erase more of her bravado; each step took her closer to the person she never wanted to be again.

She was shaking now. Not a little, but a lot.

Halfway down, her phone rang. She jumped, then checked the screen: *Uriah*. She didn't answer. Instead, she refocused the app.

There it was. The single bare lightbulb.

In the center of the room was the cell where she'd spent three years of her life. More important, near the bottom of the steps was a body, or what was left of a body after months of decay.

She was only distantly aware of the overpowering stench. Her focus was the flannel of his shirt, and how the fabric had felt under her fingertips those times when she'd both fought him off and begged him to stay. Beneath the odor of rot, she detected the cigarettes he smoked, and she remembered the way his beard had felt against her neck in the darkness.

She completed her descent, sidestepping the remains. The cell door was open. Inside, she could see a filthy blanket. A chipped ceramic plate. She stared at the rose pattern, recalled it, recalled thinking how curious for someone so cruel and evil to have a plate with a delicate rose pattern.

She turned and left.

Without examining the rest of the residence, she walked back up the stairs, walked out the side door, and circled to the front of the house to locate the faded numbers above the entry. A glance at the nearest street sign, then she pulled out her phone and called Uriah, who answered on the first ring.

"Did you find a body?" he asked, his voice tense.

"Yes." She gave him the address. "It's in the basement. Call the BCA. Get a crime-scene team here."

"Good work." A pause. "You okay?"

She should have felt relief. Hope for this moment had kept her going. She hadn't realized that until now. This moment, recognized or unrecognized, had been the driving force of her days. Find the house. Find the man.

But instead of relief, all she felt was horror, along with a sick compulsion to go back downstairs and rub her face against the flannel of the dead man's shirt.

That would be certifiable.

She'd gotten away. She'd escaped. Why couldn't she have left it at that? Why couldn't that have been enough? Why hadn't she let it go, the way Uriah had suggested? Her captor was dead. He'd been dead for months. And proof of his death changed nothing. *Nothing.* It didn't erase the brutality she'd suffered. Instead, finding the body brought her suffering back with a clarity that was cruel beyond cruel.

Now . . . *now* he was alive again. Even though he was lying down there in a puddle of grease and bones, he seemed more alive right now than he'd seemed since her escape. It was as if she'd dug him up, breathed life into him, and brought him back to her.

She used to find it frustrating when victims refused to press charges against a person who deserved to be put away. Now she understood their thinking. Acknowledgment brought it back. It meant there was no walking away. No starting over.

Part of her wanted to run home. Not even get on her bike—just run. Just feel the sidewalk under her feet, feel her arms pumping and her lungs burning. Another part of her wanted to circle the house, go back inside, return to the basement, and lock herself in the cell.

Of the two choices, returning to the basement seemed the most appealing.

"Jude? Talk to me. Are you okay?"

She'd forgotten about the live phone in her hand. Uriah repeated his question. She wanted to tell him how she was feeling, but it was too hard to explain, and she wondered if putting the words out there, sharing her feelings with someone else, would bring with it another level of real. She couldn't take any more real right now.

She thought about leaving. Wondered if she should stay. How long before the crime-scene team got there? She should talk to them. She didn't want to talk to them. She didn't want to see their reaction to the house. She didn't want to see their reaction to the place she'd lived for three years. From now on, whenever they saw her, talked to her, they would imagine her here, and their very awareness would further imprint this place on her, stamping it into her very marrow.

"I'm fine," she told him, and disconnected.

CHAPTER 19

U riah pulled to the curb behind Jude's motorcycle, shut off the car, grabbed a small flashlight, and got out. He was the first to arrive on the scene.

The house was typical of Midtown Phillips, a neighborhood located north of Powderhorn and east of Whittier. Red trim, cream stucco, one and a half stories. In need of repair. Rotten wood, chipped paint. The lawn had been mowed maybe two weeks earlier, and Uriah recognized the city's yard-maintenance bill stuck to the front door. Somebody had apparently complained about the grass. A surprise, since most area residents probably wouldn't care about the criminal or weirdass next door, let alone tall grass.

He'd expected to find Jude waiting outside, but after a quick perusal of the exterior and no Jude, he took the crumbled cement steps to the kitchen and eased his way inside.

The smell of death permeated the building. Not that overpowering stench that developed soon after, but the other one, the one that came after a body rotted, after the fat melted into a puddle that never went away. That odor was every bit as bad as the other. No one would ever be able to live in the house again.

A few steps to the right were the kitchen and a doorway that led to a short hall and probably bedrooms and a bathroom. Sink piled high with dishes. A layer of dust and grime on everything. He tested a couple of switches. No power—another sign that nobody had been there recently.

Directly in front of the back door and entry area were the basement steps. Was she down there? Or had she left the house? Was she walking up the street, gulping in fresh air until the crime-scene team showed up? That's what he'd do.

"Jude?" He didn't shout. Just a conversational tone. He sure as hell didn't want to startle her.

"Down here." No emotion.

He pulled out the Maglite. Clicked it on and gave the beam a pass across the blood-spattered walls of the stairwell. He paused halfway down the steps, the glow illuminating his partner.

She stood with her back to him, dressed in black pants and leather jacket, one hand on her hip, elbow out, legs spread, looking down at a pile of fabric and melting flesh at her feet. As if she were making sure it didn't move.

"Is it him?" he asked.

"I don't know."

Her voice sounded oddly untroubled. Like somebody answering a question about whether she thought it might rain. "Maybe. Maybe not." She held her phone in her hand. The flashlight app was open, and the beam moved with her comments. "Nothing really distinguishing about the clothing. Jeans, boots, flannel shirt. Hair—not sure about that. Not with all the decay, but it looks about the right color."

"We've got the gun you shot him with, so ballistics should produce a match. And we'll run his prints, if we can lift any, and DNA through the database." He heard the sound of a siren. Why the hell were they using sirens? "Sure you don't want to go outside? Let us handle this?"

"I'll stay."

This wouldn't be easy for her.

"It feels like I never left." She turned, and he directed the flashlight beam toward the floor so the light wouldn't blind her. "I can't explain it," she said. "And I know this will sound crazy, but it's kind of like coming home." Her voice cracked a little on the last word. She was struggling more than he'd thought.

"You were here a long time," he said quietly.

"Sometimes it seems like days, and at other times it seems like I was here forever. Like I was never anywhere else." Her expression turned inward as she tried to examine what she was feeling. "There's a part of me that regrets killing this monster. He owned me, and life was simple then. Just the nothing of it. Isn't that *weird*?" She looked at him, really looked at him, something she didn't often do. In communication rather than examination. "I know it's wrong," she said. "I know it's crazy. I know he was an evil bastard. I know he should be dead, but part of me . . . part of me wants to crawl into that box." She broke eye contact and moved her light to illuminate a tiny room built in the center of the basement, ceiling to floor, the walls thick and soundproofed. "Part of me wants to crawl in there and close the door behind me."

He swallowed. "Conditioned response."

"Part of me misses *that* me." She pointed to the box. "That me was all I had at one time. That me got me through this."

He thought about the things she'd told him in the hospital. It had shaken him then, and it shook him now—being in the space where she'd been tortured *for so long*. The length of time it had gone on was especially heinous. Add to that the fact that he felt guilty for assuming her dead . . .

"It's okay," she said quietly. "It's all right."

"Don't comfort *me*. I'm not the one who deserves comforting."

"You're the one in pain."

He blew out a breath and shook his head. She'd been broken, and somehow, on her own, she'd put herself together again. And this new person was both weaker and stronger than the old one. "My pain is nothing."

They stared at each other, both reacting at the same time upon hearing sounds of activity near the house.

Leaving Jude in the basement, Uriah turned and went upstairs and outside to brief the crime-scene crew. "No electricity," he said. "Somebody needs to call the power company and get the juice back on. In the meantime, bring some portable lighting inside."

Yellow tape was already going up around the perimeter of the property, strung by a crew wearing navy-blue jackets with the letters *BCA* across the back. The tape would be there a long time. The yard would be vacuumed. Once that was done, the soil would be probed, and if anything suspicious turned up, the ground would be turned over. The house itself would be combed top to bottom.

"I want video footage of everything, especially the cell in the basement," Uriah told the tech in charge. "The shell casings on the kitchen floor? Get them to ballistics. Tell them to see if they match the gun we took off Jude Fontaine the night she escaped."

Grant Vang burst through the cluster of people, jacket flapping, out of breath, face tense. "I got here as fast as I could," he said. "Where's Jude?"

A team member emerged from the house, an uncomfortable expression on his face. "Should she be in there?" He nodded over his shoulder in the direction of the kitchen and the basement, where Jude was probably still standing over the body.

Uriah looked at Grant. "Let's see what we can do."

CHAPTER 20

Darkness was coming on with more seriousness as Jude straddled her bike in front of the corpse house. As she reached for her helmet, the phone in her pocket vibrated. Uriah and Grant were still in the basement. Since they'd only just convinced her to leave, she doubted either of them would be texting her. She checked the screen: *Lola Holt*.

The text read, *Meet me at Spyhouse. I need to talk to you.*

Located in the Whittier neighborhood, Spyhouse Coffee wasn't that far away. The message served more than one purpose. Jude would finally get that interview with the elusive and uncooperative Lola Holt, and she didn't have to go home just yet, which meant she could push thoughts of the body in the basement to the back of her mind, at least for now.

She replied to the message: *Be there in ten minutes.*

She strapped on her helmet, put the bike in neutral, and gave the kick start a downward thrust of her heel. Engaging the gears and releasing the clutch, she took off up the street.

As Jude headed to the café, her thoughts raced. She replayed her discovery of the house, her opening of the back door, the way the light from her phone had cast deep shadows, giving the blood on the walls the appearance of movement. The smell itself was embedded in her sinuses, now trapped in the claustrophobic helmet she wanted to rip from her head. Minutes passed before she realized she'd gone several blocks with no awareness of her surroundings.

Stopping at a red light, feet planted on each side of the bike, she glanced in her rearview mirror at a black car that had come to an abrupt halt just feet from her back tire. The light changed. She made a right turn. So did the car. Maybe nothing, but just in case, she slowed and made another turn while keeping an eye on the vehicle.

It followed, continuing to ride too close.

She gave the bike gas and shifted into a higher gear. The machine jumped forward just as Jude heard a series of pops that her brain registered as gunshots. At the same time, the bike balked and the back tire pulled hard to the left. She struggled to remain upright but couldn't maintain control, rider and machine crashing to the pavement. The momentum and the difference in weight separated them until they were moving side by side, finally coming to a full stop at the mouth of an alley.

Dazed, her senses and vision restricted by the helmet, she fumbled for the latch under her chin, released the catch, tossed the helmet aside, and rolled to her feet.

As she tried to get her bearings, a body came out of nowhere, slamming into her, propelling her to the ground. Before she caught a glimpse of a face, an army of feet pounded the ground and a cloth bag was tugged over her head, blinding her while her hands were pinned. She struggled, kicked, attempting moves she'd practiced in self-defense classes, but she was outnumbered.

How many assailants? Two? Three? Maybe four.

Even as she struggled to fight them off, her mind attempted to sort and rank the possible reasons behind the attack. Robbery in an area of town where muggings had become commonplace? Worse—a reason she couldn't even fully consider—was this another abduction?

One of them punched her. Someone else held her down, knee to her spine, leaning close. A man. She was sure it was a man. She could feel his hot breath reaching her ear through the cloth obliterating her vision. She tried to focus her senses. Was he someone she knew? Someone who knew her? She needed a clue—something tactile, a scent, a voice. But her assailant didn't say a word as his hand pressed against her trachea, cutting off her oxygen until she blacked out.

CHAPTER 21

U riah reentered the house after making sure Jude had left to go home. Inside, he found Vang in the bedroom, sifting through the contents of a desk.

"Look at this." In Vang's gloved hand were newspaper clippings and eight-by-ten color photos. "The guy was obsessed with her."

Uriah took a stack and began shuffling through them. Pictures of Jude in various locations. Cafés, getting in and out of her car, jogging near the lake. The photos even marked the change of seasons. Jude in shorts and tank top, Jude in jeans and sweater, Jude in a heavy coat, stocking cap, gloves. "He was spying on her for a long time," he said.

"Planning and waiting to make his move."

"What do you think? An isolated obsession? Have you found photos of anyone else?" In particular, anyone who'd been reported missing.

"Not yet, but there's a lot here." Vang waved a hand at the desk. "Maybe you could check that bottom-right drawer. I haven't been there yet."

It was stuffed tight. Uriah tugged and the drawer finally gave, photos bursting free.

"Taken with an instant camera," Uriah said. One of the cheap Polaroid knockoffs.

Vang glanced up. "Not a big surprise."

Uriah scooped up the spilled photos, then froze as his mind struggled to process what he was seeing.

Jude. Of course, Jude.

In every one she was nude. Filthy, hair matted, welts and cuts on her chest, her legs, her back, her hips. Photo after photo of degradation and impossible torture.

My God.

He swallowed.

Was the entire drawer Jude?

"Find anything?" Vang said as he moved to another area of the room.

"Not yet." Uriah didn't want Vang to see the photos. He didn't want anybody to see them. He especially didn't want Jude to see them. What he really wanted was to take them outside and set them on fire.

And yes, the entire drawer was stuffed with photos of her.

Three years of them, starting at the bottom when she was still healthy and her hair was brown and her eyes were clear. The brutal and progressive wasting of her body and mind had been acutely and systematically documented.

"Christ," Vang whispered.

Uriah flinched in surprise and looked over his shoulder to see Vang take a half stumble away, an expression of horror on his face before he turned in an attempt to hide his reaction. Keeping his back to Uriah, he said, "You could have warned me, Ashby."

Uriah thought the thing between Jude and Vang had been nothing, maybe one of those accidents they both quickly regretted, realizing it had been a mistake. Now he wondered if Vang had been serious about Jude at one time. Was he still serious? His reaction didn't strike Uriah as the reaction of a casual acquaintance, or even that of someone who'd worked with her over three years ago. Of course, Vang had been in charge of the case. The guilt of not finding her was probably eating him up.

"How well did you know her back then?" Uriah asked, fishing.

Vang turned back around but didn't look at the photos in Uriah's hand. "She was my partner." He shrugged. "How well do *you* know her?"

Was he jealous? Upset that Jude was no longer *his* partner? "Pretty hard to get to know the Jude of today."

"Yeah, she's changed. A lot." Vang snapped off his latex gloves. "I kinda thought . . . I don't know. I mean I knew she'd be messed up, but I didn't expect her to be so . . . shut off. I didn't expect her to avoid an old friend."

"It's not about you. Or me. She's doing what she has to do to protect herself."

"I know."

"Hand me one of the large evidence boxes," Uriah said before anybody else happened into the room. "I'll put the photos inside and seal it. I don't want Jude to see them or know they exist."

Vang passed a box to him. "I gotta get some air."

After Vang left, Uriah boxed everything up and attached an evidence seal. Wondering if he was going to pass out or throw up, he thought about Jude, the Jude he knew today, not the Jude in the photos. He felt reawakened anger toward Ortega for bringing her on board, because how could anyone ever recover from the torture and brutal dehumanization he'd seen in those photos? How in the hell?

CHAPTER 22

J ude's return to consciousness was slow and confused.

For a brief moment she thought she was back in the cell. But no. She could hear the sounds of far-off traffic. And weren't those voices? Outdoor voices? Conversation and laughter?

She tugged off the cloth bag and rolled to her back. Above her were night sky and towering buildings.

Still in the alley.

She turned her head, her vision slow to follow. Blinking the world into focus, her eyes tracked across an expanse of redbrick alleyway, coming to a stop when she spotted her upright bike with her helmet hanging over one handlebar.

It seemed like a mugging, but her bike hadn't been taken. She patted the pocket of her jacket and felt the shape of her phone, her wallet alongside it. Her gun was still strapped to her waist.

She rolled to her knees and shoved herself upright. The ground tilted, and she put out a foot to steady herself. Every time she moved, the ground shifted. Like someone who'd just blown a .40 on a Breathalyzer test, she aimed for her bike. She managed to straddle the machine and remove the helmet, which was oddly heavy, from the handlebars. And then she noticed that the strap was sticky.

In the light cutting into the alley from the street, she stared at the object in her hand, her brain denying what was in front of her.

The pressure in her ears changed, became hollow and thick until the slamming of her heart seemed to come from both her chest and head. Sounds beyond the alley, sounds of nightlife, grew muffled, and lights dimmed.

She let out a gasp and dropped the helmet. It hit the brick of the alley and rolled away, leaving a trail of blood.

She stared at the blood for a long moment, then pulled out her phone.

Broken.

She turned the key on her bike and tried to kick-start it. Nothing but a disheartening click. That's when she smelled gas.

She got off the bike and picked up the helmet. Carrying it like a basket, she began walking toward the sounds of laughter.

CHAPTER 23

I t was Friday night in the Whittier neighborhood of Minneapolis. Bars and restaurants were packed, and people strolled and staggered into the streets. The party bus waited to take some of them to another area of town, and couples struggled to find keys, fighting over who would drive and who should call a cab.

"Oh my God. Look at that woman," Fatima, one of the less inebriated of her bunch said. She'd been reluctant to go out after hearing tales of how the streets were so much more dangerous now, but it was her birthday, and her friends had coaxed her into celebrating. Now her earlier unease was back.

People in her group looked up to see a tall woman with short white hair coming toward them on the sidewalk, her gait weird. Not really a stagger, but faltering. Like she was walking in soft sand, or like she was really, really tired, or really, really drunk.

Her pants were torn. She had a gash above one eye, and blood down one side of her face and neck. Dirty motorcycle jacket, black boots, black helmet in her hand.

She's been in a wreck, Fatima thought. She looked down the street, expecting to see flashing lights and maybe smashed cars.

A few girls laughed, and one shouted and clung drunkenly to the guy next to her. "Are we missing the Zombie Pub Crawl?"

The strange woman lurched closer, and the laughter that had erupted with the pub-crawl comment faltered. Fatima went still, and her boyfriend's arm tightened around her waist.

The woman reached a streetlight and paused.

"Is that blood?" One of Fatima's friends, the girl who'd talked her into coming out tonight, pointed to the helmet.

It *was* blood, Fatima decided. A lot of it.

Her boyfriend leaned close. "Call the cops," he whispered.

"That's fake," her friend said.

"Where's the camera?" somebody else added. Nervous laughter moved through the crowd, and Fatima began to hope that this *was* a stunt, and someone was recording it, and it would get a million hits on YouTube tomorrow.

The woman with the white hair heard the comment about calling the cops, and her focus shifted sharply to Fatima and her phone. She began moving toward the young girl.

Fatima slipped free of her boyfriend, pulled out her phone, and made the 911 call. "There's something weird going on," she told a male dispatcher. He had a calm, cool voice that made her want to believe everything was going to be fine. "There's a woman . . ." How did she explain this? "There's blood, or at least I think it's blood."

The woman was closer now, and Fatima took a step back, her heart slamming in her chest. The white-haired woman had brilliant blue eyes, but it wasn't the color of her eyes that made Fatima's mouth go dry. It was how direct they were, how intense. Like she was staring right into Fatima's soul. Or like Fatima was the prey.

Did she look familiar? Had she seen that face somewhere?

"What's the situation?" the dispatcher asked. "Are you in danger?"

Fatima's hand shook, and she said faintly, "It's that girl. The cop who was abducted, then escaped. Jude somebody." The news had been full of the story, and for a while linked articles kept popping up in her Facebook feed. She tried to remember what she'd read. Something about kidnapping and torture.

The woman lunged and grabbed the phone, tugging it from Fatima's grip, bringing it to her ear, telling the operator her name. *Jude Fontaine.* That was it. The words *detective* and *homicide* made it to Fatima's brain as she stared in horror at the woman in front of her.

Detective Jude Fontaine must have felt her fear, because she looked up, made that weird deep eye contact, reached for Fatima, touched her arm, gave it a gentle *it's okay* squeeze while nodding in a way meant to be reassuring.

Fatima pulled in a shaky breath, relaxed a little, looked down at the helmet in the detective's hand, and screamed.

Two hours after finding those godforsaken photos, Uriah was finally heading home from the crime scene, trying to forget the images seared in his brain. If he had anything to say about it, Jude would never know the pictures existed. He'd been surprised she'd opened up to him as much as she had, but if being in the house had made her relive her captivity, he couldn't imagine what seeing the chronological documentation of that captivity would do to her.

With one hand, he autodialed her number on his phone. She'd seemed steady when she left, but trauma could take time to sink in. His call went straight to voice mail. He was thinking about swinging by her place to check on her, when his phone rang.

The call was from a cop named Emanuel who worked in the Whittier neighborhood of Minneapolis.

"Just thought you might want to know that your partner was found walking down the street an hour and a half ago," he said, "with a severed head in her helmet."

The cluster of cop cars wasn't hard to miss even though the processing taking place in front of the popular Minneapolis hangout wasn't typical of a crime-scene investigation. There was no yellow tape, no team combing the location.

Uriah pulled to the curb, turned off the ignition, and dove from his car. He scanned the area for Jude, didn't see her but spotted Emanuel, the cop who'd called him.

"Detective Fontaine?" Uriah asked.

"In the portable crime lab." The officer gave him an over-the-shoulder thumb toward one of the white vans. "She's a cool one. I think she's less shaken than anybody here, but I guess after what she's been through, a severed head might seem like a picnic, know what I mean?"

Uriah made no attempt to hide his annoyance at the guy's insensitive comment. "I'm pretty sure a severed head would upset anybody. She's just learned to hide her reaction. And speaking of the head . . ."

An officer wearing latex gloves flipped the lid on the plastic-lined cardboard box she held in her hands. Inside was a bloody motorcycle helmet. Jude's helmet. And even though Uriah was a homicide detective, even though he'd seen more than his share of death, his mind struggled with the image presented to him. Because for a normal human, pure evil was hard to recognize when you saw it, and even harder to comprehend.

Looking up at Uriah from inside the helmet was the head of a girl with thick eyeliner and shiny dark hair. A girl he'd spoken to that very afternoon.

Nausea washed over him.

"Recognize her?" Emanuel asked.

"Yeah." Uriah stared even though he wanted to turn away. "Lola Holt."

CHAPTER 24

As Uriah stared, the lid went back on the box, and the officer carried the evidence away. "I'll contact the parents," Uriah said. The fact that Lola Holt was dead just hours after he and Jude had talked to her wasn't lost on him. "Any sign of the body?"

Emanuel rested a hand on his belt. "We've got officers working the area where your partner was attacked, but nothing yet."

A dead body was hard enough for family to deal with, but a severed head and no body?

"Someone shot Fontaine's motorcycle." Emanuel gestured up the street. "They jumped her in an alley a couple blocks from here. Most of the BCA team is there. You'll have to see the scene. Her bike was there, keys in it. Nothing taken. She still has her phone, although it's broken."

"Find any shell casings?"

"Not yet. Bullets pierced a fuel line and back tire."

"So maybe they were aiming for the bike and not Jude."

"Kinda looks that way. Bike is evidence. Got a tow truck on the way to collect it."

Someone caught Emanuel's eye, motioning him over. Uriah turned and approached the white van where Jude was being processed.

"She's about done," a member of the crime-scene team said upon spotting Uriah. "We've bagged and tagged her clothing and shoes. That's about all we can do."

"Thanks."

Inside the van, Jude sat dressed in blue scrubs, a white cotton blanket around her shoulders, a cut above one eye. "Did you see my helmet?" she asked.

"Yeah." He sat down on the bench next to her. "I saw it."

"It's her, isn't it?"

"Pretty sure. We'll have to wait for the parents' ID to make an official announcement to the press."

"Anyone find the body?"

"Not yet. What happened, Jude?"

Without looking at him—maybe eye contact would have been a distraction—she related how she got a text from Lola Holt and went to the café to meet her.

"You were lured there. Somebody was watching for you."

"I agree."

"See anybody?"

"No. My head was covered too quickly."

"What about a voice? Sounds?"

"Nobody said a word."

"Why didn't they kill you? That's the big question. People with no qualms about killing and decapitating a teenage girl, yet they let you live?"

"I don't get it either. As far as Lola Holt goes . . . maybe they're sending the other girls a message. Speak up and the same thing will happen to you." She slumped against the wall of the van, head back. He could almost feel her exhaustion.

"Somebody must have seen us with her this afternoon," Jude said. "No wonder she was so afraid." Pause. "This is our fault."

"We were doing our job. And if she'd opened up to us, there's a good chance this wouldn't have happened."

"I know, but I can't help but feel we could have handled it differently."

"What about the attack on you?"

"A warning? A game? I'm someone who'd guarantee a lot of media attention."

He'd been thinking the same thing. "The press will be all over this."

The crime-scene tech appeared at the back door. "We're done here. You're free to leave," she told Jude. "I'm sorry, but your clothing might have to remain evidence for quite some time."

Jude pushed herself upright, stood a moment to stabilize, then stepped out of the van unaided while Uriah watched, ready to jump in if she needed help, knowing she wouldn't want it.

"I'm gonna catch a cab and go home," she said as soon as her feet hit the ground.

Barely past midnight, but a few confused birds were singing in the darkness.

"I'll give you a ride and put a couple of guards on you. Whoever did this is still out there."

She didn't argue, and for once she seemed too exhausted to pick up on the signals he was undoubtedly sending, this time about those goddamn photos.

CHAPTER 25

At Jude's place, Uriah checked for signs of forced entry, but the apartment seemed fairly safe. Fourth floor, one way in, a thick metal door with an impressive dead bolt. Jude was asleep on the couch by the time the two plainclothes officers showed up, so Uriah woke her with orders to lock the dead bolt behind him.

After leaving Jude's apartment, Uriah drove straight to the Holt house, where the door was answered by a man in his late forties dressed in plaid pajama pants and a white V-neck undershirt. Charles Holt. His wife, Donna, the woman Uriah and Jude had met the day they'd stopped by in hopes of interviewing Lola, appeared behind her husband, hands busy tying a white robe, hair flat on one side of her head. They'd both been asleep.

Cops practiced this stuff. How to break bad news to people. Uriah had actually taken a seminar in which officers tried out different methods on one another. The big takeaway? There was no single best style other than delivering the news clearly and concisely. Thing was, people knew. They knew before you told them. That's what Uriah had learned not only in practice, but also firsthand. Because he'd been on the other side of that door.

It didn't help to take it slow, chat a moment, have them sit down. You had to get the news in while you could, before the brain began creating its own story. He understood how that worked too, when you know what's coming is going to be bad so you start grasping for a lesser kind of bad. Maybe a loved one maimed but not dead. And you start imagining how you'll care for that maimed person, and how that person will deal with the severity of her injuries. Those were the bargains you made. Or maybe it was a way for your brain to ease you in, a lesser horror before the full-blown truth.

Uriah preferred to tell people straight out. Clearly. Plainly. And that's what he did now. Not only the news of Lola Holt's death, but the circumstances, because there was nothing in the world that could lessen that blow. No amount of buildup, no sitting down.

The Holts clung to each other, shock mirrored in their faces. They turned, and with awkward, jerky motions, they moved deeper into the house to drop to the couch, all the while muttering words of denial and disbelief.

He knew that part too, and what came on the heels of denial. Pain, followed by fog. Without the fog, a person would break into a million pieces.

"Let me drive you to the morgue," Uriah said. Neither of them was in any shape to get behind the wheel.

His offer took a while to sink in. He could wait. And then they finally disappeared to get dressed, then reappeared to awkwardly gather belongings: a light jacket for a cool night, a purse, billfold—all part of a life that no longer held any meaning.

Uriah didn't remember how he'd gotten to the morgue when Ellen died. There was a big blank spot in his memory. Cops came to the door, and the next thing he recalled was being at the morgue. Like he'd teleported there.

"Lock the house behind you," he reminded the couple.

Keys were found, the door locked.

Uriah rarely questioned his line of work, but he was questioning it big time tonight. This was one of those moments when any job on earth had to be preferable to what he was doing right now.

He put the Holts together in the backseat, where they clung to each other in a silence broken only by sobs. After signing in at the morgue, he led them down a fluorescent hallway to a small room designated for viewing. When the night-shift assistant pulled back the sheet, Uriah could almost feel the room tilt.

Nothing could have prepared the parents for the sight of their daughter's severed head. There was no way for the human mind to process the horror. And that's what it was. Not only had these poor people lost their daughter; they'd lost her under the most horrific of circumstances.

"Is it her?" Uriah asked quietly. He was like the scene director, gently prodding the actors forward. At the same time, he heard the tremor in his own voice. No shame in that. Shame came when there was no tremor. That's when a guy had to start worrying.

Lola's father nodded, his mouth a grimace of pain. Beside him, his wife let out an anguished wail before buckling. Uriah managed to break her fall and ease her the rest of the way down while the husband stood and watched, his brain unable to grasp what was going on right in front of him.

Was there a limit to how much the mind could endure? If so, this couple deserved oblivion.

The husband finally kicked in, reached down, and helped Donna Holt to her feet; then they both stood there, too stunned to contemplate their next move.

Uriah felt a little woozy himself. Maybe it was the similarities between Ellen's suicide and the Holt girl. That knock at the door in the middle of the night. The deaths of two young women who'd had their lives in front of them. Same morgue. Those similarities confused Uriah's brain, and for a fraction of a second he thought he was there to identify his wife's dead body.

But no.

That was over.

That had already happened. He'd lived through it. He'd shattered, but now he was back. Not the same, but back.

The kindest gesture Uriah could offer right now was to leave the Holts alone with their grief. He thanked the assistant and led the couple from the room. Outside, he put them in a cab and sent them home.

CHAPTER 26

Standing outside the Holt home in the stark morning light, waiting for an answer to their knock, Jude glanced at her partner, noting the paleness of his skin, the dampness of the hair around his face, the hint of stress at the corners of his mouth. In the ride over, they'd decided Uriah would do the talking since he'd already established a rapport with the couple, but now Jude could see he was in no shape to question them. She felt a vibration coming from him, an inner trembling even though outwardly he appeared calm and in control. She guessed his reaction had something to do with the wife he'd lost. He talked about Jude not being ready for Homicide, but she wondered about him. His buried emotions lay close to the surface, and every bad thing that happened seemed to increase his vulnerability. His state of mind might be invisible to others, but it was there, hard for her to ignore, but too personal for her to address.

Jude heard footsteps from inside and said, "I'll do this." Along with the questions, she planned to watch both parents closely since everyone was suspect, especially family.

The door was answered by Charles Holt.

She pulled out her badge and introduced herself. "I believe you met my partner earlier. We know it's a bad time, but we'd like to ask you and your wife a few questions." Jude dropped into the role of compassionate cop. Not that her compassion wasn't real. Not that she didn't feel their pain and feel a familiar echo of sorrow and sympathy, but at the same time her life now was about looking at the world through a window. She felt more of an observer than a participant—a good thing in this situation.

"Have you found the body?" the man asked.

"No." Jude tucked her badge and leather case back into her jacket.

"We need to make funeral arrangements. You need to find the rest of her." The father's voice cracked on "the rest of her."

"We're trying," Uriah said.

The guy stared too long, then seemed to remember why the detectives were there. "My wife is upstairs sleeping."

"Maybe we could just start with you," Jude said. "Maybe she'll feel like seeing us before we leave."

Grieving people tended to either comply without question or lash out in anger. Mr. Holt complied, and Jude and Uriah stepped inside.

The interior had brightly colored walls, eclectic décor, plants that climbed to the ceiling, turned, and headed back to the wooden floor. Bohemian, artistic. And, in this moment, almost cruelly joyful.

They sat down on a couch in front of a coffee table. "I made this," the man said when he noticed Jude unconsciously trace fingers across the wooden surface. She hadn't realized she was doing it, and now she pulled her hand away.

"It's beautiful," she told him.

"I'm not sure my wife will be able to talk to you. She took something to knock her out."

"I understand." Jude had no real ties to anyone, but she could imagine what it might be like. She still remembered love even though she didn't think she wanted to experience it again. She didn't even know how it felt to have a pet. There was the roof cat she fed, but she thought of him in the way she thought of the plates that had been in the apartment when she arrived. He belonged to no one. That was the best she could do, and it worked for her. For now. Maybe forever. The mere act of allowing herself to have such thoughts brought a fresh wave of sympathy for the Holts that she couldn't allow herself to feel. Sometimes the world was just too much.

"Lola was everything to us," the man said. "Everything. My wife couldn't have children," he went on to explain. "We tried for years; then, after we gave up, Donna got pregnant. Our daughter was a treasure. A gift."

"I'm sorry." Right words for the situation. The only words, really.

"I feel like we let her down. We *did* let her down. We weren't paying attention."

"It's not your fault," Uriah said.

"But it is. A parent's job is to protect his child. I had one important job to do, and that was to keep her safe."

From above their heads came the sound of movement. A dull thud, a door opening and closing, footsteps that faded before becoming more pronounced.

"What are they doing here?"

Heads turned.

Halfway down the stairs stood Mrs. Holt. She was dressed in a pair of pajama bottoms too frivolous for the turn her life had taken, along with a vintage T-shirt with the white text partially worn away. Her eyes were red rimmed, her face puffy. "Why did you let them in?" she shouted at her husband. "They can't be here. Not in our house!"

Uriah got to his feet. "Sorry for the intrusion. We just need to ask you a few questions; then we'll be on our way."

"I don't care why you're here. Get out. Now."

"I understand, but—"

"Unless you have a daughter who's been decapitated, you *do not* understand." She raised her arm, the movement revealing a revolver she aimed at Uriah. "Out!" she screamed. "Get out of my house!"

Mr. Holt gasped. "Donna!"

The gun shifted to point at him. "I want them out of here."

Jude stood up slowly, table in front of her, couch behind. The gun shifted, and now the barrel was pointing at her chest. She felt no fear.

Trembling arm, shaking gun, tears and anger and hatred. "You're the reason my daughter is dead," the woman said. "Coming around here. Chasing her at the funeral. Yes, she told me about that." Each word was delivered with a thrust of the weapon. "You put her in danger, and now she's dead. Because of *you.*"

Jude couldn't argue. It *was* her fault. If she'd been more discreet . . . If they hadn't chased Lola in front of the whole world, at an event the killer had most likely attended, then the girl might still be alive. She started to repeat her earlier apology but stopped herself. *I'm sorry* was for bumping into people. *I'm sorry* was for misunderstandings, not murder.

"Donna." The husband, the broken husband, took a step toward his wife. The gun pivoted.

She was still standing on the stairs, too far for Jude and Uriah to rush her. "Do either of you have children?" she asked them.

Jude shook her head, and Uriah echoed the movement.

"Did you hear that?" The words were shrieked to her husband. "They don't even know what it's like! They don't even know how it feels! Our daughter would be alive if they hadn't put her in the spotlight, if they hadn't drawn attention to her."

With that accusation, the gun barrel shifted again, discharging this time, the sound deafening. The couch exploded; white stuffing floated in the air.

Now that it had happened, now that the trigger had been pulled, Mrs. Holt released a bellow and came roaring down the stairs, gun braced in both hands as madness and grief took over and she fired one shot after the other.

In unison, Jude and Uriah dove behind the couch. Lamps shattered. Photos crashed to the floor. The husband let out a cry and dropped. Above everything was the woman's high-pitched wail.

In those adrenaline-saturated seconds, as a series of thoughts rampaged through Jude's brain, taking her from one rejected plan of action to another, she found herself thinking, *Good for you.* She found herself siding with the mother, cheering the mother, while at the same time knowing this had to stop.

From way out there in the world, beyond the ringing ears and the mad sorrow, came the scream of sirens.

Someone had called the cops.

Shots fired.

The woman must have heard the sirens too, because her feet pounded the wooden floor as she moved toward Jude and Uriah with purpose and intent, leaving the detectives no choice.

They jumped to their feet, weapons drawn, arms extended as Uriah shouted for her to stand down.

The front door burst open, and uniformed officers poured in.

In that moment there was nothing more chilling and *heartbreaking* than the desperate click of the firing mechanism repeatedly striking the empty chamber. Donna Holt continued to pull the trigger, the clicks the only sounds in the room until a moan broke through.

Attention shifted to the bleeding husband on the floor. One of the officers called for an ambulance while Jude rushed to the side of the injured man and Uriah helped restrain the woman.

Maybe their lives hadn't been perfect. Maybe the husband was having an affair, and maybe his wife longed for something more and resented the hours he spent at work or in his woodshop. Maybe the teenager was a narcissistic brat who talked back to her parents and snuck out at night, because that's what teens did. But even if their lives hadn't been perfect, they'd never get a chance to fix what was wrong, never get a chance to work it out or forgive or find the peace that came with time. They would be forever locked in this moment, and this loss would inform every breath the couple took for the rest of their lives.

"I'm sorry," Jude whispered to the man on the floor. She could no longer depersonalize. This time she felt the words. This time she directly linked the words with a pain deep in her gut. "I'm so sorry."

CHAPTER 27

L et's talk about Detective Fontaine." Ortega leaned a hip against her desk and crossed her arms. Uriah didn't sit down but instead remained near the closed inner-office door. Just hours earlier he and Jude had been diving behind the couch at the Holt house.

Beyond the glass walls, Jude and Grant Vang were deep in discussion, probably about the Holt and Masters task force they were putting together.

He had to give Vang credit for keeping his cool around Jude. He didn't act weird after seeing the photos. Uriah wasn't sure he could say the same thing about himself. He'd seen Jude shoot him a question mark a few times. She was picking up on something. If she asked what was going on, he'd lie. She'd probably pick up on that too. But no matter how well she was handling her return to life and work, he was pretty sure she wouldn't want to know those photos existed and that he'd seen them.

"I made a mistake," Ortega said. "I shouldn't have let her come back. You were right. It seems cruel now." She shrugged as if to highlight her point. "Maybe it would have been fine if things had been fairly normal around here, but nothing has been normal for quite some time. It's been one damn thing after the other. I can't imagine what kind of impact all this is having on her. Finding the house and the body, followed by the attack and decapitation, then the unfortunate drama that took place with the parents."

Sometimes Uriah thought Ortega was too sensitive for the job as chief. She'd brought Fontaine in because she felt sorry for her. Now she wanted to get rid of her for the same reason. She didn't seem to understand that jerking her around was worse.

"I saw Fontaine after she was attacked," Uriah said, "and she was handling it well. Cool as always."

"In public," Ortega said. "Who knows how she is at home. And, if she's truly unaffected, then that also makes me question her mental state." She circled her desk and sat down. "I'm thinking of telling her to take two weeks off, then maybe giving her six months' full pay and a benefit package." She looked at him. "Unless you can convince me otherwise. How does she seem to you? Out there in the street?"

"Fontaine's not *right*. I doubt she'll ever be *right*. But who here is? Once any one of us has a homicide or two or three under our belts, aren't we all existing and working with a new understanding of just what the world is capable of? And aren't we all at least a little closer to a meltdown? But she's focused. Nothing distracts her. So far, she's kept impressively cool when the situation calls for it. I'd hate to see her go."

"I didn't think I'd ever hear you defend her."

Surprised him too. "I was worried about her at first," Uriah admitted, "but I think her experience has actually made her a better cop and maybe made her better equipped to deal with whatever is thrown at her."

"*If* she doesn't crack."

"We're all at risk of that."

"Okay. I won't pull her, not yet anyway, but you're going to have to keep an eye on her." She seemed relieved that she didn't have to deal with telling Fontaine to go home for good. "Send her in. I want to talk to her in private."

"Detective Ashby said you wanted to see me." Jude stood in Chief Ortega's office wondering if she was about to be fired.

Sitting in her chair, Ortega fiddled with her pen. Her nervousness didn't bode well for Jude. "How are things going?" the chief asked. "Any second thoughts about being back here?" Her desk was littered with framed photos and leafy plants that Jude didn't know the names of. *A plant might be nice,* she thought.

"It's uncomfortable at times, I'll admit it," Jude said. "And I'm worried that my celebrity—for lack of a better word—might have been behind the death of the Holt girl. That makes me question whether I should be here at all." Maybe that's what this meeting was about. Maybe Ortega was having the same thoughts.

"You were held captive for three years. I don't know what I'd do in your situation, but I think I might want to get as far away from police work as possible. Maybe go to Disney World or take a trip to Paris. Have you ever been out of the country?"

Yep. About to be fired. "A trip to Ireland with my father and brother when I was little. I don't remember much about it." A trip meant to be a distraction after the horrific death of Natalie Schilling.

"Maybe you should think about traveling. Life moves so fast, you know."

"It kind of feels like it's not moving at all."

"What do you want, Jude? You must want something. Forget the travel idea. What do you want right now? For yourself? Spiritually? Emotionally? Just day to day?"

Jude thought about buying a plant, but did she have enough nurturing left in her to care for it? "I want what I can't have," she decided.

"And what's that?" Ortega clicked her pen, and suddenly Jude felt as if she were visiting the department psychologist. She glanced around the desk, wondering if Ortega had received an updated report. There was no file in sight, but maybe the woman had tucked it in a drawer.

Jude focused on the question, looking for the truth within herself. What *did* she want? "My old home, my old bed, my dishes, my clothes, my books," she decided with sudden clarity. And Eric. "That's the only thing that kept me going when I was in that place. The only thing that kept me alive. Thinking about getting back there."

Ortega smiled a little, and Jude got the idea her honesty had made her boss happy.

"Sit down, sweetie."

Jude sat, a bit surprised by her own words and the truth of those words.

She still carried the memories of happier days with her just like she'd carried them with her when she was in the cell, *her* cell. Maybe that's why she'd had the urge to go inside and close the door yesterday. God, was that only yesterday? With all that had happened, it felt like weeks ago.

Would going back inside the cell have felt like a do-over? Would it have given her the chance to reset her escape to return home to that warm welcome she'd dreamed of? Unrealistic, of course, but the brain often rejected logic in favor of desire.

"Have you gone to see him?" Ortega asked. "Eric?"

"Not since the night of my escape." She'd tried not to think about that night. It was something the department psychologist had asked about too.

"Maybe you should. Talk to him. It might bring some closure."

"Or it might hurt all over again."

"Would you be open to seeing him?"

"I don't know. Maybe."

"The reason I brought it up is because he's called, asking about you. He wanted to know how you were doing. He wanted your phone number, but of course I didn't give it to him."

Ortega leaned forward, elbows on her desk. "One of the reasons I called you in here was to tell you that I'm having a cookout this weekend. My husband got a new grill, and he's anxious to crank it up." She rolled her eyes. "He's crazy about that stuff. I don't know why. But Detectives Vang and Ashby will be there. Harold, from Evidence. You should come."

"Is it mandatory?"

"Absolutely not. But I like my detectives to get together after hours. I'm not talking about going to a bar, but homey stuff. You have to have balance in this job; otherwise the cases will consume you." She rummaged around in her desk, found a piece of paper with writing on it, added something, and passed it across her desk. "My address. Saturday, four p.m. until who knows when."

Jude accepted the paper. It had the police-department logo in one corner, Chief Ortega's name across the top, her home address, and a series of numbers that looked familiar.

A cookout. Men in aprons. Kids, and maybe dogs running around. Jude didn't even know if she was ready for a plant, and here Ortega was, offering an even larger taste of normal. Something about it seemed the worst possible thing for her to do. "I don't think I'll make it, but thanks for the invitation."

"The phone number?" Ortega asked, pointing. "It belongs to Eric."

Eric.

"I've wondered what he did with all of my things." Maybe that's what he wanted to talk to her about. "I have to be honest," Jude said as she folded the paper. "I thought you called me in here to let me go."

"I just wanted to chat and see how you were doing," Ortega said.

It seemed impossible, but Ortega was easier to read than Uriah. She'd obviously called Uriah in to get a report, which meant he must have said something favorable.

"Try to enjoy some things," Ortega said. "Even if it's just a damn good latte from the café around the corner. If you need to talk, I'm here. And think about the cookout."

Later that afternoon, Jude, Uriah, and Vang spearheaded a meeting to brief beat officers on the Holt case. The meeting was held in a second-floor conference room with a low ceiling, fluorescent lights, and rows of flimsy chairs that threatened to buckle under some of the larger cops.

On the wall at the front of the room was a large corkboard that depicted what Jude liked to think of as the genealogy of a crime. The board contained a map of the city, photos of the victims, along with crime-scene images. Other details, such as information that matched both the Holt and Masters murders, ran along one side, to be built upon by task-force detectives and beat cops alike.

Almost all departments had moved to digital files that could be accessed through their VPN, or virtual private network, but Jude still liked the old-fashioned and what some might consider outdated use of the wall.

A few theories were tossed around, many conflicting. The one thing everybody seemed to agree on was that Lola Holt's head had been left as a warning to anybody who might consider coming forward with information about the murder of Delilah Masters.

"Tip-line phones will be active in a few hours," Jude told the officers. "So be prepared to respond to those calls."

The briefing was short, not over ten minutes.

"Hopefully we'll have more information next time," Vang added as he passed briefing sheets to the men and women leaving the room.

"Notice anything unusual?" Uriah asked once it was just the three task-force members left in the room.

Vang glanced around and shrugged. Jude immediately knew what Uriah was talking about. "They were scared," she said. "The cops were scared."

"Why?" Vang asked.

Uriah explained. "They're thinking the severed head wasn't just for high school girls who might be tempted to speak up. It was a warning for us too. All of us."

CHAPTER 28

J ude hadn't attended a press conference since her return from the dead. That's what she was calling it nowadays. Return from the dead.

This time around, when Chief Ortega insisted she put in an appearance, she didn't fight it. She was beginning to understand the ramifications of trying to maintain a low profile. After a point, people got tired of giving her space while their curiosity intensified. She'd still not granted anyone an interview. Now, due to the amped-up horror, those same people were salivating with curiosity while the locals wanted to know who was looking out for them.

Sometimes press conferences were held on the sidewalk in front of the Minneapolis Police Department main doors, but this one was taking place in the more controlled surroundings of the pressroom, with its low ceiling, fluorescent lighting, and business-style setting. The state and US flags designated the official space behind the typical cluster of microphones. In the crowd, Jude spotted familiar media faces from the local news outlets, along with some not-so-familiar faces she suspected were national.

Chief Ortega positioned herself behind the mic, with Jude and Uriah to one side. "We'll begin shortly," Ortega told the crowd of reporters. "We're waiting for one final person." The words were barely out of her mouth when a commotion drew all eyes to the door. In walked the governor of Minnesota, trailed by his entourage—including Jude's brother, Adam Schilling.

Her mouth went dry and her stomach clenched.

She'd seen her father on the news several times, recently and not so recently, but she hadn't been in close proximity since she was a teenager. She shot Uriah a silent question: *Did you know he was coming?*

He responded with a slight shake of his head.

She wanted to leave, to run. Instead, she managed, almost mindlessly, to participate in the presentation of facts, followed by the Q&A.

Her father reassured the crowd that everything was being done that could be done, and nothing would be overlooked. "Minnesota Bureau of Criminal Apprehension is one of the best in the country," he said.

Dialogue shifted to his political agenda and his plans to support the mayor in his plea for increased funding in all areas of police work, including getting more officers back on the streets. Then the press conference wrapped up. Before Jude could make an escape, her father cut behind Chief Ortega to grab Jude by the elbow, a big white smile on his face as cameras snapped, capturing the two of them together. Father and daughter.

"Jude. I'm happy to see you," he said. "I was relieved and thankful to hear you were alive." He might have been gray and in his sixties, but he exuded vitality and the appearance of someone who ate right and ran several miles a day.

She knew she should reply. She knew the world was watching, waiting for her response—which was exactly what this was about. Behind her, she felt Ortega's presence, even though the chief wasn't within her field of vision.

Jude got it. She suddenly understood why it was so important that she be here even though her participation was disruptive. The press conference had been about this moment, about introducing Jude to the world as a stable woman related to a powerful man. A good daughter. The public would be reassured that she wasn't the crazy cop who'd briefly brought shame to the governor by emancipating herself.

People were horrified by the recent murders, and the decapitation of Lola Holt had sparked terror in the heart of every citizen. They needed to be reassured that Jude could handle whatever was thrown her way, and that her history, old and new, was just that—history. Personal issues would not get in the way of the investigation.

While Jude loathed insincerity of any kind, she was no longer a child and she now knew how to play the game. She returned the governor's smile and reached for him, a hand to his shoulder. Leaning in, she smelled the fabric of his expensive suit, smelled the sunblock that was doing its part to protect his aging skin. The flatness of his eyes and the taut muscles in his cheeks transmitted a different story the photos and video footage wouldn't tell. And then she did something that took even her by surprise. She leaned in close and kissed him. Just a brush of her lips against his cheek. When she pulled back, she saw confusion and anger in his eyes.

And now she realized that this hadn't been about a show of solidarity, at least not for him.

"Good to see you, Father."

"Yes . . ." He was at a loss for words.

He'd probably agreed to come, braced for a confrontation. Maybe he'd even hoped to prove she was unfit for duty. She'd never been able to figure him out, and today he seemed as much of a mystery as ever, proof that her years in the basement hadn't left her with superpowers.

She smiled and moved away, ignoring the reporters and the microphones shoved in front of her. Outside, she turned her face to the sun and began walking. Inside, she was quaking.

A shout came from behind, followed by the sound of running feet. "Detective Fontaine! Please. I have to talk to you."

With no change in gait, without turning, Jude said, "I don't talk to reporters."

The woman caught up, walk-jogging beside Jude. "I'm not a reporter. My name is Kennedy Broder. My boyfriend was Ian Caldwell. He was a police-beat reporter for the *Trib*." When the name failed to register, she rushed to explain: "A little over three years ago he met with you, and a few hours later he was dead."

CHAPTER 29

Jude halted in the middle of the sidewalk, surprised to see that Kennedy Broder was more girl than woman. Short, wearing skinny jeans, black Converse sneakers, and a purple beret on her chin-length red hair.

"I've been trying to get in touch with you ever since I heard you were alive," the young woman said.

Jude was a master when it came to evading the press and curiosity seekers. This person was just one of hundreds who'd apparently tried to reach her after her escape.

"Back when you disappeared," Kennedy said, "I tried to tell the cops about my boyfriend, tried to tell them there was some connection, but nobody listened."

Jude urged the girl out of foot traffic. A short distance away, people waited in line for the noon food truck.

"I remember him now," Jude said when they reached the shade of a towering stone building. She and Ian Caldwell had met at a coffee shop in Uptown. "I'm sorry about your loss."

Here was another person seeking closure, looking for answers, looking to make sense of a thing that would never make sense—the death of a loved one. And yet Jude felt the need to say something that would give the young woman a clear picture of that day. "We grabbed a coffee and sat down," Jude said. "As soon as he introduced himself, his phone rang. He said he had to go, and he left. That's all there was to it. We didn't even have time for a conversation." She gestured and shook her head in an attempt to drive home the lack of conversation they'd had. "I'm surprised I even remember him."

Jude glanced down the sidewalk, saw Uriah moving through the crowd, a question in his eyes.

"You never knew why he wanted to meet with you?"

"No."

The girl stared, unwilling or maybe unable to accept what she was hearing. She'd had so much riding on this moment, and she'd been waiting for so long. "I kept hoping you might know something. He was investigating a missing girl named Octavia Germaine."

Octavia Germaine . . . Why did that name sound familiar?

"I don't know much about the case, but she's never been found. I always wondered if his murder had something to do with her."

"I don't even deal with missing persons," Jude said. It didn't make sense. Kennedy must have been confused. "How did he die?"

"He was beaten and robbed."

Highly unlikely that it had any connection to his meeting with Jude. People were beaten and robbed in Minneapolis every single day, and young males were often the targets.

"They never found who did it," the girl said. "I *want* them to find who did it. And I always had this idea—this *hope*—that you might know." Her eyes glistened and she bit her lip. "I wasn't even around when it happened. I feel horrible about that. We were taking a break from each other, and I was in Portland staying with friends."

"I'm sorry," Jude said. "I wish I could help, but I can't."

The girl produced a missing person flyer and handed it to Jude. Octavia Germaine was a pretty girl, about sixteen, with straight dark-blond hair. And now Jude remembered why the name sounded familiar. Germaine's photo had been in her desk. And was now locked in the evidence room.

"I don't know why I even brought it," Kennedy said, then turned and walked away.

Uriah strolled up, a red-and-white fast-food container cradled in one hand, paper bag in the other. "I got extra for you." Then, "What was that about?" He pointed behind him where Kennedy's purple beret could still be seen, much smaller now as she melted into the crowd.

Jude told him, folding the photo of Octavia Germaine and sticking it in the pocket of her jacket.

"You've said you don't remember your abduction. I'm wondering if you're missing more of that day. Maybe missing pieces of your visit with this Caldwell guy."

"That's what I'm wondering too."

"You don't know why he wanted to talk to you?"

"No, but I do know you were right. I shouldn't be here. In Homicide." What happened in there with her father had once again brought home the fact that her history, long ago and recent, was compromising their investigation. The press wasn't going to forget her story or who she was. "And I'm pretty sure Ortega is thinking about letting me go. I don't blame her."

She expected him to agree.

"Are you afraid?" he asked. "Is that what's really going on? Because fear is nothing to be ashamed of. Fear will keep you alive. *Lack of fear?* That'll kill you. You were attacked. You found a head in your helmet. I mean, come on. That's some messed-up stuff."

At least he didn't say it had happened on top of everything else. "I *am* afraid," she said. "But not for the reasons you think. We have a girl who might be dead because of us. *That* scares me."

"We were doing our job. Being a cop means collateral damage."

"I'm not one of those people who thinks one or two deaths is worth it as long as you save twenty lives in the process," she said. "One death is one too many. One death is unacceptable and unforgivable. And a young girl—a young, sixteen-year-old girl? We should have put a watch on her."

"We can't put a watch on everybody."

Realizing they were still standing on the sidewalk, they began moving in the direction of the parking garage and their unmarked car. Uriah offered her the paper bag. She shook her head. "Maybe later."

"Then take it while I eat this thing," he said, indicating the falafel in the red-and-white tray.

She took the bag.

"I know it's none of my business, but want to talk about what's going on between you and your father?" he asked between bites, eating as they walked. You'd think they were at the state fair.

Seeing her father seemed to have flipped a switch in her brain, and she was surprised at the anger still vibrating in her. And knowing the circus had been partially orchestrated by Ortega? That pissed her off too.

"Weren't you seven or eight when your mother died?" Uriah asked.

"Old enough for decent recall."

"Kids get things mixed up all the time. When I think of some of the stuff I believed when I was a kid—"

"You're just like the rest of them. I was eight, not two or three. An eight-year-old has the ability to understand, especially on an emotional level."

"I'm just trying to put things together."

"Don't overwork your brain. The man is evil. Take my word for it. Or don't take my word for it. Go back in there and kiss his ass like the rest of the city."

"Whoa." He stopped, surprised by her anger. Yeah, seeing her father had definitely lit a fire in her.

"Okay. I'll tell you what happened so you can dismiss it like everybody else. My parents had a huge fight. A short time later, my mother was dead. I saw my father standing over my dead mother, a gun in his hand, a satisfied smirk on his face."

"And your brother?"

"He was there. And that's the story, isn't it? That he was shooting cans and my mother walked into his line of fire. My dad took the gun from him when he arrived on the scene. Makes sense, right? Don't tell me people fight. Don't tell me I was a kid and misread what happened. Or that anguish can sometimes look like a smile. I've heard it all before. Now let's never talk about this again." She could see he wanted to ask more questions. She could see the disbelief he couldn't hide from her, along with the compassion.

Their phones buzzed simultaneously, indicating a text. They pulled out the devices and checked their screens. A message from the BCA: *We have a match on the body collected from the basement. Information is being sent to Homicide over your secure network.*

"Let's find some privacy to check the file," Uriah said once the car was parked and they were on the second floor of the Minneapolis Police Department.

In one of the private meeting rooms, Jude closed the door as Uriah settled himself in front of a computer and logged on to their VPN. Jude stood behind his chair, eyes on the monitor. An authentication password followed by a few key clicks, and a man's face, along with his rap sheet, filled the screen.

Those eyes . . . Large pupils surrounded by tangled brown hair. Jude reached blindly for something, anything, her hand grabbing at the edge of the table.

"Hey." Uriah wheeled out a chair. "Sit."

She dropped into the seat and waited for the blackness to recede. His hand on the back of her neck forced her forward until her head was between her knees. Uriah's voice finally cut through the roar in her head, and a minute later she straightened, her vision clear, her face and body drenched in sweat.

"I take it that's him," Uriah said.

"Yeah."

Uriah got up and returned with a cup of water. With a trembling hand, she took a long drink. It helped.

He had a name. The man who'd done such awful things to her. He had a name. She looked back at the screen. This time seeing his face didn't bring on a faint, but it made her heart slam, made her mouth go dry all over again.

Humphrey Salazar. She could read him, feel the anger he'd felt moments before the camera had captured his emotions. She'd been at the receiving end of that anger many times.

Humphrey. She would never have guessed such evil would have a name like Humphrey. Even Salazar seemed innocuous.

"You sure it's him?" Uriah asked.

"I know that face. Every line, every muscle."

Uriah leaned back in his chair, one arm on the table. "You did it, Jude. He's dead. He can't ever hurt you again. Or anybody else, for that matter."

"Yes." Until that moment, she hadn't realized how much of her captor she carried with her. How he'd been living under her skin and in her very marrow. But now, knowing he was no longer a breathing thing—*thing* because he could never be a man, never be human—she could wash him off. No, not for good. Not completely. She would never be completely free until she herself was dead, but what was happening inside her felt almost like a rebirth.

But then she remembered . . .

"What?" Uriah asked.

It seemed she wasn't the only body reader in the room.

"Nothing." Yes, she wanted to think this was it. That it was over. She wanted to think that Salazar was the most evil person she'd ever encounter, but someone was killing young women, decapitating them. It didn't get much more evil than that.

For some reason, maybe because she didn't want to ruin this moment of triumph, she decided not to share her thoughts. Instead, she reached for the keyboard and logged out. "I think I'll have something to eat now."

Uriah pulled a falafel from the bag, unwrapped it, and slid the paper-lined foil across the table. "Foxy Falafel is the best."

Jude examined the red cabbage inside the pita bread. "I've never had one of these."

"That's criminal."

She took a bite. Her expression must have gone from doubtful to pleased, because Uriah said, "Good, right?"

Jude's phone vibrated, indicating a text. She checked the screen. It was a message from Evidence. They were releasing her bike, and apparently someone had even repaired the fuel line.

CHAPTER 30

own the street from Jude's apartment, Grant Vang sat in an unmarked car munching on an energy bar while watching people enter and exit her building. His partner in surveillance was a green kid named Craig who was positioned in the alley in another car. Nobody was getting in or out without being seen.

It had been four days since Jude's attack, and so far they'd spotted no unusual activity unless you counted a drug deal and a couple having sex in a car.

Surveillance was being pulled soon. The money and especially the manpower just wasn't there. At that point, Jude would have the option to hire someone herself or move to a more secure area—maybe an apartment attached to the skyway, like the place Uriah lived.

Vang was overqualified for surveillance, and Ortega had originally tapped another officer, but when Vang offered, Ortega gave him the job even though he was already stretched with the task force. Maybe she figured he wanted to help keep an eye on one of their own. She was right about that. And he particularly wanted to keep an eye on Jude.

His phone rang. He glanced at the screen, then back at the apartment building while he blindly hit the "Answer" button. "Hey, Jude."

His own little lame joke that he'd kept going for years. He wasn't sure if she'd ever thought it was funny, not even back when she still had a sense of humor. Hard to believe she'd once been one of the craziest in the department. And by crazy, he meant crazy in a fun way.

"I'm inside," she told him.

Five minutes earlier he'd watched her motorcycle come up the street, turn, and head down the alley, where it entered the building from below. Her instructions were to report to him as soon as she was in her apartment.

Dependable, efficient Jude Fontaine. Definitely a different person from the one he'd known years ago. She'd seemed almost a kid back then. But she'd been a good detective, one of them. She'd joke around and hit the bars after her shift. Hang out. She'd also enjoyed sex, maybe a little too much.

No hanging out or sex going on now. Well, maybe she and Ashby shared a drink or two, but even that idea seemed remote. From what Vang could tell, she went straight home when she got off work. She had no other life. Work, home.

"The space is clear," she said. "And I've locked the dead bolt."

The building was more secure than it looked. Cameras in the halls, dead bolts on the doors, underground parking that could be accessed only with a code.

He told her good night.

Time dragged, but midnight finally came. A car pulled up behind him and shut off its lights. Vang checked the rearview mirror and recognized his shift replacement. Eager to get the hell out of there, he turned the key in the ignition and took off. Twelve hours straight, hardly moving, peeing in a jug. He wasn't sure how people did this kind of thing full-time.

Instead of going home, he headed straight for the all-night gym on Lyndale, parked in the lot, swiped his passkey, and went inside. In the locker room he tugged his T-shirt over his head.

Was he putting on weight? he wondered, eying his profile in the full-length mirror. Was that possible? Could a guy put on weight in a few days?

He pinched the flesh on his belly. Nothing worse than flab on a skinny guy. Then he ran his fingers across the scar on his biceps. He'd gotten it when he was sixteen. Gang fight. He'd lived, but his brother had died.

Shortly after that, he'd decided to become a cop. A kid's stupid idea, but his Hmong mother and grandmother were still so proud that even today he couldn't admit it had been a mistake. And maybe it wasn't. It gave him an acceptance he wouldn't have otherwise.

His phone buzzed and he checked the screen. Not a call this time, but a text from Jude: *Thanks.*

She knew he left at midnight.

His reply: *Anytime.*

He still had a weakness for Jude Fontaine.

CHAPTER 31

The light turned green. Jude toed the bike into first gear, let out the clutch, and shot through the intersection, her floral-print skirt threatening to come loose from under her leg where she'd tucked it. In her backpack was a bottle of wine purchased for the cookout.

What was she doing? A summer dress. Wine. Cookout. When Uriah sent a text reminding her of Ortega's invitation, she'd tried to ignore it. But at Target she'd found herself looking at the dresses, and she found herself trying one on, and she found herself fantasizing about going somewhere in different skin. Before she knew it, she was in the checkout line paying for the dress.

I can always return it.

And then she was at the liquor store, shopping for wine.

I can always drink it myself.

The thing was, not going was cowardly. She knew that, and she wouldn't allow herself to be a coward, not even when it came to something as harmless as a cookout. So here she was, on her bike, heading for Chief Ortega's place in Tangletown, a neighborhood that felt like old, solid Minneapolis, a neighborhood that felt safe and hadn't suffered the ravages of blackout looting.

The house ended up being a pale-blue Victorian that sat on top of a hill overlooking Minnehaha Creek and a jogging path. She shut off the bike and settled it on the stand. Adjusting her backpack, she took the steep cement steps to the Victorian. At the door, she paused, hand hovering over the doorbell.

Push the button. Don't run.

It took a while, but a small man with dark skin and gray in his hair eventually answered the door. He was wearing a red apron, which led her to believe this must be the infamous grill master.

She shrugged off the backpack, unzipped, and produced the wine, holding it out to him as if it were an offer required to gain entrance. "I'm Jude Fontaine." *Shouldn't have come.*

He smiled. "Welcome, welcome!" He motioned for her to follow him inside. "Everybody's in the backyard. I just stepped in to grab more barbeque sauce, when I heard the doorbell."

It was kind of him not to point out that of course he knew who she was. His wife was chief of police. He read and watched the news. "Can I use your restroom?" Jude asked.

"Down the hall on the left." He pointed. "When you're done, just come this way to the backyard." He pointed again.

She nodded, spun around, and strode to the bathroom, closing and locking the door behind her.

At the sink, she turned on the water, then flushed the toilet. Checked the mirror to see if she looked as weird as she felt. The mascara and lipstick—another impulse buy—looked ridiculous. She pulled tissue from a box, wiped what lipstick she could from her mouth, and tossed the tissue in the trash container. The cut above her eye was healing but still there. Probably should have gotten stitches.

Taking a deep breath, she forced herself to leave the bathroom and walk down the hall to the kitchen. Through the big window above the dining room table, she saw Uriah, Ortega, and Vang. They were sitting in lawn chairs drinking and talking while three young girls tore around the yard, screaming.

Jude felt a stab of something deep in her belly. She tried to pinpoint the sensation, catch it as it flew away, dismissing it when she couldn't place it. Another shout, another laugh. There it was again. That stabbing pain. When she finally recognized it for what it was, she inhaled in surprise. Minutes earlier she'd felt panic, but this was fear. Deep, inexplicable fear. The kind of fear that had no solid foundation, the kind of fear that was faceless and nameless and made no sense. And it came from looking through a kitchen window at a family.

A door opened, and Uriah stepped inside. Jeans, T-shirt, empty beer bottles in his hand, along with a glass containing melting ice and an abused lemon. "I heard you were here." He put the empties and glass on the counter, scrutinizing her, taking in her dress, but more than that, her mental state. She could tell he hadn't been drinking, and guessed the empty glass was his.

"You okay?" he asked.

"I can't do this." She dragged her hand through her hair. "Tell Chief Ortega I said thanks for inviting me."

"Too soon?"

Relieved that he understood, more relieved that he didn't seem set on trying to talk her into staying, she nodded. "I thought I could experience a normal day, normal life. Thought it might even be nice, but I can't be here."

He processed that with a nod. "I like the dress." The words were matter-o'-fact, like saying the dress was at least a nice thing about this moment.

She looked down, spotting her black boots. The boots were the only things that felt right.

"I'll walk you out."

Every step toward the front door made her feel better. Once outside, she pulled in a deep breath. Behind her, Uriah leaned against the doorframe, arms crossed. And then it seemed he just couldn't help himself. "I hear there'll be homemade ice cream."

She smiled at the unspoken plea for her to stay, turned, and walked away, a moment later hearing the soft click of the door closing behind her.

On her bike, she dug through her backpack and found the piece of paper Chief Ortega had given her a few days ago. She stared at it, then pulled out her phone, entered the number, and hit the "Dial" button.

When Eric answered, his voice was distracted.

"It's me," she said. It wasn't lost on her that those were the exact words she'd spoken to him the night she'd escaped.

"Jude." The pain was still there, laced with caution and maybe a little hope.

"I wondered if you'd like to meet for coffee."

"Now?"

"Now."

"Just like the old days, right?" Eric asked.

He wanted it to be, and maybe Jude wanted it to be, and maybe it could be. They were sitting in an Uptown coffee shop, both of them with lattes, sun streaming past the plants in the window, falling across the bistro table. The door had been propped open with a hand-painted chair, and she could hear the corner musician strumming an old Replacements song as the smell of bus diesel mixed with the scent of roasted coffee beans. Through the window, she saw hipsters standing on the curb smoking cigarettes beneath a telephone pole layered in years of staples and ragged flyers, while street punks pedaled past on tall bicycles.

They used to come here together. When he'd suggested this place, she'd balked, but then she'd thought maybe it was the right thing to do. She'd been deliberately avoiding the familiar, but maybe it was time to embrace it, face it head-on.

Eric wouldn't stop staring; she stared right back. His face was the same, yet different. His light-brown hair was longer than it had been, and he had a hint of a beard. So far, he hadn't taken a single sip of his coffee, and she wondered if it was because he didn't want to mess up the leaf design.

He'd already told her how nice she looked, and he was the second person to compliment her dress.

"Are you still a physical therapist?" she asked.

"Yeah," he said with satisfaction.

They'd met when she was investigating a homicide. A drug deal gone bad that had played out in the middle of the street. He'd stepped forward and spoken up when the rest of the witnesses had been afraid to. That had impressed her. He did what was right. Was that what this was about?

"I did look for you, you know. I did wait for you. The police thought you were dead. Everybody thought you were dead."

Or maybe it was about absolution. "It's okay. I understand."

The heavily tattooed waitress with jet-black hair and torn tights appeared and asked if they needed anything else. Jude liked that she probably thought they were just any other couple. Maybe two people on a coffee date. She'd come to realize she preferred interacting with strangers because there was none of that awkward weirdness that went along with the people who knew her history.

Once the waitress left, Eric leaned forward, elbows on the table, shirtsleeves pushed up. "I want you to come home."

His words were unexpected—from coffee to this. "What about her?" They both knew who she was talking about.

"She's gone. After you returned, it just wasn't the same with us. Our relationship quit working. We both realized it pretty quickly. She's been gone a couple of months."

"Are you just doing this because you think it's the right thing?"

"I'm doing it because I want you back in my life." He reached across the table and brushed her knuckles with his fingertips, cautiously at first. His touch was unexpectedly familiar. She liked that. When she didn't pull away, he grasped her hand. "Just give it a try. What do we have to lose?"

"When?"

He laughed, gave her hand a squeeze, and released it, as if he knew holding on too long might make her uncomfortable. With a shrug and a smile, he spread his arms wide. "Now. Today."

"I have to think about it." Did this make *any* sense? But then, did *anything* make sense? "I signed a six-month lease."

"Move anyway. Keep the apartment another month; then sublet. It's not like it's going to cost you any more to move in with me. I've gotten raises in the past few years. I can support us both. You wouldn't even have to work."

Her face must have changed, because he rushed to say, "Unless you want to work. I'm just saying that you don't have to. I was surprised to hear you'd returned to Homicide. Surprised you'd gone back at all but also surprised they let you so soon."

"You aren't the first person to mention that."

"So what do you say? I think it would be good for you. To get you in a familiar, safe environment. It'll help with the healing. And I'll be there for you. Who do you have now? Who do you talk to?"

"I've been trying *not* to talk to people."

"That's not good, Jude."

She took a sip of coffee. "I don't want anybody to take care of me or pamper me."

"How about a backrub? Would that be okay?"

She laughed.

He gave her a contemplative look, then said, "Come home. We belong together."

Nothing about this new existence felt right, and Eric cared about her. He wanted her. That counted for something. Maybe Uriah had been right. Maybe she needed to find the person she used to be. Maybe she could be that person again. This was a chance for a do-over, a chance to play out the movie in her head. "I'll come."

The words were no sooner out of her mouth than her phone vibrated in her pocket. She checked the screen: *Uriah*.

"I've got to get this," she said with apology in her voice as she turned away slightly to answer.

"Just got a call from the Hennepin County Sheriff's Office," Uriah said. "A headless body has been found north of here, not far from Saint Cloud."

She glanced at Eric. "Female?" was the only word she risked speaking.

"Yep. I'm getting ready to drive up there."

They were city detectives. Unlike the sheriff's office, they didn't have statewide jurisdiction, but if the body belonged to Lola Holt, Jude wanted to see the crime scene.

"Pick me up at my place in fifteen minutes."

"Will do."

They disconnected. She put her phone away and grabbed her backpack. "I've gotta go," she told Eric. "I'll call you."

CHAPTER 32

Going "up north" was a summer tradition for people in the Twin Cities. It was one of the things that made living in such a frigid state worthwhile. On Friday afternoons the interstate was clogged with cars heading north; Sunday meant bumper-to-bumper traffic as people returned to their jobs and city life.

Jude had ridden up Highway 10 north of Saint Cloud often as a child, but she hadn't been this direction in years. Now, as she watched the landscape roll past her window, she spotted familiar landmarks, like the billboard for the touristy gas station where they used to stop for snacks on the way to the family cabin. The sign was still the same: a kitschy wooden cutout of a black bear and cub.

Uriah was driving. They'd flipped a coin and he'd "won." She'd been glad about that, but an hour into the trip she wondered if it might have been better for her to be behind the wheel so she could just concentrate on the road.

Instead, her mind drifted and she found herself thinking about the scrapbook she'd put together after her mother's death. As a child, she'd saved newspaper clippings about the shooting, along with the obituary. She'd even saved flowers from the funeral. When she got older, she added photos of the cabin, along with drawings and snapshots of the surrounding grounds. Now, thinking of the scrapbook, she wondered where it was. Still at Eric's?

"I don't want to stop here," she said when she saw that Uriah intended to pull into Black Bear Station. She couldn't deal with more memories right now. "I think there's another place a few miles up." Yet at the same time, after all these years, she had an overwhelming urge to see the family property where her mother had died.

Without a word, he shut off the blinker and accelerated.

Fortunately there *was* another place to get gas. They filled up, grabbed some snacks, and hit the road again. Fifteen minutes later the GPS led them to the crime scene.

The terrain was typical of the area. Hilly, with a dense field of evergreens flanked by acres of woodland and white-trunked birches. The weedy dirt lane running alongside a broken barbed-wire fence must have seemed the perfect place to dump a body. Or maybe the killer had panicked. It happened more often than not.

There were several cop cars on site, parked in disarray, most belonging to county deputies.

They pulled to a stop and got out.

The temperature was at least ten degrees cooler here than in the city, a little too chilly for no jacket, but the sun was warm. And the air, filtered by the Boundary Waters and untouched landmass, was so pure it was like breathing stars. Even the colors and shadows were deeper and more intense.

They had to question a few people before being directed to the officer who'd found the body—a middle-aged man in a brown deputy uniform.

"People take this route when riding bikes to the Boundary Waters," Deputy Pruett told them after they flashed their badges and introduced themselves. "It's a big deal in the summer. A bunch of riders stopped along the highway, and there it was. A hand. Course at first they thought it was rubber. Some Halloween thing. But nope." He passed the bagged, severed hand to Uriah, whose reluctance to take it was obvious. Not because it was a hand, but because, like Jude, he was probably horrified by the lax treatment of evidence.

"So I went home and got my hunting dog, let her get a good whiff, and off she went."

"Where was the hand in relation to the body?" Jude asked, accepting the bag from Uriah and exchanging a concerned look. She hoped the BCA arrived soon.

"Two miles away. I just got lucky. Thought about this piece of woodland that's easy to access from the highway and brought the dog here. I'm guessing whoever did it forgot to get rid of the hand and just gave it a toss as they drove down the road."

"That seems a likely theory," Jude said.

She didn't mention that the dog might not have been a good idea either. The area had been compromised, with dog prints as well as boot prints everywhere. Even now, officers were milling back and forth, and it was obvious the lane that led to the woods had been traveled by so many vehicles that it would be impossible to get a tire print. The BCA had their work cut out for them. They'd also have to set up containment at both sites—the shallow grave and the location along the highway where the hand had been found. Judging from the processing of the crime scene so far, Jude felt doubtful Pruett had marked the highway location.

The officer led them up the lane, past cops leaning against cars, all waiting for the BCA to arrive, most looking queasy and disturbed by what they'd seen in the woods.

The brush was dense, and thorns snagged their clothing as they walked. "It's over there." Pruett pointed to a mound of soil in the distance located in deep shade surrounded by trees. "And yes, I dug around. Know I probably shouldn't have, but I wanted to make sure it was human before I called it in."

He put a fist to his nose and strode away, leaving them alone.

Beneath the sweet, sickening smell of rotting flesh was the unmistakable odor of gasoline. The body had been dropped in a trench, doused, set on fire, then covered with dirt. "Burned on site," Jude said. "And *both* hands are gone." Female, but impossible to tell the age. "Only half the body is charred, so I'm guessing they were in a rush."

"This might be the most disturbing thing I've ever seen." Uriah made an anguished sound as he stared down at the charred, headless flesh. "Standing here, looking at this? Makes me thankful I don't have kids. The world's gone to hell. And right now, at this moment, I want to walk away. Just get in the car and drive. Go up to the Boundary Waters, maybe. If you've never been, you should go. Maybe we should do that right now. Drive up to Ely, rent a canoe."

"Why did you become a homicide detective if not to stop people from doing bad things?" Jude asked.

He turned his back to the body and took a few steps away, moving upwind. "My dad was a cop. I always admired him, saw him helping people. For some reason I had this naïve idea that I was going into a noble profession. But you know what? Eighty percent of people hate us. *Hate us.* We can't even mingle with the rest of society, and the only people we can really hang around with are other cops—other cops everybody hates. And then we have to deal with this kind of thing, with the kind of people who do this kind of thing to others. And people hate us. How does that make sense? In what other occupation are people so despised?"

"Lawyers?" Jude suggested.

"I don't think the percentage of hatred is as high as it is for cops."

"You're probably right."

"How would that break down?" He took a few more steps away from the body. "Cops, then lawyers. What comes after lawyers?"

"It has to be something to do with cable companies."

"Or how about landlords?"

"They'd probably be in the top ten."

"So yeah . . . when kids are little and talking about growing up to be a fireman or a policeman, they don't say they want to grow up to be the most hated man in town." He shook his head. "I guess I got kind of offtrack. How'd this start?"

"You were glad you didn't have kids."

"Oh, yeah."

"Think it's her?"

"It's impossible to tell, but I'd bet the farm on it."

"Why would someone be so blatant with the head, then attempt to hide the body? Does that make sense?"

"It would if the killer thought the body might give up some clues."

"What about the hands?"

"A half-assed attempt to get rid of prints? I'm guessing the perpetrator planned to cut her up even more, then decided to burn the body instead. And *that* wasn't even done right."

They heard an engine and looked up to see the white BCA van lumbering up the dirt lane. It pulled to a stop, and the crime-scene team exited the vehicle, carrying their processing kits.

"I'm going to assume we're all on the same page in suspecting the body belongs to Lola Holt," said the head of the team, a man named Scott James. "We should have a DNA match in a couple of days. When we have the results, someone will contact you."

Jude passed him the bag with the hand, then moved away to an area of privacy and pulled out her phone, relieved to see it had three bars. She scrolled through her contacts and called Charles Holt. When he answered, she asked if he was driving.

"I'm still home recuperating from the gunshot wound. Plan to go back to work tomorrow."

"I want to let you know about something before it hits the news," Jude said. There was no way to soften the blow, so she didn't even try. "A headless body has been found in a wooded area northeast of

Saint Cloud. We won't know the identity of the victim until DNA tests are run."

Mr. Holt let out a choking sound, and Jude imagined him reaching for support.

"There's nothing you can do at this point," Jude said. "I just wanted to let you know before you heard it somewhere else. I'll contact you as soon as we get results."

Jude disconnected and let out a breath.

An hour later, she and Uriah were heading back for Minneapolis when Uriah unexpectedly exited the highway. "I need a drink," he said in answer to the question on her face.

"You haven't been drinking."

"How do you know?"

"I can tell."

"Crashing the wine cellar in my old house was a wake-up call. I decided I'd better leave the booze alone, but after what we just saw out there this seems like a really good time to start again."

The car bounced into the parking lot of a bar called Crossroads. The wood-sided building was long and low and almost looked like someone's home except for the neon beer signs in the windows.

Uriah cut the engine and pocketed the keys.

"I'm moving back in with my boyfriend," Jude said as they got out of the car and slammed their doors.

He paused long enough to give her a look. "Is that wise?"

"Maybe. Maybe not."

His thoughtful stare continued until she began to think he was never going to speak. "Good for you," he finally said. "When are you moving?"

"Soon."

"Need any help?"

"No. Thanks. I don't have much."

"I suppose not."

"I have mixed feelings about it."

"It doesn't have to be permanent. And not living alone is a good idea. It'll be safer."

They walked toward the bar. "We used to talk about having kids," Jude said.

"Really?" He sounded surprised as he held the door open for her.

It was one of those entryways common in Minnesota. Two doors, the first leading to a small five-by-five vestibule that buffered the frigid air when it was forty below zero.

"Is that so strange?" she asked. "Me? Kids?"

Inside, the bar was cool and dark, no other customers except for one guy in a plaid shirt sitting at the end of the counter watching a soap opera on the television.

"You with a baby? Kinda."

"Thanks."

"The world is too messed up for kids. If you set out to have kids, you have to hope things are going to change. You want to give them a better future."

"There have always been evil people," she said as they slid into a booth that afforded them some privacy. "There will always be evil people. That will never change. How you fight them, *if* you fight them, is key. I think for us, for people involved in what we just saw out there in the woods, the secret to life is in the moments. We can't look back, and we can't look at the big picture. It's too much. It's just too much. We have to focus on whatever the headlights illuminate and nothing more."

"So you think you have a calling."

"Not a calling, but purpose. I'm going to find the person or persons who did this to Lola Holt."

"She's already dead. It's already happened. We didn't stop it. We weren't able to keep it from happening."

"I'm sorry." Sorry he was in pain. Sorry Lola Holt was dead. Sorry they weren't any closer to finding the killer or killers.

"I have to admit that the atrocities perpetrated against women have been getting me down lately. And I know it seems selfish of me to dwell on my own feelings in light of what you've been through, when I'm only looking at it from the outside, but there you go. I'm a selfish bastard."

The bartender put paper coasters down in front of them. Jude ordered a Coke, Uriah a whiskey.

Two drinks in, he began talking.

And then it came out. Why he'd gone to his old house. "Did you know my wife committed suicide?" he asked.

"I heard that."

"For a long time I blamed myself. She was taking classes at the University of Minnesota. I was working long hours. There were times she wanted to go out, wanted to talk, wanted to have sex, and I wasn't there for her. But then it seemed like things got better." Without looking at her, he took a drink.

"Did she leave a note?"

"Nope." He emptied his glass. "Ellen was just a small-town girl. I dragged her up here. She didn't want to move. She was homesick. Afraid of a lot of things, and I think my job amplified that. Shined a light on the possibilities. I talked her into going back to school, maybe getting a degree. Things got better for a while. She seemed happy." He shrugged. "I don't know what happened. Worse, I don't know why I didn't see it coming. The thing that keeps bugging me, the thing I can't quit thinking about, is her suicide. Why did she do it?"

Jude spotted the server moving toward their booth. She gave her a small shake of the head, and the woman nodded and returned to the bar.

"Let's play a game of pool before we leave," Jude said, hoping to divert Uriah's attention from another drink.

It worked. He pushed his glass away. "Five bucks says I win."

While they played, as balls vanished from the table, the detectives quietly discussed the case in voices that wouldn't be overheard, each presenting theories, none of those theories satisfying to either of them.

The game was pretty evenly matched.

"Eight in the side pocket," Uriah finally said, pointing with his pool cue.

The black ball dropped. The white cue ball with blue chalk followed the green felt rail to the corner pocket—a scratch. Uriah paid up.

Fair was fair, but Jude would have preferred to win by sinking the eight ball. She tucked the bill away, slipped her stick back in the rack, and held out her hand for the car keys.

CHAPTER 33

His girl.

He wasn't coming around as much. Sometimes she filled two full journals before he appeared with a grocery bag in his arms and new batteries for the lantern. The grocery bag contained boxes of cereal and boxed milk. PowerBars and granola bars. Along with that, he brought jugs of water that she'd learned to ration. One time she ran out and began to hallucinate from dehydration. That's what he told her had caused it, anyway. And then she asked if he was some kind of doctor, and he slapped her.

She used the water to wash herself, but God, how she'd love to take a shower. Sometimes she fantasized about what she'd choose if she had the choice. Hamburger, fries, and a chocolate shake—or a shower. It would be tough.

Curled on her side on the mattress, her stomach a knot of pain, she fumbled for the lantern, for the switch, found it, turned it on.

He'd lost interest in her journals. He didn't read them anymore, but she still wrote about him. Not with the infatuation of the past, but with fondness.

How long since he'd been to see her? Weeks? She was sure it had been weeks. She was down to a few granola bars and one gallon of water.

She'd been proud of her bravery, but now she was afraid. Not afraid of him, not afraid of what he might do to her. Her fear, her stupid and real fear, was that her captor, her lover, wouldn't do *anything* to her. She was afraid that one day he'd simply decide to *never come back*.

CHAPTER 34

The headless body and hand did indeed belong to Lola Holt. Two days after their trip up north, Jude and Uriah sat at a bistro table on the outdoor patio down the street from the police station, no other patrons nearby, a corner to themselves, the just-released autopsy report between them, sandwiches on plates, Uriah with a turkey, cheese, and fresh-baked bread concoction, Jude with an avocado-and-pesto sandwich, plus dessert.

"You should try my brownie." She pointed. "It's kind of amazing."

He broke off a piece while she flipped through the report. DNA was a match, as they'd suspected.

"This is interesting." She passed the lab report to him. He read it and looked up. "Chlorine."

"Traces, not in her lungs but on her skin."

So far they'd been unable to piece together much about the day Lola had been murdered. What they did know was that she'd gone back to school after the funeral, hung out with friends at a café, and hadn't returned home.

"I'll call the father and give him the news about the match," Uriah said.

"A better idea would be to visit him in person." Jude checked the clock on her phone. "He should be at work. I say we drop in and surprise him."

"After last time? I don't know."

"I want to see how he reacts."

They finished eating, both leaving a tip as they gathered their things and got to their feet.

Mr. Holt was a mortgage broker working in a downtown office located in the IDS Center on South Eighth Street not far from the police station. Jude parallel parked the unmarked car, and Uriah swiped the department credit card at the meter. Inside the IDS Center, they checked the directory and paused long enough to get a temporary photo pass that got them through security before taking the elevator to the twenty-third floor and Holt's office.

"There are two detectives here to see you," the woman working the reception desk said into the landline phone. The reply must have been favorable, because she hung up and led the partners down a carpeted hall.

At the sight of them, Holt's face drained of color. He managed to tell them to take a seat as he dropped into a chair, the city skyline behind him.

"We have some news," Jude said from the seat across from him.

"I'm not sure I'm ready." He wiped a trembling hand across his forehead. On one arm was a gray sling. "Will this ever end? I want it to end."

The words seemed to burst out of him, ripped from a place of numb despair that went along with events the mind wasn't prepared to deal with.

What Jude didn't say was that there would never be an end. Mr. Holt would never wake up one day and feel lucky or fortunate or blessed. His heart would never again swell with the simple excitement of a new morning, and beautiful sunsets would hurt because they were sunsets his daughter would never see.

"The DNA matched," Uriah said quietly. "The body found in the woods two days ago was that of your daughter. I'm sorry." He unzipped a leather case, pulled out a manila folder, and placed it on the desk. "Here's the autopsy report." Without removing his hand from the top of the folder, Uriah leaned forward. "It contains eight-by-ten color photos. If you'd like, we can hang on to the report and just pass along the crucial information. I can put the file away. Save it for you. If you decided to take it, my advice would be not to look at it—not now. Put it in a safe-deposit box or locked file. Seeing it will serve no purpose."

"We especially don't think it would serve any purpose for your wife to see this," Jude said. From what she understood, the poor woman was back home, out on bail.

The man nodded and reached for the file, picked it up, but didn't open it. Instead, he hugged it to his chest, his mouth trembling, eyes red rimmed and glistening. "Did it tell you anything?" he asked. "The report?"

"Mr. Holt, do you happen to know if Lola went swimming on the day she was murdered?" Jude asked. "Did she possibly have a swimming class in school?"

"Not this semester. What's this about?"

"The autopsy report indicated that she had chlorine on her skin," Jude explained. "Do you have any idea why that would be? A friend with a pool, perhaps? A place she might have gone swimming, if not at school?"

"I can't think of anything. It's possible she went somewhere I didn't know about. She had a mind of her own and didn't always tell us every-thing. She was a teenager, after all."

They thanked him, gave him their sympathies, told him they'd be in touch, and left.

"Why did you tell him not to open the folder?" Jude asked as they headed for the elevators. "I'd planned to watch him as he looked at the photos."

Uriah hit the "Down" button, then turned to face her. "I know you did."

"So?"

"You remember what you told me your first day on the job? No? I do. You said kindness was maybe the most important trait a person can have."

"But it doesn't apply when dealing with a possible criminal. When dealing with someone who might be able to give us information. Parents are always number-one suspects."

"He didn't know anything. And sometimes you have to decide when to quit being a detective and just be a human."

CHAPTER 35

As the Uber pulled away, Jude approached the door of her old home with two black trash bags of belongings, one in each hand. The backpack cutting into her shoulders was stuffed with a laptop, case files, and notebooks. She'd return to her apartment later to get her bike.

It was Wednesday, early evening, three days after meeting Eric for coffee in Uptown. Another beautiful example of Minnesota weather. The air was dry, the sky was clear, temperature about seventy-five. It was the kind of day that almost made up for winter.

Eric had offered to pick her up. Begged, actually, but she'd wanted to arrive by herself, on her own. And for some reason not fully understood, she hadn't wanted him in her apartment. Not that she was embarrassed. She wasn't ashamed of the place. It was more like she wanted to keep it separate from this house and the man inside. Maybe that should have been a warning.

He answered her knock with a smile, and she thought about how different it was from the last time she'd stood on the same porch. That moment was probably forever etched in her memory. His horror. The woman whose name she still didn't know. That person had replaced Jude, and now Jude was replacing her.

"Come in!" Eric's excitement made her uncomfortably aware of her lack of emotion. Should she be feeling the same thing? Should she be *happy*?

The duplex was a two-story cream stucco. Their space was on the left, with a kitchen, half bath, and living room down, bedroom and full bath up. From the bedroom window a person could see the dome of the Basilica of Saint Mary.

"I'll take your things to our room."

He relieved her of the garbage bags and headed for the stairs while she shrugged out of the backpack, dropping it on the couch.

Our room.

"I'm making us something to eat!" he shouted from the second floor while she wandered around, examining familiar and unfamiliar objects. The couch was the same, but a floral chair had been added to the mix. New television, new lamp. The built-in bookcase was still overflowing with books, mostly hers. She pulled out and replaced one after the other.

"I tried to put everything where it used to be," he said once he was back downstairs. "Most of the stuff was in storage. I couldn't bear to look at anything that belonged to you."

She wondered what had happened to the scrapbook she'd put together on her mother.

"Say something," he said. "What are you feeling?"

What *was* she feeling?

She eyed him with the kind of scrutiny she realized made people uncomfortable. He wasn't handsome, but he was attractive, with an innocent naïveté that almost made *her* uncomfortable. And right now he was like a boisterous child, anxious and nervous and excited all at once. The emotions he exuded overwhelmed her.

"I want to look around upstairs," she said.

He started to follow.

"By myself."

He stopped, and she could see she'd hurt his feelings.

"I just need to be alone for a few minutes," she explained with a softened voice.

He nodded, seeming to understand. "I'll be in the kitchen. Come down when you're ready, and we can eat. I'm making your favorite: chicken fajitas and guacamole."

Upstairs on the double bed covered with a pink-and-green quilt, she dropped her backpack beside the garbage bags. The quilt was new. The curtains—frothy, feminine things—were new too, most likely added by the woman with no name. Shopped for and picked out and hung in much the same way Jude had shopped for linens when she and Eric moved in together.

The house had been built in the twenties, and much of the original detail was still there. The wooden floors, the crown molding, painted white, contrasting with the pale-blue walls. The walls used to be a soft beige. She liked the blue. It was peaceful.

The closet still had the vintage glass knob. She opened the door to see her clothes on one side, Eric's on the other. The dark suits she'd worn to work were there, along with boots and shoes and a red wool coat she'd gotten from a thrift shop. Vintage dresses that she recalled wearing. How could clothing feel so personal, yet so foreign?

She shut the closet and turned back to stare at the bed. From downstairs came domestic kitchen sounds, and she smelled chicken cooking.

How many times had they made love in this room, this bed? Hundreds?

She imagined how it would be tonight. The two of them, together.

It was odd, because one of the things that had kept her going during her years of captivity were the memories of them right here. His gentle ways, his teasing, the softness of the mornings together. Those were the things she'd clung to, the things that had reminded her that she was human and that two people could have something between them that wasn't painful.

But right now she felt pain.

On the bedside table was a framed picture staged at just the right angle. An image of a happy couple. The girl was on the guy's back, her head tilted to the sky, her mouth open wide in laughter.

She remembered that day . . . The photo had been taken at Lake Harriet. They'd gone canoeing, and later they'd had a picnic near the rose garden. A perfect day . . .

Her phone buzzed.

She pulled it from the small pocket of her backpack. A text from Uriah: *How's it going?*

She stared at the message. Had he known how hard this would be? She entered a reply: *A little weird.*

It was a lie. She should have said, *A lot weird.*

Uriah: *I'll bet. Let me know if you need anything.*

Jude: *Thanks.*

His texts made her feel better.

Downstairs, the table had been set with lime-colored dishes that were new to Jude. Every detail in the house was either a reminder of the life they'd once shared or a reminder of the years that had passed.

"I thought maybe we could walk around Lake Harriet later," Eric said. "Then go to Sebastian Joe's for ice cream. They still have your favorite, raspberry chocolate."

Why, he was *wooing* her. The kind of wooing where the day was a setup for the night. She needed to ease back in gradually, not just take up where they'd left off, pretending the past three years had never happened.

This was a mistake. A horrible mistake.

She supposed she had him to thank for her rapid realization. If he'd approached with caution, if he hadn't pushed so hard, so fast, she might not have known for weeks. If he hadn't put her things in their old room, if he hadn't prepared food she used to like, if every single thing he'd mentioned hadn't been referencing the old Jude . . . If the day hadn't been all about the coming night . . .

He had no idea how much she'd changed. He had no idea she would never be the person he used to know. When should she tell him this was a bad idea? Now, before they ate? Or after?

"This isn't going to work," she said, deciding to jump in without hesitation. It was a relief to acknowledge how wrong it was. Being here was like seeing herself in someone else's photo.

He stopped halfway between the sink and the table, two glasses of water in his hands. "The food? I can make something different."

"Not the food. This. You and me."

He was understandably stunned. She felt bad about that.

He placed the glasses on the table. Not just anywhere, but to the right of the plates, as if expecting the evening to continue. "I changed my life for you," he said. "I broke up with Justine. I redid the house. I got all of your old clothes out of storage. I made your favorite food."

She thought about her belongings in the bedroom, already imagining carrying them back into her apartment.

"I should have known when you didn't want help moving. I should have known when you just brought two garbage bags of belongings." Then his tactic changed. "Don't go," he begged. "Give it twenty-four hours. A couple of days. You just got here. Of course things will seem strange."

"It's wrong. Time isn't going to change that. I'm sorry, Eric. I shouldn't have called you." She turned to go upstairs.

His hand lashed out, fingers wrapping around her arm. She could feel the pressure of his fingertips as he held on, as he tried to keep her from leaving.

Any doubt she might have felt was erased by the aggressiveness of his touch. It wasn't rough, it wasn't brutal, but it was a man trying to restrain a woman, to physically restrain her, to make her stay against her will.

Sweat on his face, breathing rapid, his mouth open. He smelled like dish soap and deodorant and the onions he'd chopped for their meal together. His skin had a layer of freckles below the surface. She'd forgotten about that. You couldn't see them unless you got really close.

Without breaking eye contact, she said, "Let go of me."

It might have been the lack of emotion in her voice that made him recoil and drop his hand. Or maybe it was the fact that he was finally really seeing her, the new her. Not the young woman in the photo upstairs. Not the young woman who'd worn those clothes and danced with him right where they now stood. That woman was dead.

The surprise in his face changed as a new plan of action hit his brain. He charged to the hall closet and pulled out cardboard boxes. Like a child having a tantrum, he attacked the shelves, sweeping handfuls of books to the floor, most landing in the box at his feet while she stood and watched.

His face red, he sprinted upstairs, then returned, his arms overflowing with her clothes from the closet. He strode to the front door, opened it, and tossed everything into the yard. While he continued to purge her belongings from the house, Jude pulled out her phone and called Uriah. When he answered, she said, "I'd like to take you up on that offer to help me move."

"I thought you already moved."

"I'm moving back."

"Oh." Silence. She gave him the address even though she knew he'd been there at least once to interview Eric. Then, "Be there in fifteen minutes."

He made it in ten.

Out of the car, hands on hips, Uriah perused the litter of clothing in the front yard. "Wow."

On the porch, Jude hitched her backpack over her shoulders and strode toward his car, garbage bags in hand, all the while aware of faces in windows across the street. "Yeah," she said as she passed Uriah. "Things didn't work out."

"I see that."

Once everything from the yard was loaded in the car, they circled the vehicle. Jude was opening the door when Eric came running down the sidewalk. Judging by his expression, he was still wound tight. And God no, he was crying.

"You broke my heart twice!" he shouted. "Twice!"

Jude slammed her door and stared through the windshield while Uriah pulled away from the curb. "Self-involved little asswipe, isn't he?" he asked.

"I don't remember him that way." She couldn't keep the puzzlement from her voice. Who was that guy? How had she ever been involved with him? "And yet I have the feeling he hasn't changed. I'm the one who's changed." Interesting, to think that the thing that had crippled her and broken her and turned her hair white was the very thing that had given her a fresh and true awareness of the world around her. It didn't seem right that her new eyes had come from such a dark place.

"I clung to this for so long," she said. "It kept me from going insane when I was in that cell, but this world isn't me. Not anymore. And now I wonder if it was ever me. Even when I was living it."

"It got you through it—remembering your life here. That's something. That's a lot."

"Yeah, but it makes me sad to realize it no longer holds the same importance. In my memories, he was different. We were different. I don't know what happened. How it changed."

"It's kind of unnerving to think about how we're shaped by the darkness in our lives," he said in an echo of her own thoughts.

"That's true. I used to laugh at *South Park* and *The Simpsons*," she admitted. "The person sitting here would not laugh at *The Simpsons*."

He turned right on Lyndale. "We'll have to work on that."

Inside Jude's apartment, boxes deposited on the floor, Uriah lifted the framed photo of her riding on Eric's back. "I can't get used to seeing you with dark hair."

"Or seeing me happy?"

"I wasn't going to mention that, but yeah. When was this taken?"

She dropped a bundle of clothes on the couch and looked up. "Four years ago, maybe."

He put the photo on the coffee table and looked around. "Got anything to drink?"

"No."

"I'll run to the bar down the block."

He returned so quickly that she'd hardly gotten a chance to put anything away. "Opener?" he asked as he pulled a six-pack of brown bottles from a paper bag.

She rummaged through kitchen drawers, then handed him a metal opener with a handle shaped like Minnesota. "It came with the apartment."

He uncapped two beers and passed one to Jude. She took a swallow, then set the bottle aside to open a cupboard and pull out a can of cat food.

He glanced around, looking for signs of a pet. "You have a cat?"

"Not really." She tucked the can in the back pocket of her jeans and grabbed her beer. "Follow me."

He followed her up the cramped stairwell and onto the roof, where the sun was going down and the sky was blushing pink.

"You've got a roof," he said.

Without looking at him, she adjusted one of the white plastic chairs, placing her beer on the deck. "I sleep up here if it's not raining.

It's why I rented this place. It might be risky to live here, but it wasn't about the location. It was about the roof."

He dragged a chair closer to hers, but not too close. "And the cat? I want to know about the cat."

She tugged the can of cat food from her pocket and peeled back the metal top. "It climbs that tree over there and sleeps up here at night. It's feral, as far as I can tell." She walked across the tar paper and put the can down near a bowl of water and the thin branch that hung over the roof.

"You seem more like a dog person."

"I used to be a dog person. I don't know what I am now."

She picked up her beer and sat down beside him.

"I'm sorry about what's-his-name," Uriah said.

"In a way, I'm glad it happened. I can let it go for good. No wondering. No what-ifs."

"Hey, look." He pointed with the hand that held the beer.

Like an animal tracking a mouse, the cat was slinking along the roof, belly low, movements ranging from slow to frozen.

"Does it have a name?" Uriah asked.

"No."

"You should name it."

"It's just a cat. Just a yellow roof cat."

"I'll bet we could catch him."

"He's doing okay."

"Winter will be coming. You could catch him, have a vet check him out, and let him live in your apartment."

"Why?"

"Maybe you could use a friend."

"I don't need a friend."

"Sure about that?"

"I'm incapable of a relationship. Even one with a cat."

"Okay, then." He finished his bottle. "I'm gonna take off. I'll leave the beer. Consider it a retroactive housewarming gift. Don't get too drunk—we have another task-force meeting early tomorrow morning."

"Uriah."

It was getting too dark to see his face. "Yeah?"

"I was talking about a domestic relationship. I didn't mean a partnership was impossible."

"I know."

"Thanks for helping me move back."

CHAPTER 36

Shortly after Uriah left, Jude settled in for the night, settling in being the sleeping bag and pillow on the roof, gun and phone beside her as she found herself comforted by the faint sound of far-off music and the smell of grilling meat from the corner bar.

A few hours into the night, cold rain began to pelt her face. Once she woke up enough to realize what was happening, she gathered the sleeping bag and pillow and ducked inside the stairwell. Back in her apartment, the claustrophobia overshadowed her need for sleep. She gave up, put the kettle on the stove, and began going through the boxes left on the floor of the living room.

She wasn't sure if there was anything she wanted to keep; it all reminded her of a life that now seemed incredibly false. How could that be, when this life felt like the shadow life? And more disturbing, the only things that felt real and solid were her days in that basement. Some philosopher said the darkest place you ever live will be etched forever in your soul and you will look back on those days with a twisted sort of fondness. Those words rang with a truth she hated to validate with thought. From now on, would anything ever feel like the life she should be living? Or was that kind of existence over for her? That ability to embrace the present and allow herself to be fooled by it? To be convinced that someone like Eric was right for her?

The lamp. Should she keep it? It was a vintage design that she and Eric had picked up at Everyday People in Saint Paul. It had an orange corrugated plastic shade and three wooden legs. Not a knockoff, but the real thing. Even the bulb was vintage. When she plugged it in and turned the little knob, she was surprised to find that it worked.

She liked it; she'd keep it. If she found it made her feel bad whenever she looked at it, she'd get rid of it.

She emptied two boxes, designating one for trash, the other for Goodwill. Most of the clothes went into the Goodwill box, although she kept two pairs of faded jeans. Jeans were jeans. Neutral. She wasn't sure about the pantsuits she'd worn for work. Would she ever wear such things again? Reminders of that person she used to be? Back when she'd thought she was not only a good detective, but maybe even a great one too? Great detectives didn't get caught and held captive for three years.

She kept the two pantsuits. She'd need them for the times she'd be required to testify in court. And like the lamp, she'd get rid of them if she found they served as uncomfortable reminders of a past life. But maybe the ghosts of that life would fade and the suits and lamp would become a part of this life.

The books she'd give to Uriah.

Novels and movies no longer made sense to her. Stories that weren't true. Stories about people doing bad things to one another, or stories about people falling in love. None of that was for her.

The final box contained purses and shoes. She checked the purses—pockets, zippers—shaking them upside down, the typical dredge sifting out. Something red and bigger than a paper clip hit the floor.

A flash drive. No writing on it, not even a logo.

She picked it up but didn't recognize it. But then a flash drive was a little like finding a pencil or a pen. Before she tossed it in the trash, she wanted to make sure it didn't contain private information, like a report she'd filed way back when. She opened up her laptop and inserted the drive into the USB port.

The drive contained a single MP4 file. She hovered and clicked. QuickTime opened, and she played the video. Five minutes in, she hit "Pause," grabbed her phone, and called Uriah. When he answered, she said, "You need to come over to my place. Right now."

CHAPTER 37

J ude buzzed Uriah in. Seconds later she heard his feet pounding up the stairs to the fourth floor. She opened the door before he knocked.

He burst into the apartment, shoulders wet from the rain, out of breath. She read the thoughts that crossed his face, saw him think about touching her to make sure she was okay.

He didn't touch her. Instead, he gave her a quick visual as he closed the door behind him. The concern on his face was replaced with relief at finding her unharmed, then annoyance at finding her unharmed. She hadn't thought that her call might imply that something had happened.

"I take it you're okay." His face was sleep-bleary, and his wet hair hung over his forehead.

"You sound disappointed."

"A little. I ran two red lights to get here." As if the trip had robbed him of all strength, he collapsed on the couch, arms limp. "I'm not someone who wakes up very fast. Explorer Roald Amundsen called it morning peevishness."

"Proof that language today isn't what it used to be." She lifted her cup with its paper tea-bag tag. "Want some caffeine?"

"Got any coffee?"

"No. Sorry."

"What kind of tea? Not any of that herbal stuff, I hope."

"Earl Grey."

He rubbed his face. "That sounds as appealing as infant formula, but I'll give it a shot."

In the adjoining kitchen, she poured hot water into a mug, added the tea bag, and returned to the living room. She felt like such a hostess.

"I want to know what was so important that you called me here"—he pulled out his phone and checked the screen—"at three a.m. Maybe you don't do anything by the clock. Maybe you don't need sleep to function, but I kinda do."

He dipped the tea bag up and down, took a sip, made a face. "This is like drinking perfume. Makes me wonder if the Boston Tea Party wasn't really about taxes at all."

"Could you bitch any more?"

"I told you, I don't wake up easily."

"Not a good thing for a cop. There's still beer. You want a beer?"

"I'll suffer through. I didn't like broccoli as a kid, but I ate it anyway." He took another sip of the tea, made another face.

"I want to show you something." She sat next to him on the couch and pulled her laptop close so it was between them on the coffee table. "I was going through my old things and found a flash drive in a purse." She clicked several keys, then hit "Play."

The footage was dark, and at first it was hard to tell what they were looking at, but it soon became apparent from the splashing sounds mixed with echoing laughter that it was people frolicking in a pool.

"You brought me here to watch a pool party?"

"Wait."

The person holding the camera was positioned at a shallow end of a rectangular pool, the focus on five girls as they laughed and splashed one another. A minute later, two of the girls began making out, and the camera zoomed in for close-ups of bare breasts. Nude girls. Obviously wasted girls.

Uriah leaned closer, squinting at the screen. "They're awfully young."

"Right," Jude said. "None of them look over sixteen."

As they watched, one of the girls waded toward the person holding the camera. The girl moved up the steps, her body slowly emerging from the water. The camera lens examined her, from the patch of hair between her thighs, to her flushed face and red lips, her glassy eyes. She tilted her head and gave the videographer a sly smile.

The screen went black. End of footage.

"I think the person at the end might be Octavia Germaine," Jude said.

"The girl the murdered reporter was investigating?"

"And the girl whose photo was found in my desk." Jude produced the missing person flyer and handed it to Uriah.

"I definitely see a similarity," he said as he examined the photo of the smiling young woman.

Jude replayed the last few seconds of the video, pausing on the girl's face. "We'll have to run it through facial-recognition software to see if it's a match."

Uriah put down his cup on the table. "Where'd you get this video, and what significance does it have?"

"I don't know where I got it. It was behind the torn lining of a bag I think I might have been carrying the day I met with Ian Caldwell."

"The reporter who was killed?"

"Yeah, but I have no memory of his giving me a flash drive."

"Could he have dropped it in your bag without your knowing?"

"Maybe."

"And why would he give it to you and not someone in Missing Persons?"

"I have no idea."

He frowned. "So let's say it did come from Caldwell. So we have this reporter who somehow got footage of a missing girl at a pool party. I don't know if this means anything. Who didn't get drunk and go skinny-dipping at sixteen?"

"Me."

"I did it all the time. Not in some fancy pool, but ponds. Quarries. Lakes. It was almost a part of growing up where I lived. I have to admit I'm not sure it merits my dashing over here in the middle of the night. Say the girl *is* Octavia Germaine. That tells us nothing. I'm sorry, but without more information it feels like a dead end."

"I know it's a stretch, but I wonder if it could be in any way connected to our current homicide cases. We have high school girls; we have water, probably chlorine."

"Seems a pretty big coincidence to me. We've not seen anything about Octavia Germaine that at all links the cases. And she disappeared over three years ago."

"Maybe this is it. The link."

"The video is poor quality. I can't tell if they're in a hotel, school, or a private home. I'd like to get an ID on at least one of the other girls so we can bring her in for questioning."

"I'll get Trent in tech to enhance it," Jude said. "See if we can spot anything or anyone recognizable. Also see if any kind of time and date signature can be found. Possibly determine the operating system so we'll know what it was shot on. Anything."

Uriah got up from the couch, walked to the kitchen, and put his cup in the sink. "Let's revisit this tomorrow. I'm going home."

"Thanks for coming." She remembered the books, grabbed the box, and handed it to him. "You can have these. There might be something collectable in there."

He tucked them under his arm. "Because I'm in such dire need of books." He paused in the doorway. "Still think it could have waited until morning."

Once Uriah was gone, Jude stretched out on the couch, pillow under her head. Staring up at the ceiling, she realized the scrapbook she'd put together on her mother hadn't been in her belongings.

Outside, Uriah glanced in the direction of the unmarked car. He knew what this looked like, leaving Jude's apartment in the middle of the night after being there for not much more than an hour. But it was too risky to stop by the surveillance car to let Vang know the visit had been business. And he probably wouldn't believe it anyway. Nothing Uriah could really do about that. Hopefully the detective would keep his mouth shut. Maybe it didn't really matter. Jude existed in a mind-space that was different from the rest of theirs. Truth was, she probably wouldn't care one way or the other what anybody said about her.

Head down, Uriah ducked from under the awning. Cold rain hit his face and neck.

At home, he couldn't sleep, so he did what he'd been doing too much lately. He pulled out his laptop and went to his wife's Facebook page. Not directly to it. First he visited Octavia Germaine's, where he took some notes and checked to see if she had any friends in common with the Holt and Masters girls. None, but Germaine would have been about three years older.

Then he clicked on his wife's page.

He knew what he was doing: the pretext of work when his real purpose was to spend the few hours left until dawn going through Ellen's Facebook photos again. He practically had her page memorized now.

Like always, after looking at everything, he wanted more. Like always, he logged out of his page and tried to log in as Ellen. He could contact Facebook and get her password, but that would take a level of acknowledged obsession he wasn't comfortable with.

He glanced at the box of books he'd left on the floor near the door; then he tried a new password tactic: titles. His third attempt was the word *Wuthering* for *Wuthering Heights*, one of Ellen's favorites.

And he was in.

CHAPTER 38

Apparently people wrote to the dead. Uriah's wife had close to two hundred unread private messages, the majority from people reaching out to her postsuicide, saying things like, *I'm sorry you felt it necessary to take your own life. I wish I'd known what you were going through. I wish you'd reached out to me.*

Some messages were sent from "friends" who didn't know she was dead. *You've missed the last few book club meetings and it's your turn to host.* Or guys hitting on her: *Hey, gorgeous. U R hot.* Most attached shirtless photos. There were also the same random attempts at contact from half-naked girls.

It took a while, but he finally got through everything to arrive at the ones she'd responded to when alive.

He frowned and leaned closer to the screen.

Page after page of communication with a guy named Joseph Johnson, a philosophy professor at the University of Minnesota. Since Facebook displayed the most current messages first, Uriah followed the thread back to the beginning.

It started out harmlessly enough. Talk about Socrates and Nietzsche. But it evolved into the professor asking Ellen to meet him for coffee. And later, hotel rooms. Trips out of town.

Heart slamming in his chest, Uriah made himself read everything. Every last fucking word of their correspondence. The reason behind

Ellen's attitude change, the reason she'd gone from hating their life in the city to loving it, seemed to be because of this guy.

Uriah looked him up on the University of Minnesota website.

As he read Johnson's bio and class information, a calm settled over him. He closed the laptop and checked the clock. A little past six. He showered, shaved, put on his suit, along with his belt and badge. He checked his .40-caliber Smith & Wesson semiautomatic, making sure the magazine contained a full load before holstering the weapon. After exiting and locking the apartment, he took the seventeen flights of stairs to ground level.

Outside, the morning air had that city chill that came with the promise of a warm day. A night delivery truck pulled from the loading zone, engine laboring as it left a blast of diesel exhaust behind.

The corner café was opening.

Uriah was the first customer of the day. A large black coffee, tip in the jar, and then he was heading to the six-story parking ramp and his car. From there, he took the maze of streets through construction zones and one-ways, past the Vikings' stadium to Interstate 35 and the University of Minnesota, where Joseph Johnson was teaching an early-morning summer class on ethics.

CHAPTER 39

U riah crashed Professor Johnson's class. He was able to get away with sitting in the back of the lecture room, way up at the top, in the corner.

He could see how Ellen might have found the guy attractive. He was cocky and sure of himself, and he spoke with conviction. But he was also a cliché with the shaggy hair, scruffy beard, horn-rimmed glasses, along with a paisley shirt and dark-brown tie. Age, maybe thirty-seven.

Uriah didn't know what his intention had been in coming. At the very least, he'd wanted to beat the shit out of the person most likely responsible not only for Ellen's happiness, but also for her suicide. But as he sat there in a world that wasn't his world, a world that his wife had embraced, he was overcome with sorrow and guilt. For not seeing her. For not recognizing her needs. For leaving her by herself too much. For spending too much time working.

When the class was over and the students filed out, Uriah remained in the back waiting for the professor to finish talking to his assistant. A brief exchange, then Johnson was alone in the small auditorium. Alone except for Uriah.

"Are you all right up there?"

Johnson had spotted him. Or maybe he'd felt him sitting in the dark, staring. Uriah had the Smith & Wesson at his waist. How easy it would be to pull it out and fire. But that kind of response didn't live anywhere inside him. Instead, somewhat to his own disappointment, he found himself getting to his feet and walking down the steps, all the while keeping his eyes on the guy near the podium. Uriah could smell the academia on him.

Ellen had been a part of this world. She liked deep, philosophical conversations Uriah found tedious. "Too much navel-gazing," he'd told her. It made sense that this guy with the paisley shirt and brown tie and hair that fell over his collar would have interested her.

At the bottom of the steps, Uriah positioned himself under a light while continuing to watch the guy's face. And damn, it felt good when Johnson recognized him and went pale. Uriah pulled his jacket aside and planted a hand on his hip, revealing his gun. "To answer your question, no, I wasn't all right up there," Uriah said. "And I'm not all right down here."

Johnson lost all his cool. That was worth the trip.

"What are you doing here?" His accent said East Coast, maybe Boston.

"I want to talk."

"I don't have anything to say."

"I think you might have a lot to say." Uriah let his jacket fall closed. "How long were you and Ellen seeing each other?"

Johnson caved pretty quickly. Guns had that effect on people. "A few months," he said. Once he decided to talk, everything poured out. "I know what you think. That I'm one of those instructors who takes advantage of his position."

That was exactly what Uriah thought.

"She's the only student I've ever had a relationship with. And it just happened. One afternoon after class I found her sitting in the back of the room, crying. She was lonely. She was homesick. I talked to her. Just talked to her. And then one day we went for coffee. Friends." He shook his head. "Things just happened," Johnson said. "I made her *happy*."

"Not happy enough." Uriah stared at him a long time, trying to call up rage and outrage. Instead, everything except for one thing finally made sense. "Why did she kill herself?"

"I think the guilt got to her. She was a small-town girl. An affair wasn't even in her vocabulary. She loved you. I know that. She didn't love me. I just happened to be there for her. I wanted to marry her. I wanted her to leave you." He looked at Uriah with glistening eyes.

"Were you with her the night she died?" Pills and a hotel room in Saint Paul.

"I was. Before." His voice shook. "She told me she couldn't see me anymore, and she told me to leave. So I left. All I wanted to do was protect her. Instead, I made things worse. I'm the reason she's dead."

Uriah wanted to hate the guy, but he couldn't. Truth was, if there was anybody in the room to hate, it was himself. Wordlessly, he turned and left.

CHAPTER 40

"There." Jude pointed at the monitor. "Can you scrub that image?"

It was the morning after she'd found the flash drive, and she and Uriah were in the tech center of the Minneapolis Police Department, standing behind the basement workstation of one of their specialists, a young guy named Trent. His skill was isolating audio, but he was also good when it came to sharpening images. Jude had already put in a call to Kennedy Broder, girlfriend of the dead crime-beat reporter, to see if she could shed any light on the video. The young woman knew nothing about it.

With a few key clicks and mouse movements, Trent erased the murkiness and lightened the girl Jude suspected might be Octavia Germaine. "This is the only face I can work with," he said. "The others are too dark and far away."

"I think it's her." Jude glanced at Uriah, who was watching the screen. He'd arrived at the police department disconnected and distracted, with a strange look in his eyes.

Trent cropped out the face, created a new file, then hit the "Print" button. Across the room, a machine came to life and cranked out two copies of the photo. "I'll send a JPEG to your e-mail too." More clicking of keys.

Jude sat down at a computer terminal, pulled up the image just sent to her, and ran it through facial-recognition software. "Octavia

Germaine," she said with satisfaction a couple of minutes later. "First person to pop up."

She didn't give herself time to savor the match. "What about anything else in the room?" she asked, returning to Trent's monitor. "Something that might help us ID the location."

"Obviously an indoor pool," the tech said. "Not a school. Probably a private home." He enlarged an area. "Here's a window. Looks like some kind of sitting area. See the television?"

Uriah leaned closer. "What's on the TV screen?"

After some manipulation, they decided it was a syndicated sitcom that could also be found on Netflix or DVD. Didn't mean anything. "Too bad it wasn't the news," Trent said. "That would have helped us date the video. As it is, the footage has no time stamp. I'll send the flash drive over to digital forensics. See if they can find the creation date in the metadata, but metadata isn't always accurate, especially when it comes to something that would have been uploaded to a computer before it was put on the drive."

"What about sound?" Uriah asked. "Can you isolate anything?"

Trent brought up the audio track, clicked some keys, hit "Play," then shook his head when nothing really jumped out at him. "Sorry. I'll keep working on it, but I'm feeling doubtful."

"The walls are unconventional for a pool room," Jude said. "Did you notice that? Maybe made of stone or marble. And that sconce wall light . . . That's not something you see every day."

"I have a buddy in construction," Trent said. Key clicks. "It's a long shot, but I'll send him an image."

"Thanks." At the printer, Jude removed the photos from the tray; then she and Uriah left the room.

"That's really not much of anything," Uriah said as they headed down the hall toward the elevators. "I know you think it is, but it's not. Trent couldn't date the video, and even if digital forensics finds something, I'm not sure how much help that'll be. This isn't anything to do with us. You need to turn everything you have, slight as it is, over to Missing Persons and forget about Octavia Germaine. I don't have anything against a detective following up on something outside Homicide when we aren't working a high-profile, urgent case, but you have no business letting this clutter your head right now."

"You seemed okay with it last night."

He halted in the center of the hallway to face her. In that millisecond, she placed the scent she'd been struggling with for so long.

"I wasn't okay with it. I was never okay with it," he said. "I was just humoring you. And you know what? You aren't the only one dealing with personal shit. I'm dealing with personal shit. A lot of personal shit."

"Your wife. I know. But I thought you didn't want to talk about her."

He gestured with both hands. "That's because your story, what you went through, is so huge. It makes everything I'm dealing with trivial by comparison. I can't talk to you about what's going on in my life. I can't."

Something had happened between the time he'd left her apartment early that morning and their meeting with Trent. "I'm sorry you feel that way. I guess I understand even though I don't agree."

"Good." Relief. "So let's focus on our own cases."

"All right." A lie. She planned to visit Octavia Germaine's parents as soon as possible. She pressed the elevator button. While they waited, she said, "It's books."

"What's that?"

"The scent I haven't been able to place? It's old books. I kept thinking it was some manufactured concoction used in soap or aftershave, but it's paper and leather and glue and mildew and ink. I don't know why it took me so long to figure it out. It's in your clothes, in your suit."

The rapid change in his expression, going from confusion to annoyance, was like looking at a flip-book. He wrapped up his reaction by tilting his face to the ceiling and dropping his shoulders. "Oh, fuck me."

The elevator dinged and the doors parted.

CHAPTER 41

"I read about you in the paper," Ava Germaine said. Twenty-four hours had passed since Uriah told Jude to forget about the Octavia Germaine case. "About what happened to you," Ava said. "And I thought if you were still alive, if you got away, then maybe my daughter might still be alive. Maybe she can get away."

"I know you've gone over this many times," Jude said, flipping a notebook cover and clicking her pen. "I've read the transcripts, but I'd like to hear it from you."

Just that morning, Jude had brought up the issue to Chief Ortega, and Ortega had warned her about pursuing a fresh line of inquiry into the cold case. Not a homicide. Not their job.

"Teenage girls run away every day," Ortega had said. "If we were to dig up every case, we'd have no time to pursue homicides. Leave it to Missing Persons."

Five minutes after speaking to Ortega, Jude looked up the number for Ava Germaine and told the still-distracted Uriah that she was leaving for a dental appointment. Now here she was, sitting in a tiny Section 8 house located in the Frogtown neighborhood of Saint Paul, a few blocks from the light-rail. Fairly high-crime area, but the woman on the sofa across from her didn't seem to care about anything, least of all crime. She looked unwell, emaciated, wearing baggy gray sweatpants with food stains. Her dark-blond hair was dry and lifeless, pulled back in a ponytail. She might have been on something, because in the middle of a sentence she'd just stop talking, her face going blank.

Jude had done her homework. She knew Ava Germaine had been a well-respected psychologist with a thriving practice in the upscale Fiftieth and France business district of Minneapolis. Online photos revealed a nice-looking woman who appeared confident and in control of her life. There was nothing left of that person.

As the direct result of evil, Jude had gone through a life change, so she kind of understood. *Kind* of understood, because no one could ever fully understand what Ava Germaine was going through without experiencing it. Lola Holt's father had asked if it ever ended, like a ride gone bad that he wanted to get off. Ava Germaine was living a nightmare that would never stop. The not knowing had to be another level of hell.

With trembling hands, the woman shook a cigarette from the pack on the table, lit up, tossed the plastic lighter down, and blew smoke toward the ceiling.

"Tell me about the day your daughter disappeared," Jude said quietly.

Ava seemed eager to launch into the details—more proof that a parent never got over it, and proof that there was no need to tiptoe around the subject. It wasn't as if Jude's questions would remind her of that day. There was no way to remind her of a day she could never forget, a day that was always in her head.

She talked.

Octavia Germaine went to school but never came home. As Ava spoke, she frowned in concentration while plucking tobacco from her tongue. Jude thought about how nobody had seen the abduction. There had never been any reports of any unusual activity. Same as the Holt case.

"Something like this is hard on a marriage," Ava confided. "My husband left about eight months after Octavia vanished. I lost my business. I used to be a psychologist." She laughed. "Can you imagine?" She gestured toward herself, a sweep of hands from head to toe.

"I'm sorry," Jude said.

"I couldn't help anybody. I couldn't listen to their problems. And I couldn't leave home for work. What if she came back? But, since I wasn't pulling in any money, I lost the house in Minneapolis. Now if she comes home, I won't even be there." She took a deep drag. "I left instructions with the new owners, but for all I know someone else could be living there now." Tapping the cigarette against an overflowing ashtray, she thought a moment. "It's hard for me to keep track of time. I wonder how long it's been. That's something I should know. A good mother would know that."

"About three and a half years."

"That's right." A nod. "She'd be almost twenty now. I called the police department after I heard about your escape on the news. I asked to talk to you."

"I didn't get the message. A lot of people were trying to contact me."

"It wasn't just me trying to reach you. It was other mothers too."

"Other mothers?"

"I'm not the only one. I'm not the only mother with a daughter who's gone missing."

"Are you talking about members of the national organization? The Missing Children's Network? They can be very supportive."

"I belong to that, but I'm talking about missing girls here in Minnesota."

Jude tried to keep her voice level, tried not to sound alarmed. "How many mothers are in this group?"

"Five. There used to be seven, but it ended up one of the missing girls, Florence, ran away. And poor Katherine . . . Her body was found."

"Unfortunately, teenagers do run away. It makes it tough to sort out crime from disobedience. From the behavior of a rebellious teen." Jude placed her pen against the tablet in her hand. "This Katherine . . . Do you know how she died?"

"Suicide. Just like Virginia Woolf. She filled her pockets with rocks and walked into the lake."

Jude struggled to keep her expression neutral. "She drowned?"

"Yes. Something about her boyfriend dumping her. Girls that age are so dramatic. Everything is life and death." She let out a false laugh. "Life and death."

"What was her last name?" Jude asked.

"Nelson."

Jude wrote it down.

"Why do you care about her?" Ava stubbed out her cigarette. "She's already dead. It's my daughter you should be focusing on."

"Send me an e-mail with the names of the other women in your group," Jude said. "Phone numbers and e-mail addresses too."

"None of the others are from around here," Ava said. "Most are from northern Minnesota. I think one is from the south, near the Iowa border."

Which would explain why the cases hadn't been flagged. Communication between police departments was an ongoing issue, one that CISA, Criminal Information Sharing and Analysis, was trying to remedy. A data system that all law enforcement and all agencies within the state could access.

"Anything else you can think of?" Jude asked.

"I want to talk about you. How did you get away? That's what I want to know. I heard nobody rescued you, that you did it by yourself. But then, you're a cop. I suppose that helped."

"It was luck. Just luck."

"You killed him, didn't you? The man?" She was watching her with hope in her eyes. "The man who abducted you?"

"Yes. He's dead." Jude sat there, thinking about what Ava had just shared. Was there a connection between the missing girls? She closed her notebook and got to her feet, handing Ava a card with her contact information. "I'm going to look into this," she promised.

"Everybody always says that."

"But I mean it."

CHAPTER 42

Uriah looked up from his computer monitor to see Jude striding toward him, a stack of papers in her hand. She slammed them down on his desk so hard he felt a blast of air against his face. "All missing persons," she announced, hand on hip, prepared for a confrontation. "All girls." There was fire in her eyes. He didn't see that very often, and never here, never when talking about a case.

"I thought you went to the dentist."

"I lied," she said. "I drove to Saint Paul for a visit with Ava Germaine, Octavia Germaine's mother."

Jesus. He knew she'd gone behind his back to talk to Ortega about investigating the missing girl, and he knew Ortega had said no. That was before Jude left for the "dentist."

"We need to look into this," she said.

He reached for the stack of papers. "I'll pass it along to Missing Persons."

She flattened her hand on the pile. "No."

"You might have forgotten, but you found a severed head in your helmet, and, before that, we had a dead girl floating in the lake. We can't go running off after cold Missing Persons cases."

"You know what I think?" she asked.

"I can never begin to guess what you think, so you're going to have to tell me."

Jude grabbed a chair, placed it close to Uriah's, and sat down, her eyes drilling into his. "What if there *is* a connection?"

He had no new response for her, nothing he hadn't already said more than once.

"Between the unsolved Missing Persons cases and these new cases," she said.

She was reaching. It could happen when someone was too close to an investigation. Things became screwed up in your head. "I doubt the Missing Persons cases are connected, let alone the Missing Persons cases *and* the recent murders."

"I'm just speculating. We're thinking of the crimes as isolated, but what if they aren't? What if some, or even all, are related? We can't afford not to consider everything and follow every lead."

"You're trying to connect dots that don't even exist. On top of that, we don't have the manpower. We have to be selective and focused."

"Okay, what about this girl?" Jude shuffled the papers, then tapped the top sheet, a printout that included a photo of a pretty teenager. "She was declared a suicide," Jude said.

"People commit suicide." He managed those words with no emotion. It was as if they'd exchanged roles.

"And you know how it happened? Rocks in her pockets. And you know what else? I contacted the facility where the autopsy was performed. No lake water was found in her lungs."

Now she had his attention.

His desk phone rang. "Leave everything here," he told Jude. "I'll look at it. I promise." He picked up the receiver. The call was from Trent, their audiovisual specialist.

"Those wall sconces you wondered about?" Trent said. "You're not going to believe this. They were custom made for the governor's mansion."

Uriah was acutely aware of Jude still sitting a foot away, a question in her eyes. Jesus Christ, the governor. Was the video part of a smear campaign? It wouldn't be the first time a reporter had tried to dig up dirt on a politician. And maybe Caldwell had contacted Jude because she was Schilling's daughter and he'd known she had an ax to grind.

"More good news," Trent said. "Digital Forensics was able to lift a creation date." Even though Uriah felt no shift in his expression as Trent shared the news, Jude stood up abruptly, his reaction to the call raising her hypervigilance several notches despite his poker face.

"What's going on?" she asked the second Uriah hung up.

He told her about the sconces at the governor's mansion. He watched her process the information.

"What else? That's not all."

"Forensics came up with a creation date for the video you found." She was picking up on his reluctance to share the rest of the news, and he knew she'd put her own personal spin on the date, read too much into it. "It was made a week before Octavia Germaine's disappearance."

CHAPTER 43

Three hours later, Jude and Uriah pulled up in front of the governor's mansion, located on the tree-lined boulevard of Summit Avenue, an area of Saint Paul known for beautiful stone houses that most people could only dream of owning. Luckily, Jude had never lived there. That would make it easier since it would hold no painful memories. She vaguely wondered if her father still owned the house they'd occupied as a family in Minneapolis, and then she decided she didn't want to know.

Her father.

All of the things Jude had tried hard to bury had been brought to the surface by that one phone call identifying the sconces in the video.

Her father.

Death brought denial and blame. She'd seen it again and again in her work as a homicide detective. Denial followed by blame were almost always the first two reactions. Lack of denial could often be the "tell" in someone who was guilty. So as a cop, she understood what she'd gone through as a child and understood what had possibly been her own misguided conviction, something to cling to and believe in, something to rage at and focus on, nothing more. But now . . .

The sconces, the creation date of the video, Ian Caldwell reaching out to her when he could have contacted anybody else—why? Because she would have *believed* him. She might have been the *only* person to believe him. Now, despite the tenuous clues, she was convinced her father knew something about the disappearance of Octavia Germaine. And, if so, Jude might be the only person with enough resolve to dig the answer out of him—and she was willing to risk whatever it took to get to the truth.

As they approached the front door, she thought about the day her mother died, remembered her father's white face and the blood on his shirt and hands before he reached for Jude, sobbing, choking out the horrible news. But before he'd buried his face in her hair, she'd seen his eyes, and later, she'd seen the smile on his lips when he thought no one was looking.

The bell was answered by a tall, austere woman who led them down a hallway to a large library that also served as an office. It was what Jude would have expected of the governor's mansion. Dark wood, ceiling to floor. Bookcases packed with books; most, she suspected, had come with the house. Her father was a reader, but she didn't recall his ever reading what would be considered literature—the likes of which covered one wall. These books were meant to impress. Her dad, at least when she'd known him, had been a fan of commercial fiction, mostly of what she called guy fiction, like Tom Clancy.

Her father got up from a desk big enough to land a jet on. He came at her, arms extended, smile on his face.

She took a step back and held up her hands to ward him off. "There are no media cameras here. You can drop the father act." Without missing a beat, she pulled an eight-by-ten from a folder and presented it to him. "Have you ever seen this girl?"

Uriah gave her a secret glare. Oh, yeah. He'd tried to talk her out of coming. Once he'd given in, his plan had been to run the show and do the talking while Jude gauged her father's reaction to the photos. To be fair, her objection to the plan was something she'd failed to mention on the ride over.

The governor accepted the photo of Katherine Nelson, the girl whose death had been ruled a suicide, held it in his hand a few seconds, then passed it back. "It's possible we met, but I meet so many people. I do seem to recall when she went missing. It got a lot of media attention." He shook his head. "A sad situation."

Jude went for the folder again. When her father saw she wasn't done, he waved them toward two deep leather chairs. "Sit down, please."

Uriah sat in one of the chairs. Jude preferred to stand since it was a power position, but she reluctantly joined her partner while her father took a seat on the other side of the desk. This time she produced a photo of Octavia Germaine. Because the desk was so big, she shoved it at him. "How about this? Does this girl look familiar?"

His breathing changed almost imperceptibly. Jude glanced at Uriah to see if he noticed. No reaction.

A knock, then the office door opened and the woman who'd led them down the hall stuck her head inside. "The car is leaving in five minutes," she announced.

The governor's relief wasn't hard to miss, and Jude wondered if he'd given his secretary instructions to interrupt them.

Probably.

"The photo?" Uriah said, pointing.

"Oh, yes." The governor scrutinized it, then put it down with another shake of his head. His forehead was beginning to shine with a hint of perspiration. "I don't know. What's this about?"

"It's about a girl who disappeared over three years ago." Jude leaned forward. "A girl who was here a few days before she vanished. She attended a pool party."

His camera face faded. "More than once, aides were found to be having parties at the mansion when I was away at my cabin. That's common knowledge, because the press caught wind of it. Yes, it's entirely possible the young woman was here." He looked at Uriah. "Jude has been trying to blame me for her mother's death for years. And now it sounds like she wants to blame me for some missing girl. My daughter is unstable. You realize that, don't you?" Still looking at Uriah. "I feel heartsick about what happened to her, to us, and I've kept quiet about her problems out of respect for my deceased wife, but don't force me to make my daughter's mental health public knowledge."

"I seriously doubt you'd do that," Jude said. "Whether people believe it or not, it will reflect poorly on you. Publicly humiliating your own daughter. And I've heard rumors you might try for a Senate seat."

"If you keep pushing me, if you don't let these . . . these delusions drop, I'll call a press conference and put everything out there. You won't have a job, and you won't be able to show your face on the streets of Minneapolis or Saint Paul."

During the governor's tirade, Uriah had gotten to his feet. "Jude. Come on. We're done here."

He was mad. At her. There was also something else about him, something new. Her father had managed to plant fresh seeds of doubt when it came to her sanity. Maybe even more than doubt.

She'd seen it before. Phillip Schilling had the ability to make anyone believe anything, but she was surprised Uriah had been taken in by him.

She collected the photos, watched her father stand. He reached into his suit and tugged at his vest. Even though he gave off the aura of cool, she could smell his nervous sweat. He was afraid, and he was hiding something.

Jude had a final card to play, a card that would probably seal her own fate rather than his. "You're right. I'm unstable." Standing, she reached to her belt, unsnapped her holster, and pulled her gun free.

Was it possible she'd planned this confrontation long ago? Before they got the call about the video? It felt so scripted, so deliberate. Had she thought about it while on the roof staring up at the sky? Or thought about it when she was in the box in the basement? Maybe. She wasn't sure. That possibility alone made her wonder about herself. Was her father right? Was this all just the delusion of a crazy child, now a crazy woman?

Every second felt like ten. She had time to thumb off the safety, time to cradle the weapon in two hands and aim it at her father's chest. "Tell me what really happened that day in the woods."

Uriah's speed seemed too fast for the slow and heavy thickness of the room. His arm drove her hands skyward at the same time his body propelled her to the floor.

A gunshot exploded. As she and Uriah fell in slow motion, she had time to wonder where the bullet had lodged. Probably not in her father. Maybe in a wall, or in a book, or in the ceiling.

She hoped it hadn't hurt anybody. The only person she wanted to hurt was the man standing behind the desk with a ridiculous expression on his face. She almost laughed. She might have laughed for real if the air hadn't been driven from her lungs as she hit the ground, Uriah on top of her.

She wanted to tell him that she wouldn't have killed the governor. It was just a threat to make him talk, make him finally confess to killing her mother or knowing something about a missing girl, or both. But in truth, she wasn't sure she wouldn't have shot him.

Uriah was looking at her, his face very close. She felt the need to say something. "Where's a grassy knoll when a girl needs one?"

He closed his eyes, then reopened them. Did he almost laugh? No.

Someone removed the gun from her hand—Uriah, maybe. And then he did something unexpected. He smoothed back her hair, and spoke words just for her: "It's okay."

But he was wrong. It would never be okay. Never. Those were the thoughts she transmitted to him while she looked into his eyes. She saw compassion there, and pity.

"I'm sorry this happened to you." He was blaming himself.

"He's lying about Octavia Germaine," she whispered.

"How do you know?"

"I can read him."

"You can't read people, Jude. You can't read dead girls, and you can't read living people."

From somewhere came the sound of pounding feet.

Uriah rolled off her, and once the weight of his body was gone, hands grabbed her arms and she was jerked to her feet. Her father's staff had mobilized. She was surprised to see that one of the men holding her was her brother, Adam.

She held his gaze for a few long minutes, waiting for him to say something. When he didn't, she looked down at the eight-by-ten of the missing girl where it had escaped the folder and now lay faceup on the floor.

Uriah cuffed her as sirens drew near.

"Have you seen that girl?" she asked Adam, pointing her chin toward the photo.

He blew air through his nose, ignored her question, and turned to Uriah. *What did I tell you?*

After passing her to a police officer, Uriah gathered up the prints, folder, and Jude's gun. As she was led away to a squad car, she spared one final look at her father and brother, who stood watching from the front door of the stone mansion.

Maybe she *was* crazy. Maybe she'd always been wrong about what had happened to her mother. But it was too late to change her mind, and too late to let go of the conviction she'd carried two-thirds of her life.

She smiled, feeling calmer than she'd felt in years. A firm hand touched her head, and she was pushed into the caged backseat of the squad car.

CHAPTER 44

Your father isn't pressing charges." Uriah had followed the squad car to the underground booking area of Hennepin County Jail, figuring Jude would at the very least get a reprimand from the judge and be sent home. But her father had pulled strings, and she was being released without charge.

In the basement loading and unloading area, the handcuffs were removed. Uriah grabbed her by the elbow and steered her toward his car. With Jude in the passenger seat, he took the exit ramp. When the automatic door opened, he turned onto Fourth Avenue.

"Of course he's not pressing charges," Jude said. "Pressing charges would mean media attention. He doesn't want this getting out. You don't believe me, but he was lying."

"Because you know him so well."

"I do."

"Really? You haven't lived with him or had anything to do with him since you were sixteen."

"That doesn't mean I don't know him."

"Okay, say he was lying," he said, deciding to humor her. "What do you think he's covering up?"

"He knows something about Octavia Germaine. He did not react like an innocent man." She gave him a hard look. "Did you just roll your eyes?"

"Yes. Because you've got it in for your father. When you were a kid, you mistakenly decided he killed your mother, and now he's Mr. Evil. You're seeing guilt where there is none. And if the guy's acting weird, why wouldn't he? He's being questioned by the daughter who accused him of murder and damaged his reputation when he has aspirations of running for Senate. I'm sure he's worrying about what you might decide to say to the press. A few sentences could ruin every chance he has of being elected."

"Are you siding with him?"

"There are no sides. You need to let go of the past. Not easy. Believe me, I know, but it's clouding your thinking. If every case that comes along leads you to him, then—" He cut himself off.

"Then what?" she asked.

"Never mind."

"I'll say it for you. Then I'd better quit Homicide. That's what you were going to say, right?"

Eyes on the road and traffic, he asked, "Would you have killed him?"

"Are you asking as a detective?"

"Off the record. Completely off the record."

A long silence, then, "I don't know."

Uriah turned onto the lower level of the Washington Avenue Bridge. Once they crossed the Mississippi River, the bridge dumped them out on campus, the Frank Gehry–designed Weisman Art Museum on the right, ultramodern light-rail train on the left. Students crossed the street in front of traffic as if they were strolling through a park.

"Where are we going?" She'd unfortunately realized they weren't heading toward her apartment or the police station.

He hit the "Safety" button, locking all doors and windows. "I have orders to put you under a seventy-two-hour mental-health hold."

"You're kidding."

"I couldn't be more serious." Minutes later he pulled into the emergency entrance of the University of Minnesota Medical Center. He parked in patient loading and unloading, dove from the car, circled, and opened her door. "Get out."

"Were those my father's orders?"

"Chief Ortega's. And you won't be coming back to the department once you're released. I'm sorry, Jude. You weren't ready for this. Today was proof of that. And honestly, I don't think you would have ever been ready."

"You son of a bitch."

He was prepared for her to bolt. She didn't. Inside, she signed the forms put in front of her, and she let a nurse lead her down a hall to a thick door that locked behind her.

Maybe she knew this was for the best.

Uriah watched, wondering if she'd look back. She didn't. No, he didn't suppose she'd give him that satisfaction. Along with her father, he was now the enemy.

Back in the car, he pulled out his phone and called Chief Ortega. "It's done."

CHAPTER 45

J ude left the mental-health unit of the University of Minnesota clutching a white paper bag containing her medication, along with several sheets of instructions and contact numbers.

During the seventy-two hours, they'd given her some heavy-duty meds to reset her brain. Jude thought of it more as shutting her off. And that was okay. More than okay. But now, with the medication singing in her veins and pressing her to the ground, she had to get home. Once there, she'd crawl into bed. But how to get home? Her motorcycle was still in the police-department parking garage. That left a cab, or Uber, or light-rail. All seemed impossibly hard.

Someone called her name.

She turned her head and the world swam. A hand caught her arm, and a young voice said, "You okay?"

She blinked the scene into focus. In front of her, with concerned eyes, stood a college student. Curly hair, beard. She nodded. He let go, then strode away, back to campus and student life.

She hadn't liked the feeling of a stranger touching her, but the fact that he'd stopped and voiced his concern made her throat burn. Kindness still existed. She had to remember that. It was important. It was the thing she'd preached to Uriah, the thing she'd lost track of in her return to police work.

Good people still existed.

Not everybody was evil.

The voice she'd heard moments earlier repeated her name.

She turned her head in the direction of the call, slower this time, with only a slight amount of dizziness, zooming in on a man leaning against a car, arms and ankles crossed.

Grant Vang.

She'd expected Uriah. She couldn't have dealt with him right now. She wasn't sure she'd be able to deal with him ever again. And she wouldn't have to. Chief Ortega had stopped by the hospital yesterday . . . or had it been the day before? Whatever the day, Ortega had reiterated what Uriah had already told her.

"We're letting you go," Ortega had said. She'd gone on to explain that they'd arrange for Jude to receive a medical pension. "I take full blame for what happened. You should have never come back and should have gone on disability to begin with. We'll get it straightened out, and you'll be taken care of. If you live modestly, you should be fine."

Jude had wanted to ask what would happen if she lived immodestly.

Grant was waving now, and Jude moved toward him. In her mind, she saw herself shuffling along, and she would have laughed at the image she conjured up if she'd had the energy.

He opened the passenger door. "Hop in," he said. "I'll give you a ride back to your apartment."

She got in. Grant slammed the door, rounded the car, and settled himself beside her.

"Seat belt," he reminded her as he pulled away from the curb.

She managed to fasten herself in. Outside her window, students moved up and down the wide sidewalk, heading to class or dorms. That life seemed so remote and alien, yet so comforting. She could understand how some people remained lifelong students. It was an insular world. How could that not be wonderful?

"I heard you were getting out this afternoon," Grant said, "and figured you might need a ride since your bike is still in the parking garage. And, well, you shouldn't be riding it right now anyway."

"No."

Her brain kept stopping—at least that's what it felt like. Or maybe it was more like floating away, because she'd suddenly find herself back in reality, in the car, riding down the street.

At her apartment building, they took the elevator to the fourth floor, where she unlocked and opened her door. In the living room, in the center of the coffee table, was a cardboard box full of things she recognized from her desk at work. She regretted not getting that plant.

"The building manager let me in so I could drop off your stuff," Grant explained. "I figured you might not feel like going back there." He crossed the room and opened the refrigerator. "And I got you a few things." Like Vanna White, he gestured at the shelves. "Milk, juice, eggs." He let the door close, then opened the cupboard above the sink. "Cereal and bread here. Sorry, but your laptop is gone. Police-department issue, so I had to collect and return it."

"Thanks for everything." She put down the bag of medication and unzipped her purse.

"You don't have to pay me back," he said, seeing what she was about to do. "It was no big deal. I wanted to help."

"You're a good guy."

"Yeah, well." He smiled. "I try." He glanced around. "Want me to stay awhile? I can."

"I'd like to be alone."

He nodded. "If you need anything, just call or text. You have my number."

"Okay."

Once he left, she remembered the cat.

From the cupboard, she retrieved a can of cat food and filled a small jug with water. Then, even though her body and mind wanted nothing more than to crawl into bed, she forced herself to leave the apartment and climb the narrow, steep stairs to the roof.

Someone was already there, standing near the edge, looking down at the street. At the sound of movement, he turned, and she recognized Will Sebastian, the building manager. "Glad to see you're back," he said. "I fed your cat while you were gone."

Both the food and water bowls had been replenished. "Not my cat."

"Whoever it belongs to—I fed it."

She put the can of food and jug of water on the table. "I've never seen you here before." Although the cigarette butts had been evidence of his visits.

"I usually come up during the day, not at night like you."

He probably knew she slept on the deck. That wouldn't be happening tonight. Setting up camp would be too much work.

Will crossed the roof to come closer. "When I got out of jail," he told her, "I couldn't stand small spaces. But some guys can't stand to be in the open. Up here? They'd freak."

Feeling dizzy again, she said, "I gotta go. I gotta lie down." She reached for the heavy metal door, tugged. Above her head, Will held it open, joining her in the stairwell, the door slamming behind them.

She didn't like that sound.

On her floor, he followed her into her apartment, spotting the white paper bag with the pharmacy logo. "What do they have you on?"

Was it that obvious? She picked up the bag, ripped through the staples, and handed him three prescription bottles. Who was she kidding? Of course it was obvious.

He read the labels and passed them back. "That's some serious stuff. That's the kind of cocktail they give people in mental wards."

An antipsychotic, a tranquilizer, and sleeping pills. "If the shoe fits . . ."

"I've taken the tranquilizer," he told her. "Maybe half that amount, and I was a vegetable. Almost catatonic. Took time to adjust. Not that

I'm trying to tell you not to take it," he said, seeming to realize his comment wasn't the best thing to say to someone in her situation. He passed the bottles back. "Didn't mean that the way it sounded. Just saying you might have trouble functioning for a while."

"I don't have anything to do anyway." She dropped to the couch. With a sluggish gesture, she slammed the prescription bottles down on the table. "I've been fired."

"Oh, man. Sorry to hear that."

"Don't worry. I'll still be able to pay rent."

"I'm not worried. Half this building is empty anyway."

"I need to sleep, so . . ."

"I'm gonna watch out for you until you're back on your feet," he said. "Just a friend looking out for a friend. Whatever you need, day or night, give me a shout. Okay?"

"Okay."

Once Will was gone, she shook a pill into her palm, popped it, and washed it down. It hit fast. Minutes later, she was flat on her back on the couch, beginning to experience the catatonia Will had mentioned. Her cell phone rang. It took forever to retrieve it from her back pocket.

She stared at the name on the screen: *Uriah Ashby*. As she watched, the phone finally stopped ringing and the name finally vanished. Moments later she heard a text tone. Ignoring it, she tossed the device aside and closed her eyes, waiting for blackness to engulf her.

CHAPTER 46

Everything was better. That's what Jude decided almost a week after her release from the hospital as she wandered through the farmers' market near her apartment on a bright Sunday morning.

She didn't even care that she hadn't answered Uriah's calls or texts. He was a part of her old life, her life as a cop, as a detective. That was no longer relevant. That person was gone, and the brief period she'd spent investigating murders now seemed like a dream.

What had she been thinking? To go back there?

What had *they* been thinking, to allow her to return?

She stopped to examine some particularly red tomatoes. "How much?" she asked, lifting the green cardboard container.

"Five dollars."

Jude reached into the messenger bag slung across her chest, opened a small zip purse, pulled out a five, and passed it to the woman behind the table, who tucked it into her yellow apron pocket. Dirt-caked nails dumped the tomatoes into a bag and handed the bag to Jude.

She hadn't been ready to go back. She would never have been ready, she thought as she weaved her way through the crush of shoppers.

Now, whenever she turned on the tiny television she'd picked up at a thrift store, when she saw the report about another homicide, any homicide, she knew it had nothing to do with her. Even when the press got hold of the most recent chapter of her own story, along with photos taken the day of her release from the hospital—close-ups of her clutching her white prescription bag—even then she didn't care.

She didn't even mind sleeping inside anymore. That was an improvement, right? When she thought back to her nights on the roof, she recognized it for what it was: the behavior of a crazy person.

She still went up there once a day to feed the cat, but that was it. She put the food in the cat's bowl and dashed back down the stairs, afraid if she stayed too long she might revert to the person who thought it was okay to sleep on a roof.

But seeing press about her father still bugged her. She hadn't moved past that. The nasty event at his place had only succeeded in making him more popular. Afterward, with no mention of the gun she'd pulled, only that she'd flipped out, he'd held a news conference in his office and explained that his daughter had problems and that she'd had problems for years, but her abduction had intensified them. She wasn't to blame. Maybe the mental-health system was to blame. And maybe society was to blame for the way they shamed people with mental-health issues. But if anything, what happened had helped shine a light on the issue. And he promised to make mental health a top priority in his political career.

People applauded.

The public loved him.

As Jude had watched his face on the TV screen, she'd found herself wanting to love him too. She remembered how she *had* loved him at one time.

Before leaving the farmers' market, she bought a bouquet of freesia from a Hmong child in a print dress and white flip-flops. Jude lifted the blossoms to her nose and inhaled their sweet scent—and felt nothing.

This was what women did. Bought flowers in the market to take home and put on the table. Tomorrow she would go to a book-club meeting at the library. Tonight she would watch more knitting tutorials on YouTube. And maybe Will would stop by with food, or maybe he'd ask if she wanted to go to a concert in the park or take a stroll around the lake.

And she would go. Because it was normal.

At the corner, she pushed the "Walk" button and waited for the light to change.

"Detective Fontaine!"

Jude turned to see a blond woman in jeans and a turquoise hoodie hurrying toward her. When the woman got close, Jude felt her stomach drop. *Ava Germaine.*

The grieving mother had left maybe twenty voice mails. Jude hadn't responded, and after the first three she'd begun deleting them without listening.

The light turned, and the green walk icon appeared, along with the numbers counting down the seconds. Jude ignored the woman and stepped from the curb, moving quickly.

Ava Germaine ran to catch up, a white shoebox with a pink print wedged under her arm like a football. Halfway across the street, she fell into step beside Jude. "I've been trying to get in touch with you," she said breathlessly. "I left messages."

Three seconds remained when they reached the opposite sidewalk. Jude's apartment was only blocks away. She didn't want Ava to follow her there, but it seemed apparent the woman wasn't going to give up. Jude took a deep breath, turned, and faced her.

She looked different from the last time. Not as disheveled, and maybe her hair had been cut. She was wearing makeup.

"I'm not a cop anymore. And you've probably seen the news. I should never have gone back to work."

"You're the only person to contact me in two years," Ava said. "You're the only person who gave me hope."

False hope was what Jude thought, but didn't say. She felt very little anymore, but she felt bad about the false hope. "I'm sorry," she said. "You need to talk to someone in Missing Persons."

"I have! They nod and act like they're taking notes that I'm sure they throw away as soon as I leave. They *don't care*."

"I don't think that's it . . ." The truth was, they'd done all they could do.

"Can't you keep looking?" Ava asked. "Even though you aren't a cop, you can keep looking, right?"

"I'm sorry."

"I don't have much money, but I can pay you a little."

"It's not the money."

Ava was acting as if Jude were someone who could fix her life, who could save her, who could bring her daughter back. Jude horrifyingly caught herself almost asking the grieving mother if she'd thought about taking up knitting. Instead, she thrust the flowers at her. "Here."

Maybe they would help. Maybe giving them to her would some-how absolve Jude of the wrong she'd done in contacting her. But in reality, if anything, the cloying scent would probably forever embed this moment into both their brains, marking the day Jude finally and fully grasped just how messed up she was, and the day Ava Germaine realized nothing and nobody was going to do anything more to help her. What Ava didn't know, and what she'd probably never admit to herself, was that her daughter was dead.

All the cops knew that.

Forty-eight hours unfound, and the abductee had most likely been murdered. Three and a half years?

Jude was the rare exception. Jude's very existence had given the poor woman hope in more ways than one. By visiting her and making promises she could never keep. By merely breathing.

"Take this." Ava shoved the box into Jude's hands. "It might help you find Octavia." She turned and ran away, leaving Jude standing in the middle of the sidewalk, staring at the shoebox while church bells rang in the distance.

CHAPTER 47

I nside her apartment, Jude put the shoebox on the coffee table, unsure of what to do with it. Stick it in the closet? Shove it under the couch? Certainly not open it. Even as she had these thoughts, she took note of the brand on the box (Skechers) and the shoe size (six and a half).

She found herself contemplating the physical characteristics of the girls who'd gone missing, thinking about what she knew and what she'd need to know if she were working the case. Thinking about how the missing girls compared to the recently murdered girls.

But she was able to let it go.

She walked to the kitchen, filled a glass with water, and downed her medication, taking it a little later in the day than usual, a trick she'd learned when she had something planned for the morning. Once the medication hit her system, it was hard to function for several hours, and half the time she couldn't remember what she'd done or where she'd gone. The doctor said she'd get used to it, but so far that wasn't happening.

Now that her brain had been reset, she knew her behavior at the governor's mansion wasn't that of a sane person. And whenever she bothered to think about it, she questioned everything she'd done and felt since her mother's death. Even her behavior after her escape. Going back to Homicide. Claiming she read bodies and people. None of that was going on now, not since starting the medication.

Back in the living area, she dropped to the couch, pillow under her head, intent on riding out the next hour or so on her back. She glanced over at the shoebox. And then she reached for it, placed it on her stomach, and lifted the lid.

She assumed the belongings had been vetted by Ava and not just grabbed and randomly boxed years ago by the missing child. Child. If Octavia were still alive—highly unlikely—she would no longer be a child. She'd be nineteen. Old enough to vote. Old enough to serve in the military.

Jude sifted through the photos. Pretty girl with straight dark-blond hair and a perfect smile. Photos of her with other girls. Photos of her with boys. One particular boy's face was repeated in several snapshots.

If Jude were working the case, she'd ask Ava about Octavia's friends, maybe even interview them if they still lived in the area.

In the box, she found a wrist corsage that had crumbled, along with a leather key chain from Black Bear Station. Probably half the teenagers in Minnesota had something from Black Bear. It was a popular stop on the way to the North Shore.

Near the bottom of the box was a journal with butterflies on the cover. Life interrupted.

The box and its meager contents represented that point in a girl's journey when the world was waiting, when anything and everybody was possible, and love and happiness were inevitable. Sixteen.

Even though Jude's own life had been a crazy mess at that age, she could still recall the feeling of magic and hope and promise.

She opened the journal.

The handwriting was youthful, round and big, and Jude imagined the dark-blond girl sitting cross-legged in bed, a soft smile on pink lips as she wrote.

Checking the date, she noted that the first entry was about a year before Octavia vanished. She put the shoebox aside and settled in for a read.

Stuff about friends and boys and classes, but mostly friends and boys. Losing her virginity, getting drunk for the first time.

About halfway through the journal, Octavia began talking about sneaking out, along with telling her mother she was staying at a friend's when she was really going to parties in and out of town.

Up until that point, the journal had felt like a true journal—an outpouring of everything in a young girl's heart, no secrets. But once Jude reached the halfway point, things seemed to change. Maybe Octavia had gotten tired of journaling, or her life had become too busy, but there seemed to be something evasive about the entries. The references to out-of-town parties were still there, but they contained no details. And boyfriends, previously mentioned by name, were now just an asterisk.

In one entry, she talked about coming home with scratches on her arms and legs from "some kind of thorny bush." Her mother had questioned her about the scratches, and Octavia had concocted a story about falling into the rosebushes at her friend's house.

The scratches seemed significant, but maybe it was the drugs. They were saturating Jude's system, making her body heavy, dulling her mind. She struggled to keep her eyes open, struggled to keep her thoughts on track.

She played this game every day. She didn't have much time. Before passing out, she grabbed her cell phone, scrolled through the names, and placed a call to Ingrid Stevenson at the medical examiner's office.

Surprisingly, Dr. Stevenson herself answered.

"I'm following up on the decapitation case," Jude explained.

Silence, then, "I thought you no longer worked in Homicide."

Jude lied. "I'm only part-time," she said. "I've been retained to continue with the Masters and Holt investigation. It was decided that it would be better to keep me on rather than bring in new people this late in the game." Did that make sense? Was she making sense?

She must have sounded convincing, because Dr. Stevenson asked what she could help her with.

"I'm looking through my paperwork." Jude made a rustling sound with the pages of the journal. "Did Lola Holt's body have scratches on the arms or legs?"

"Give me a second while I bring up those files."

Jude heard clicking keys and imagined Ingrid in her office, in front of a monitor.

"Lacerations on parts of her legs that weren't burned."

"Care to speculate on them?" Her words were getting a little slurred. She sat up, swinging her feet to the floor. The apartment tilted. She closed her eyes and tipped her head back, waiting for the room to stabilize, all the while taking shallow breaths through her mouth.

"My guess is some kind of thorny plant. Possibly buckthorn, which has become a real problem up north."

They talked a little more; then Jude thanked her and was ready to disconnect, when Ingrid said, "I'm glad to hear you're still on the case. The news made your story sound pretty dismal."

"You know how the media likes to exaggerate everything."

"Right." The ME laughed. "I can't recall a single piece about me that was accurate, and yet when I watch the news I find myself accepting what I'm hearing as fact. I have to quit doing that."

Jude thanked her with only a slightly thick tongue. She was putting the journal back in the box, when a thin chain caught her eye. She pulled out a necklace and held it high.

It was a heart design she'd seen before, this one with the name Octavia engraved on it. *He gives them all engraved necklaces,* she thought, dropping the chain back in the box, slamming the lid, and passing out.

CHAPTER 48

J ude woke up on the couch, disoriented and sluggish, with only a faint memory of the contents of the journal and her call to the medical examiner. Coffee and a shower didn't help, and she was pretty sure it wasn't supposed to.

That evening, she recognized the sound of Will's knock and unlocked the door to let him in.

"Want to go for a motorcycle ride?" He walked to the kitchen and checked to make sure she'd taken the medication from the days-of-the-week container, flipping open a lid, closing it with a snap. While there, he began rinsing dishes. Seeing him puttering around in her apartment didn't seem at all unusual anymore.

"What did you eat today?" he asked over his shoulder.

"I picked up something at the farmers' market." Had she? She couldn't remember. She'd lost weight, and he was always checking to make sure she'd eaten. It was something she forgot to do—another side effect of the medication.

"What about that motorcycle ride?"

He meant a ride on *his* bike. No way was she alert enough to ride hers, which was back downstairs after Will had picked it up from the police-department garage. She didn't know if she liked riding with him. Maybe. Maybe not. "I think I'm going to stay in and knit."

He laughed and shook his head. "You and knitting. That cracks me up."

"It's good for me."

"I'm sure it is."

"You should try it." Her weak attempt at light conversation wore her out.

"I'm gonna go for a bike ride. Want me to feed the cat before I leave?"

"I can do it."

"Don't forget your sleeping pill."

"I won't."

He approached her, stopping a couple of feet away. Sleeveless denim vest, hair tied back, tattoos. Over six feet tall and over two hundred pounds. It was sort of funny what a mother hen he was. "I'll check on you tomorrow morning. Call if you need anything. Don't forget to charge your phone. You keep letting it run down. There's ice cream in the freezer. Eat some of it before you go to bed. You need the calories."

She nodded and he left.

Once he was gone, she retrieved a can of cat food from the kitchen cupboard and took the stairs to the roof. With a metal spoon, she emptied the can into a bowl of unknown origin. It had just appeared one day. She figured Will must have picked it up from the pet store.

Done serving up the cat food, she heard a motorcycle leave the building's underground parking garage. She walked to the edge of the roof and watched Will's bike pull away and roar down the street. Her gaze tracked to a car she'd first noticed a few days earlier. Department surveillance had been pulled, but the beige vehicle was sitting in the spot where Grant Vang used to park. And somebody was in it.

Probably nothing. Maybe nothing. Hopefully nothing.

Her brief stint back in Homicide seemed like a dream, seemed far away. Even finding the head in her helmet no longer seemed real. Just something she'd seen in a bad movie.

She remembered Uriah. He seemed clearer than everything else, but she couldn't forgive his betrayal even though she knew he'd just been doing his job. Maybe that was what bugged her. *Just doing his job.* His taking her to the hospital with no attempt to defend her or warn her had underscored his lack of loyalty to his own partner.

Thinking about it, she pulled her cell phone from her jeans and scrolled through the short list of names, stopping when she hit Uriah's, pausing briefly before deleting him with a single stab of her finger.

The cat didn't show up to eat.

The stars came out and she didn't care.

She went back downstairs to the apartment, picked up her knitting needles, and began watching a YouTube tutorial on her phone. Fifteen minutes later, she tossed the needles and yarn aside. Maybe she should take up painting instead.

In the kitchen, she popped open the top of Sunday's medicine compartment, filled a glass with water, and dumped the sleeping pill into her palm. And it came to her that this life wasn't all that much better or different than her life in the basement.

From the kitchen, she could see the corner of the shoebox poking out from under the couch. Those scratches . . . Somebody should follow up on those scratches . . . And the necklace. The necklace could be significant.

She should call Uriah. Then she remembered she'd deleted him. And really, would he even care? Did he have time to follow such a flimsy lead?

No.

But she had time.

She carried the sleeping pill to the bathroom, tossed it in the toilet, and flushed.

A lot of time.

A few hours later, she was lying in bed unable to sleep, regretting the flush of the sleeping pill, thinking about getting up to take one from the brown prescription bottle on the kitchen counter, when she heard a key turn in the lock.

Her initial instinct was to reach for a weapon, but her handgun had been taken from her, something that seemed unwise considering the history of people wanting to do her harm. She was poised to slip from the bed to hide, when she caught a whiff of the familiar—an alchemy of exhaust fumes, beer, cheap cigarettes, and male body odor.

Will.

She remained in bed, eyes open just a slit, barely breathing.

She heard the door close, heard soft footfalls as he made his way to her room.

When he reached the doorway, he stood there, a dark silhouette against the lighter darkness that was never completely dark due to streetlights.

A friend, just coming to check on her?

Or something more sinister?

He stood watching for a full five minutes, his breathing heavy; then he left, turning the key in the lock behind him.

She exhaled. Would she ever feel safe anywhere again? Would she always feel victimized? She picked up her phone and thought about calling Grant. Then she remembered the car across the street and put the phone aside. She couldn't trust anybody. Only herself. And she wasn't even sure about herself.

CHAPTER 49

His girl.

He *finally* came. She'd barely dug into the food he'd brought when they ripped off their clothes and fucked the way they used to. In the dark, she tugged the mask from his head so she could kiss him without the knit material in the way. They kept at it for hours, until he couldn't get it up anymore. That made her mad, because fucking was the only thing in her life, the only thing that broke the monotony. She tried to arouse him, but nothing worked and he passed out on his back on the narrow bed.

He'd never fallen asleep there. Never.

She tiptoed to the lantern, turned it on, and moved silently back to the bed, holding the light high.

She had no idea how long she'd lived in the small room. Judging by the stack of journals, she'd guess years. Most of that time had been spent with a specific mental image of her captor in her head. She'd clutched that image to her, obsessing over him when he was gone, swooning over him when he was with her.

If one of those composite artists had come along, she would have described him down to his last hair. The color of his eyes and the shape of his jaw and lips.

So who the hell was this stranger lying naked on the bed in front of her? Not the man of her dreams.

He looked nothing like her man. *Nothing.*

She stared, willing his face and even his body to change. He *had* to change.

Crazy thing, it was a face she recognized. How weird was that? But then, this was her first glimpse of human features in years. Was her mind playing tricks on her?

No, it was him. She was sure of it.

He was asleep. She could leave. What was to stop her from just walking away? Find his keys, find his car, drive off, blow her parents' minds when she walked in the front door of their house.

She was still trying to figure out a plan when his eyes opened and he stared up at her, his expression going through a series of transformations as he realized the seriousness of the situation.

She could see him.

She could identify him. And then she realized what that meant for her. If he didn't kill her, it meant he could never let her go. Ever.

"It doesn't matter," she whispered, hoping to placate him. "I wanted to see you." She lowered the lantern. The shifting of light and dark made his face change, made him look even scarier. "It's okay. I'll never tell anybody. I'll never say anything."

"No, you won't."

He sat up. And even though it made no sense since she'd already seen him, he grabbed the ski mask and pulled it down over his face.

Like an executioner.

She backed to the wall, accidently knocking over a stack of journals—words that represented her life, her *love.*

Sometimes she thought of herself as an adult, sometimes a kid. While she'd been imprisoned, she'd matured, but she also knew she'd become twisted and stunted. At times, she saw her present life as some sad commentary on the role of women and how men needed to control them. Because was this mess much different than that of many women who *weren't* kept in small rooms? At other times, she saw the situation as simply a crazy guy doing crazy things.

He came at her, slowly, with purpose, his eyes reflecting the light from the lantern.

When he was close enough, she screamed, ran at him, and swung the lantern at his head, where it connected, taking them both by surprise.

She'd always been so docile.

And she'd loved him. Maybe she still loved him or could love him again, his face, in her mind, already turning back to the face she'd created for him years ago.

The lantern hit the floor and the room went dark. She felt a rush of air, felt his hand hit her, shove her. A foot connected with her stomach, and she went down, landing on her back. Her journals avalanched around her, and she thought about how she'd need to restack them, and it would be such a job. And then she began to wonder if she'd live to restack them. If not, what would happen to them? All those words? Her words? Words of love and hope.

"You're older than I thought," she said faintly. Just an observation, more for herself than for him. "Too old for me, anyway."

Her last comment really fired him up. "If anybody's too old, it's you." He kicked her again, but she was still glad about hitting him. Maybe she'd laugh about it later if she was still alive, especially the sound the lantern had made against his skull.

CHAPTER 50

Jude went cold turkey.

It wasn't too bad, maybe because she hadn't been on the medication that long. The only real negative was being unable to sleep, but she faked it when Will came around for his nightly creepy viewings. And she faked a thick tongue, and she faked being disinterested in everything.

"I'm too tired," she'd tell Will when he asked if she wanted to do anything.

Three days.

That's what it took to begin thinking clearly.

On the third day, she headed down to the parking garage and her motorcycle, but when she turned the key in the ignition, nothing happened. She got off the bike and checked all the places she'd been taught to check.

The spark plug was gone.

It wasn't something that would just fall out; it took a special ratchet to remove it. And with the bike parked in a secure area, the list of people who might have done such a thing narrowed pretty quickly.

She'd been telling herself she was crazy, telling herself she was indeed paranoid and that her mind had snapped after her years in the basement—or even before that. Here was proof that someone didn't want her to leave. But maybe it wasn't connected to anything other than the nutjob who managed her apartment building.

She took the stairs to the first floor, and the first floor to the entry area with the rows of mailboxes embedded in the wall; then she was out through the double doors. To the left and down the street was the beige car.

Footsteps coming up the sidewalk from the other direction, and there was Will striding toward her, a look of concern on his face.

She let her shoulders slump, let her face go lax.

"What's up?" he asked, reaching over her head to grab the door and hold it open.

"I was going to go out." She passed a hand over her forehead in what she hoped was a gesture of confusion. "But I don't think I want to."

"It's a great day. We could walk around the lake."

His words were so harmless. *So harmless!* Once again she began to doubt herself. A walk around the lake would be nice.

But he came into her room at night.

Yes, to check on her.

Was that so wrong? So threatening?

Yes. *Yes!*

"I'm too tired," she said.

He nodded, conveying his understanding.

"I'm going to watch TV, then go to bed."

"Okay. I'll be up later to see how you're doing."

Of course he would. "Oh, hey." She pretended to suddenly remember something that wasn't very important. "I was in the garage checking on my motorcycle, and it wouldn't start. Maybe you could have a look at it."

"I should have told you. I pulled out the spark plug because I'm going to replace it. I didn't say anything because you haven't been riding it anyway."

Not a shred of guilt. And it made sense. A new spark plug.

Later, when he showed up at her apartment, she let him do the dishes and feed the cat. She promised to take her pill, but once he was gone she flushed it down the toilet. She pretended to sleep when he came in to watch her. Once he was gone, she bailed out of bed, tugged on her boots, shrugged into a black hooded sweatshirt, grabbed her backpack, and stuffed it with belongings and clothes, along with the shoebox Ava had given her.

Packed, she slipped from her apartment and took the stairs to the roof, pulling the hood over her white hair. A furtive look at the street revealed no surprises: the car was still there, and someone was inside. She spotted the glow of a cigarette.

Keeping her knees bent and head low, she ran to the tree on the opposite side of the building, grabbed a branch, and climbed down, pausing on the lowest limb, high above the alley. She took a deep breath and let go, dropping and rolling to the bricks below.

Bruised but no bones broken, she shoved herself to her feet. Adjusting the straps on her backpack, she stuck to the darker shadows as she moved down the alley, away from the apartment and away from the person in the car.

She headed for the nearest ATM, withdrew all she could in a twenty-four-hour period, pocketed the cash, then pulled out her phone and stared at it a moment before dropping it to the ground and smashing it with her boot heel.

CHAPTER 51

Jude needed to go north, to the area where the Holt girl's body had been found. Not far away were the cabin and property where her mother had died. Logically, she understood that the two were very likely unrelated, but the close proximity of the Holt girl's body to the Schilling property, plus the necklaces that might have come from the nearby Black Bear Station . . . Flimsy clues at best, but still clues. Then again, maybe it was simply a strong desire to go back to the place her mother had loved, the place where her mother had died.

She thought about stealing a car or buying a cheap junker. She thought about hitchhiking or hopping a casino bus going north. In the end, she did something that was maybe more foolish than any of her ideas. She took a city bus to Ava Germaine's house, careful to keep her hood up and head down.

Under cover of darkness, she knocked softly on the front door until she heard a sound. The porch light came on, and maybe Ava did or didn't check the peephole.

"Who's there?"

"Jude Fontaine. Detective Fontaine."

The door opened and Jude slipped inside, closing the door behind her. "I need your help."

She didn't go into detail, because how did any of it make sense, and how did her actions make her seem anything but paranoid? And maybe that's all they were. Maybe that's all they'd ever been. "I need to get out of town, and I need a car."

Fluffy slippers. Gray sweatpants, standing in a house that smelled like cigarette smoke. "What's happening?" Ava asked. "Where are you going?"

"Northern Minnesota. All I can tell you is that I'm following a lead."

"About Octavia?"

"Yes."

Ava pressed a shaking hand to her mouth while staring at Jude with shining eyes. "I want to come with you."

"You can't." No attempt to soften her response.

Seeming to accept that she would get no more information from Jude, Ava rummaged through a jacket that had been tossed on the couch. She retrieved a set of keys, removed two from the ring, and pocketed them before handing what remained to Jude. "You'll need to get gas. There should be about a third of a tank in it."

Jude closed her fingers around the keys. "If anybody traces me to your house, say I made you give me the car. And don't tell them where I went."

"It's parked on the street," Ava said. "The silver Corolla. It was Octavia's. I kept it in the garage, and then I lost my job and my house and my own car fell apart, so I started driving hers. I hated that. I wanted her to come home and find it how she left it."

The car represented a mother's hope. "She'd just gotten her license. She was so proud of that car. Seemed extravagant at the time, but I thought having her own car would keep her safe." She burst into tears but quickly got herself under control, kept talking. "It seems like it just happened, and it also seems like it happened years ago. And life . . . It's like I'm moving through somebody else's dream. Do you know what that feels like?"

"I do."

"Did you read her journal? Did you see where she said she went to parties up north in the woods? I didn't even know she went up there until I read about it. And that wasn't until after she was gone. I had no idea she was so secretive."

"Most teenagers are."

"I guess so." Ava opened the front door and stood aside. "Be careful. And if you don't find her, I'm still thankful you listened to me. I'm thankful you took action." She thought of something else. "You're like Joan of Arc."

"Wasn't she insane?"

"That's what they say."

Jude surprised herself by laughing. Then she turned and jogged to the car, hitting the "Unlock" button as she approached. She tossed her backpack on the passenger seat, dove in, and took off down the street.

The drive was fast and uneventful. Ninety minutes later she pulled into Black Bear Station, filled the tank, then went inside. The interior lighting was weird the way it always was in the middle of the night—the kind of light that made you feel stoned even when you weren't. The place was empty except for a clerk behind the counter sitting on a stool, his dark head bent over a comic book.

In the back of the store, Jude found the engraving machine, surprised but not surprised that it was still there. The necklaces looked the same, choices of gold or silver hearts, circles, or ovals.

She fed money into the machine, pressed the correct letters, and watched the device mechanically etch the necklace. When it was finished, she scooped it from the metal cup. She was no forensics expert, and she'd have to compare the two necklaces, but it looked identical to the one she'd found in the shoebox, maybe identical to the one found on Delilah Masters's body.

And what does that prove?

Nothing.

Slipping the chain around her neck, she attached the clasp. At the counter, she bought water and granola bars, paying cash for everything, including gas. She considered showing the clerk an old photo of Octavia but didn't want to draw attention to herself, especially given the remoteness of his being of any help on such a cold case.

"Cool name," the comic-book kid said with a nod to the necklace as he dropped the change into her palm. "Have a good one."

"You too."

Thirty minutes later, she turned up the lane that led to her father's property. Jude was surprised she'd found it so easily, without the help of a GPS. But even though she hadn't returned in over twenty years, she'd gone back in her mind many times.

The lane was overgrown the way untraveled paths got in the north country, but not so overgrown as to indicate no traffic. The parallel tire paths were dirt; the center strip, tall grass that brushed the undercarriage of the car. The headlight beams bounced as the tires rolled over the uneven surface. She checked the clock on the dashboard. It would be dawn in three hours.

Before reaching the cabin, she cut the headlights and engine. A quick search of the glove compartment turned up a flashlight. She thumbed the switch, grateful to see the battery wasn't dead.

Out of the car, she closed the door but didn't latch it. If someone was in the cabin, she didn't want to announce her arrival with a slam. Flashlight pointed at her boots, backpack straps over her shoulders, she began walking down the lane, noting the lack of fresh vehicle tracks.

Round a turn and there was the cabin. A quick skim of the flashlight beam revealed no vehicles. She approached the building the way she'd approach a crime scene, with care, taking note of the dirt on the wooden steps and porch, along with the lack of shoe scuffing. No one had been there in a while.

The front door was locked. No surprise.

She peered inside the windows for telltale signs of security detectors mounted on framework, or motion sensors in ceiling corners. Not seeing any obvious clues of an alarm system, she grabbed a log from a nearby stack and smashed it against a window, shattering the glass.

After pulling out the biggest shards, she tossed her backpack through the window, then climbed in after it. Once inside, she felt for a wall switch, faintly surprised when a table lamp responded.

The cabin was smaller than she remembered, with an extremely low ceiling. The size made her wonder if she was in the right place, but as she moved about she came upon things she recognized, like the "before" picture on the living room wall. How strange that the family photo was still there.

Jude's father stood behind her, hands on her shoulders. Her mother was there, and Adam. *One happy family.* She looked more closely at her mother. *Had* she been happy the day the photo was taken? Yes. It was in her face, in the way she stood. No matter what had transpired the day she died, she'd been happy in the "before." That was real.

The cabin was nothing fancy, especially for a governor. She had to give her father credit for not selling it off to buy some fancy, expensive property in one of the more popular areas. Wood interior, built in the fifties, if she remembered correctly. Dark, with a musty odor combined with something organic—probably the septic system. The cabin had a living and dining area, kitchen, and three bedrooms. Directly in front of her was a rustic wooden table that could seat eight. No landline phone, no Internet.

Being there felt surreal, and she had to remind herself of her mission, of the girls with scratches, and the necklace, and her plan to search the area as thoroughly as possible. All so foolish.

The bed in her parents' room was something that could be found in a lot of northern Minnesota cabins. It had a frame made of logs, and a mattress covered by a plaid quilt. She forced herself in deeper, picked up a pillow, pressed it to her nose, and inhaled. Not her mother's scent. Relieved and disappointed, she put the pillow back and continued her assessment of the cabin, pausing when she reached what had been her bedroom, with its even lower ceiling and sense of a room that might have once been a porch.

Good God. The spread was the same, pink and purple. How insane was that? It was almost as if the place had gone untouched just to mess with her. For a moment she thought about going back to the car and driving away. Away from Minnesota. Away from her father and the place where her mother had died. Away from reminders of Homicide and the man who watched her when she slept and away from men who attacked women in the street and men who chopped off young girls' heads.

She hated being a victim. Maybe that's what this was about. Taking a stand. Breaking a window. Pulling a gun on her father. Badasses weren't victims.

From somewhere beyond the cabin came the sad and haunting cry of a loon. She hadn't heard that sound in years.

She left the bedroom and unlocked the back door, stepping through the mudroom and off the porch, moving in the direction of the loon's cry. The path to the lake was overgrown; the grass brushed her knees and soaked her jeans as she made her way to the water's edge to stare at the moon the way she had years ago. She remembered standing in the same spot with her hand gripped tightly by her mother's. Sleepy, in pajamas, wanting to go to bed while at the same time knowing the moment was special.

She passed the flashlight beam around the shoreline. The dock hadn't been put in the water. Instead, it was waiting nearby, in need of repair, the boat probably long gone. Looking back, she realized their life seemed so scripted, so false.

She returned to the cabin, put her backpack on the table, unloaded the shoebox, and dug out the necklace. After removing the one she'd made at Black Bear, she compared the two.

Identical.

What did it mean, if anything?

She drank a bottle of water and ate a granola bar. Then, exhausted, she dropped across her childhood bed and fell asleep.

CHAPTER 52

For Uriah, every waking, sleep-deprived moment was about the murdered girls. Challenging his concentration were thoughts of his wife. And yes, Jude. He felt bad about the way things had played out.

He needed sleep. If he could just grab a few hours, then maybe his brain would function better, but his very desperation kept what he needed most from happening. Now, at 5:00 a.m., he gave up. Rather than think about the case, he forced his mind in another direction so when he returned to the puzzle he'd hopefully see it in a different light.

In the kitchen, he scooped coffee grounds into the coffeemaker, filled the reservoir with water, and hit the "On" button. While the coffee dripped, he moved through the dark apartment, keeping the light subdued. He put a vinyl record on the turntable, then perused the bookcase for something old, maybe a classic.

The books Jude had given him weren't organized and had been shelved in a hurry to get them out of the box and off the floor. He spotted the copy of *Through the Looking-Glass*. He suspected it was a first edition, complete with black-and-white etchings. It might be something Jude would want back.

He pulled it from the shelf and opened it carefully. On the title page was an ornate bookplate. The thick paper rectangle, with the name *Natalie* handwritten below a lithograph of a young boy reading under an apple tree, had obviously been attached by an inexperienced hand long after the release date. He'd guess within the last twenty or thirty years.

Maybe it was because he was sleep deprived, maybe it was because of what had happened with Jude and Ellen, not to mention the case that was weighing heavily on him, but he felt a wave of melancholy.

Uriah had this thing about antiques, especially when it came to books and music. Old books and old music comforted him, yet sometimes they made him overwhelmingly sad because they were reminders of the passage of time.

No kids.

No dog.

Ellen, dead.

His parents were getting old.

What did he have?

His job.

His job and this room full of melancholy things. And out there in the street, young girls were being murdered, young girls who would never get older and never discover who they were and never one day mourn the passage of time.

They should all have a chance to mourn.

He wasn't doing his job.

Yesterday he'd talked to Ortega about bringing in the FBI. Should have been done earlier, but they had to prove the Holt and Masters murders were connected.

From the kitchen, the coffeemaker let out a final burst of steam while the scent of medium roast from Peace Coffee filled the tiny apartment. That scent was comforting too. He could be standing over a dead body with a cup of coffee in his hand and one whiff would soothe him.

Such a stupid thing.

With care, he turned the pages of the book. The action stirred up another fragrance he loved: old books, old paper. He smiled a little, recalling Jude's pronouncement that it was his particular scent.

Even though he knew the odor was a toxic combination of degrading paper and mold spores, he inhaled. He'd heard of people developing lung diseases from living in close proximity to old books. A strong argument for e-books, he supposed.

He had the urge to give his father a call but had to remind himself that it was too early. His dad had never brought his work home, and Uriah found himself wondering if his father had cases he'd never solved, cases that ate away at him.

Because evil also grew in small towns.

Another turn of the page revealed an article cut from the *Star Tribune*. The paper had yellowed, and the folds, when Uriah put the book aside and opened the clipping, were impossibly flat. Hard to tell if the paper had been folded and unfolded hundreds of times, or if being pressed inside the book had created a sense of repeated viewing.

The piece was about a thirteen-year-old girl named Hope DeMars from Minneapolis, who'd gone missing twenty-seven years ago.

Uriah carried the clipping into the bright light of the kitchen to get a better look at the photo. Pretty girl with straight blond hair and a beautiful smile. She looked a little like the girl in the lake.

He opened a drawer and dug out a magnifying glass—a gift from his mother, because, in her words, "What detective doesn't need a magnifying glass?"

He focused the glass on the girl's necklace. A heart, engraved with her name.

In the living room, he opened his laptop. Taking advantage of open-source intelligence, he Googled the girl and brought up more articles, more photos. In many she was wearing the necklace. Then he pulled up articles on Jude's mother's death, which had taken place on their property in northern Minnesota. The twelve-year-old Adam

Schilling had been in the woods shooting cans when Natalie Schilling walked into his line of fire. According to the article, Jude was inside the cabin when the accident occurred. On the surface, there was nothing implausible about the story. Gun accidents happened far too often.

Uriah returned to *Through the Looking-Glass*, this time going through the pages one at a time, checking for anything he might have missed. When he reached the last page, he started to close the book and felt a shift—like something sliding.

Another search of the kitchen drawer produced a paring knife. He wouldn't have felt bad destroying a new book, but an antique? It hurt. Feeling a great deal of guilt, he revisited the title page, running fingers across the uneven bookplate. With the knife blade, he loosened the edges of the paper and lifted it free, revealing and uncovering a cheap gold necklace. He picked it up by the chain and held it close enough to read the engraving on the heart. *Hope.*

His breath caught. What did it mean? Who'd put it there?

"My mother collected books," Jude had said.

Had the necklace been hidden there by Jude's mother? Suddenly all the random threads that previously seemed to have no connection now formed a relationship. The murdered girls, a young teen named Hope, and yes, maybe even the reporter and Octavia Germaine.

The necklace changed everything.

He pulled out his cell phone and called Jude's number.

Out of service.

She probably hadn't paid her bill.

Uriah spent the next hour putting together different scenarios, the most alarming dealing with Jude's mother. If she'd had a missing girl's necklace in her possession, then her life could have been in danger. It could mean Jude had been on the right track. Maybe not about her father's involvement, which still seemed far-fetched, but about her mother's death not being an accident.

An hour past dawn, dressed in a black suit and tie, Uriah headed to the Hennepin County Sheriff's Office Crime Lab, where he requested to see the evidence from the death of Natalie Schilling.

The clerk performed a search on her computer. Without looking up, she said, "It was destroyed five years ago."

"Destroyed? At whose request?"

More key clicking. "Minneapolis Police Department and signed off by Judge McCall."

Not that unusual. Evidence wasn't kept forever, especially when that evidence hadn't involved a murder case. There was only so much space.

"Thanks."

In the fluorescent hallway, his cell phone vibrated. He checked the name—Ingrid Stevenson—and hit "Answer."

"I just faxed you the results of the hair analysis on the Masters and Holt girls. They both had GHB in their system."

GHB, a schedule 1 controlled substance, was a date-rape and sexual-assault drug. It was also a party drug, so the girls might have taken it willingly.

"It's possible she drowned because she was high on GHB."

"Thanks, Ingrid. Anything else?"

"Got a call from Jude Fontaine a few days ago."

"Really." Not something he expected to hear.

"We had an interesting conversation about flora. I'm sure she'll tell you about it when you see her."

"Jude Fontaine is no longer a detective with the Minneapolis Police Department."

"She said she was still on the decapitation case."

"Well, she isn't. She's out completely, so if you get another call from her, don't disclose anything."

"I'm sorry." He could almost feel her mortification through the phone.

"Don't beat yourself up. She can be convincing. What about flora?"

It took her a few moments to pull her thoughts together after getting the news about Fontaine. "She asked if Lola Holt had scratches on her legs. I told her yes."

Why was Jude asking about the Holt case? "Anything else?"

"We discussed the area where the body was found. It's a county known to contain dense buckthorn. The DNR recently launched a battle to eradicate it, so it's had a lot of press."

Uriah remembered the thorns that had ripped their clothes at the Holt crime scene. He thanked Stevenson and hung up. Then he headed for his car and Jude's apartment.

CHAPTER 53

U riah walked up the sidewalk in the direction of Jude's apartment, pausing when he reached the undercover car and the private detective. They'd pulled Vang off surveillance, citing lack of funding, so Uriah had hired a PI to keep an eye on Jude, at least for a while, until he was convinced she was no longer in danger or no longer a threat to the governor. He knocked on the trunk of the car, and the PI, a young guy named Tyler Ford, lowered the window.

Bending at the waist, Uriah said, "Any action?"

Tyler shook his head. "She hasn't been in or out today." He checked his watch. "It's barely past eight. That's early for her. If I see her at all, it's usually not till late morning."

Outside Jude's apartment building, Uriah didn't get a response when he pressed the "Call" button for her unit. Since she hadn't replied to any of his text messages, he was pretty sure she wouldn't want to talk to him.

He tried the building manager. The guy took his time but finally responded with a curt "Yeah" through the ancient intercom system.

Uriah introduced himself. After a moment, the door buzzed and he stepped inside. Just off the lobby was an apartment marked *Manager*. Under that was the name Will Sebastian.

Before Uriah could knock, a big guy with long hair and a lot of tattoos opened the door. Looked like Uriah had gotten him up. Puffy face, morning breath. Without a hello, he stood there, hand high on the doorframe, eyes suspicious.

"I need to see Jude Fontaine." Uriah flashed his badge.

"I know who you are, and I'm pretty sure Jude doesn't want to see you."

"That's irrelevant." Without waiting for the confrontation that was brewing, Uriah took the stairs to the fourth floor. When his repeated and loud knocks went unanswered, he checked the roof, then returned to her apartment, where the manager now stood in front of her door.

"Unlock it," Uriah said.

"Can't do that." Without taking his eyes off Uriah, Sebastian knocked hard and called Jude's name.

"She might be in trouble," Uriah said. "She might have overmedicated herself. Unlock the door."

The tattooed guy raked back the long hair that had escaped his ponytail, let out a sigh, and dug a set of keys from the front pocket of his jeans.

Together the men searched the small space.

"Not here." Sebastian seemed agitated by the discovery.

There were signs of a hasty departure. Open drawers, open closet, open cupboards. On the kitchen counter were three prescription bottles.

Uriah read the labels. "Wow." Strong stuff.

"I think she quit taking that," Sebastian said. "I suspected it, anyway."

Uriah gave him his card. "Call me if you see or hear anything, day or night." Then he jogged down the stairs and exited the building. On the street, he paused at the private detective's car and the open window. "You might as well go home."

Tyler craned his neck. "Huh?"

"Jude Fontaine is gone. Probably slipped out last night or early this morning. I won't be needing your services any longer."

"Oh, man." Understandably sheepish.

As Uriah watched the car pull away, he tried Jude's phone again and got the same inactive message. Then he put in a call to the department's private-data specialist. "I need somebody to run Jude Fontaine's credit cards." The specialist was young, and he was good, and he was fast when it came to subpoenas. "I also need phone and bank information for the past forty-eight hours."

Thirty minutes later, as Uriah pulled his unmarked car into the police-department parking ramp, he had a response to his request.

"No credit card purchases," the specialist said. "But it looks like she might have maxed out her ATM card. Two withdrawals, both within a few blocks of each other. Both shortly after midnight. No trail after that. Nothing on her phone since a couple of days ago, and that was to someone named Will Sebastian."

Uriah thanked him, then called the chief of police.

"Fontaine has gone dark," he told Ortega. "Killed her phone and maxed out her ATM card." He added something he didn't want to add. "Someone needs to contact the governor and advise him to stick close to home today. His life could be in danger." Maybe Jude just wanted to disappear and start over, but that seemed unlikely. Not when her obsession with her father had only intensified over the years.

After ending the call to Ortega, he sent a text to Vang, filling him in on the situation.

Uriah pounded on the front door of a rundown shack in Frogtown, a neighborhood that had slipped back into neglect after the light-rail began running, and was now one of the higher-crime areas of Saint Paul.

The woman who answered looked like she'd been beaten down by life. Tired hair, giving off the scent of cheap cigarettes. She hadn't been awake long either. He flashed his badge, introduced himself, and said, "I need to speak to Ava Germaine."

"I'm Ava Germaine."

Uriah could be charming and persuasive, and ten minutes later, suspicions confirmed, he was walking swiftly to his car, phone to his ear, talking to Molly, his information expert at MPD. "Find out if the governor still owns property up north."

As he slid behind the wheel of the unmarked car, he heard the click of a keyboard, followed by Molly's reply. "He's owned the same property for over thirty years. Fifty acres and a three-bedroom cabin on a lake east of Little Falls. It's less than two hours from Minneapolis and not a great area. You'd think the governor would have something on the North Shore." More key clicks. "But then again, if I lived in the governor's mansion, I'd never leave town." He was just about to stop her personal commentary, when she added, "Back when I was in high school, they used to hold parties there for his aides. Let me tell you, that place is something."

"Did you go swimming, by any chance? Was it a pool party?"

"God no! It was boring and lame and formal. Are you kidding?"

That lead quickly snuffed, he said, "Molly, I need the property address."

"Oh, right!" As she gave it to him, Uriah entered the location into his vehicle's GPS.

"Thanks." Before she could launch into another story, he disconnected, then made another call, this one to order an APB on Jude, giving the dispatcher color, make, model, and license of the car.

CHAPTER 54

Lying on her back in her old room, fully dressed, bed still made, boots on, Jude woke to the sound of scratching mice in the ceiling above her head. The clock beside her read 9:45 a.m. Could that be right?

Considering what had transpired on the property and how the event had broken the family, she was surprised to find a measure of comfort waking up in her childhood bed. So much time had passed, and she'd all but erased her own history, but there was something reassuring about knowing her younger self had actually slept here and played here. Being in the cabin shifted the boundaries of who she was and expanded her recent definition of herself.

As she stared at the ceiling above her head, trying to zero in on the location of the gnawing mice, she noticed an anomaly in the wooden slats.

A crawl space.

Until that moment, she'd completely forgotten its existence, her only memory of it being her dad reaching into the black hole, pulling down boxes when Jude was maybe five or six.

Out of bed, she grabbed the chair from one corner of the room, dragged it across the floor, and placed it below the area in question. Standing on the chair, she pressed against the ceiling, and a section popped loose to reveal the framework of a drop hatch, her action disrupting and silencing the mice.

The hatch sat freely within the frame. It had no handle; the only way to access the space above was to push it up and out of the way, which she did.

A long-lost but familiar scent drifted to her through the opening, a scent she couldn't place, one that stabbed at her chest and made her throat go tight.

Once the square of wood was heaved aside, she groped in the darkness, her fingers coming in contact with the edge of a metal box. She continued her blind search, this time touching the tattered edges of a large book. She grabbed it, pulled it free.

Standing on the chair, she stared at the object in her hands, now understanding why the smell had seemed so familiar and why it had brought with it an echo of pain. Her scrapbook. The scrapbook that had been missing from her belongings.

She flipped through pages, pausing on photos of the cabin taken by her young self, as if the images might solve what she'd considered the mystery of her mother's death. Her first case. Her first unsolved case.

Eric must have found it in her things and given it to her father. It seemed the only plausible explanation. What it was doing here was a mystery.

Allowing herself no time to speculate further, she tossed the book to the bed and went back for the metal box, dragged it toward the opening, and lifted it free.

She recognized it too. Gray, something designed for legal documents, secured with a padlock. In one corner was a yellow smiley face. She remembered the day she'd put it there, sitting at her father's desk in their Minneapolis home. He'd been working. She'd come in to see him, and he'd lifted her to his lap. She'd tried to put the sticker on his cheek, but he'd laughed and pushed the lockbox toward her.

And now here it was. The box from her past, from a childhood that had seemed perfect for a short time.

She stepped from the chair and carried the box to the dining room table. Using the poker from the woodstove, she broke the lock and opened the hinged lid.

At first glance, the contents appeared to be what someone might expect. Manila envelopes that most likely contained paperwork associated with the property. Except that on top of a stack of envelopes was a Polaroid Land Camera, along with two packs of film. Even though Land Cameras were obsolete, the film could still be found in pawnshops and on eBay.

She'd always called them serial-killer cameras. It was a cliché, but serial killers liked to document their crimes, and Polaroids were one way to avoid detection. Keeping a record of kills was part of the obsession. They needed the visual, needed the documentation.

Pictures, or it never happened.

Just like other people wanted photos of vacations.

With growing dread, she opened the first envelope. Inside was a snapshot of a teenage girl wearing a gold heart necklace.

CHAPTER 55

J ude didn't recognize the girl in the photo. She was standing against a mildewed cement wall, barefoot, wearing a light print dress—something that could have been manufactured anywhere within the past ten years. The image was bad, blurry and dark, so it was hard to tell if her body had any telltale signs of abuse.

Where had the photo been taken? It looked like a basement—something the cabin didn't have. Years ago there had been another structure on the property, but it was long gone, bulldozed, the basement filled.

Her eyes went to the girl's throat and wrists. It would take someone in Digital to reproduce the image and clean it up. Maybe then it would reveal something. But Jude didn't need to see marks or bruises or lacerations. The girl's body language said it all.

Her smile didn't reach beyond her mouth. Happiness reflected in the whole person, in the muscles and the nerves and eyes. Instead, the slope of the teen's shoulders spoke of exhaustion, the tenseness in her limbs—of terror. Her eyes were flat, devoid of readable emotion.

Her fear might not be apparent to most people. Others might see a happy, pretty girl.

Jude needed to get a forensics team up there. She shouldn't touch anything else. But who would believe her? Who would come? And wasn't it possible that she'd just happened upon a photo of a young girl? Somebody's crush? Maybe a family secret. A love child?

Unlikely.

Jude placed the photo beside the necklace on the table and opened the next envelope.

Another girl.

This one she recognized.

Octavia Germaine.

The pose was similar to the previous girl's. Dark, taken in front of the same cement-block wall. False smile on the young woman's face. Bare arms, bare legs. Another bad photo that revealed no signs of violence.

But those eyes.

And her entire body. One of her hands was open wide, clawlike, as if she were grabbing for more than air, her knuckles sharp and defined. Her other hand was partially hidden by her skirt, but not so hidden that Jude couldn't see that it was clenched into a fist. And the way she held her head was stiff, as if she couldn't relax enough to portray a natural pose.

She put the photo aside, fell back in her chair, and let out the breath she'd been holding. Still no solid proof of anything, although a photo of Octavia should be enough to get a team on site.

She continued and things got worse. She found the heartbreaking evidence she needed. There were photos of four dead girls, along with four necklaces that slid into a tangled pile on the table.

All of the photos were similar, taken in what appeared to be a heavily wooded area, which led her to think the burials had most likely taken place nearby, on her father's property. All of the bodies were wrapped in clear plastic, dropped into a trench, the plastic pulled away to reveal the girls' faces. The similarity of pose led Jude to believe that the burials were somewhat ceremonial, as if the killer were honoring them, at least in his own sick and evil mind.

None of the dead was Octavia.

Jude's pulse raced. Was she still alive?

Who'd hidden the box there? Her father? Adam? Someone else entirely? One envelope left.

It was obviously old and had been on the bottom of the stack a long time. Very flat, and the manila had turned dark. When she pulled it from the box, it had that smell of age, of old paper and dust and hidden spaces.

She tilted the envelope, and photos slid to the table, six in all. Like a fortune-teller, she lined them up in front of her.

Not what she'd expected to find.

Her vision darkened at the edges, and her head roared. She braced her arm against the table, hoping the support would stop the shaking of her hand. It didn't. Instead, the shaking moved up her arm until her entire body trembled.

The photos had been taken a long time ago, back when Jude was eight years old.

Photos of her mother lying on the ground, her eyes blank with death. Salacious photos, as if the photographer wanted to get her from every angle.

In the chaos that followed the bullet to the heart, her mother's blouse had been ripped open, maybe in an attempt to save her life or in an attempt to make it look like someone had tried to keep her alive. Her breasts were bare and covered in dark, dried blood, the gaping gunshot wound to her chest the star of the show unless you considered the blankness of her eyes.

Now she knew why the scrapbook had been hidden in the ceiling along with the lockbox. The killer was keeping all of his victims in one special place.

Jude mentally flagged Phillip Schilling as the prime suspect, especially considering the inclusion of the scrapbook, but any decent detective would say what she'd found wasn't hard evidence. It might have been in the Schilling house, but it didn't mean it belonged to her father.

Jude swiped at the photos, driving them into a pile, then turned the stack facedown. She couldn't look anymore. Once they were out of sight, she let out a loud sob and pressed a hand to her mouth. She'd sensed that the cabin held secrets. Deep, dark secrets. But nothing could have prepared her for this.

CHAPTER 56

J ude gathered up everything. Not quickly, although she felt a sense
of urgency. She was careful to replace the photos in the correct
envelopes, careful to touch only what had to be touched. When
all the items were returned to the box, she closed the lid and placed
the horrific memorabilia in her backpack, along with the shoebox and
the Octavia necklaces. Evidence should remain at the scene, but she
couldn't risk leaving it behind.

Trying to ignore her shaking legs, she left the cabin through the
front door and headed for the car. She'd destroyed her phone, so she'd
have to drive somewhere to call the sheriff's department, who in turn
would have to call the BCA. Not Minneapolis Police Department jurisdiction, but she'd let Ortega know too. Hopefully the chief would pass
the information to Uriah.

A minute later she took the turn in the lane and saw her borrowed
car where she'd left it. She slowed her approach, stomach sinking, until
she was close enough to confirm that all four tires had been slashed.

On a hunch, recalling Jude's comment the day they'd driven north
to the Holt crime scene, Uriah exited Highway 10 and pulled into
the parking area of Black Bear Station. Inside, he flashed his badge,

introduced himself, and produced an iPhone photo of Jude taken at the Minneapolis Police Department on her first day back. "Has this woman been in your store in the past several hours?"

The white middle-aged clerk looked at the photo and shook her head. "Maybe earlier. My shift starts at seven."

The bell above the door rang, and a heavyset guy with straight dark hair entered. "Hey, you got my check?" he asked the woman behind the counter. "I gotta make a car payment."

The clerk opened the cash register. "You should ask Teddy," she told Uriah, nodding toward the new guy on the scene. "He was working when I clocked in."

Uriah showed Teddy the photo of Jude.

"Yeah, she was here. Around three. Something like that. I thought it was weird because she went to the back of the store and bought a necklace from the engraving machine. Usually only kids or high school girls do that."

The woman behind the counter handed him his check. He eye-balled it, folded it, and stuck it in his wallet. "She had the necklace on when she came up to the counter. I told her I liked the name Octavia."

"Octavia?" Uriah asked. "You sure it was this woman?" He held up his phone again so the guy could get another look.

"Positive. That white hair is hard to miss. Plus, she was kinda cool and tough. I wondered if she was maybe in a band."

Uriah thanked him, then hurried to his car, restarting the GPS directions as he sped out of the parking area.

CHAPTER 57

Hands gripping the straps of the backpack that dug into her shoulders, Jude dove into the woods, ducking under tree limbs and jumping over rocks and small downed trees in her race to reach the highway and put distance between herself and whoever had sliced her tires. At one point she paused to listen for sounds of pursuit. When she turned to resume her flight, she heard a distant rustling of leaves—followed by a series of pops.

In the city, when people reported shots fired, they often said they mistook them for firecrackers. This was like that, but louder. Three rapid rounds.

It's weird how the brain reacts to such things. Even when she felt the white-hot pain rip through her biceps, even when she felt the warm blood running down her arm, she found herself thinking it was ridiculous for someone to waste fireworks on such a sunny, cloudless day. Faced with the obvious, the brain still rejected aberrant behavior. A fraction of a second later, reality sank in. Someone was trying to kill her.

She ran, cutting through saplings, looking for terrain that would afford the most cover. From behind came the sound of snapping branches. She skidded down a slope, hit the bottom of a shallow ravine, her boots pounding the ground, buckthorn tearing her pants and scratching her arms and legs like it had scratched the girls. She stumbled, faltered. Pausing for a second, just a second, she pressed her back against a tree and squeezed her eyes shut against the pain.

Maybe it was her heavy breathing, maybe it was the roaring in her head, but something drowned out the sound of approach. She never heard him coming. Suddenly someone spoke her name. She recognized the voice even though it was one she hadn't heard much in the past several years. But he'd always had a distinctive way of saying Jude—with a teasing tone of disdain.

She opened her eyes, blinked, struggled to focus. Her brother stood in front of her, a gun in his hand.

"How did you know I was here?" She'd been so careful.

"Your boss, or I guess I should say ex-boss, warned us, said you could be heading to the governor's mansion," he told her. "But when I heard you'd been flagged as a person of interest, I called my contact in the police department and he said you'd been asking about the area where Lola Holt's body was found. From that it was easy to figure out you were probably coming here."

Blood dripped from her fingers and splashed on her boot. Her vision was edged with undulating darkness. *Adam. How could that be?* "You murdered those girls." Why hadn't he been on her radar? *Because I've been too obsessed with my father, that's why.* Had Adam murdered Lola Holt too? Delilah Masters? What about Octavia?

"I made too many mistakes," he said.

At first Jude thought he regretted his crimes, but no . . .

"I should have taken permanent measures with you from day one."

Permanent measures. "Are you saying you were behind my kidnapping?" Her opinion of him had been low, but she'd never have thought him capable of being responsible for her years of torture.

"I knew Ian Caldwell had something on me." As if expecting her to understand, he told her the reporter had bragged about how he planned to supply Jude with evidence. That's when Adam had decided it was time to be proactive. "I was going to kill you along with Caldwell, but Vang came up with the kidnapping idea."

"Vang?"

"My contact. Without him, I couldn't have been certain you were no threat after you escaped. Vang assured me you didn't remember anything about Caldwell."

Before she could begin to process the deceit of Grant Vang, Adam spilled the rest, from his part in the decapitation he'd hoped would warn Jude and the girls away, to admitting to being one of the four who'd attacked her in the alley. He seemed proud of everything except the bungled dump of Lola Holt's body.

Jude's mind struggled, searching for a plan. If she collapsed and played possum, maybe she could turn this around and get his weapon. Before she grew weaker, she pushed herself away from the tree and took a step closer. He didn't seem to notice. "What about my mother?" She had to know what happened that day in the woods. "Why did you kill her?"

"It was an accident!" His face twisted in almost comical torment.

"I don't believe that. I saw the photos." Her voice dropped, taking on a pleading tone. He was going to kill her. He might as well tell her the truth. "I need to know."

"You wouldn't understand!"

"No, probably not." Then, "How did you get the scrapbook?"

"Eric. He thought the family would want it."

"Did Father know the truth about our mother's death? Did he know about the girls?"

A sound came from the nearby woods, and they both turned their heads to see Uriah Ashby step from the landscape of trees and under-brush, a man out of context, incongruously dressed in a suit and tie, his weapon drawn. Apparently the whole world knew her whereabouts, and the gunshots must have fine-tuned Uriah's search.

Jude forced her focus back to the immediate situation. She'd trained for just such a scenario, and Uriah likely had too. He might have even stepped into this encounter with that training in mind. A second cop enters a highly charged scene and diverts the assailant's attention long enough for the first cop to act. Practice was supposed to make what happened next almost muscle memory, but in her present condition Jude lacked confidence in her ability to follow through with the dance.

Adam reacted in the most ideal and expected way possible. He turned his body toward Uriah, the handgun following his shift in stance and vision.

With no time to think, only to deploy the maneuver, Jude dredged up the strength to kick and shove hard and high, her boot connecting with Adam's thigh. He went down, his semiautomatic, pointed in Uriah's general direction, firing in rapid succession, the blast echoing through the woods, the smell of gunpowder floating on the air as shell casings bounced on the ground.

In the chaos of noise, it was hard to tell if Uriah had fired at all. That was until Adam dropped straight to his knees, where he remained a stretched second before pitching face forward into the leaves.

Uninjured, Uriah lunged, kicking the weapon from Adam's limp hand. The gun slid across the dirt as Jude collapsed, watching the two men through a haze of pain.

"Is he dead?" she gasped. *Octavia. I didn't ask him about Octavia.*

Uriah rolled Adam to his back, exposing a puddle of blood and stained soil. He checked for a pulse, then ripped open Adam's shirt to reveal a chest wound.

How odd, Jude thought. That he would die out here in the same woods as their mother, and from the same kind of gunshot wound. The ultimate karma.

Uriah let out a breath. "Yeah." She could see that he was already doubting his reaction, wondering if he'd fired too quickly.

"You had no choice," she said. "You or him."

"I know." But still, he doubted.

She crawled to where the backpack had fallen during the alter-cation. She grabbed it, hugged it to her chest with one arm. Things got blurry, and she crashed to her back. "The sky is so blue. Doesn't Minnesota have the bluest sky?"

Uriah left the dead body to crouch beside her. With one finger, he began loosening the knot in his tie.

"I can't believe you got dressed up for this," she said.

He let out a grim laugh. "What's in the pack?"

"Evidence that will blow your mind."

"You can loosen your grip on it. I don't think it's going anywhere."

She let the backpack slide from her hand. "Octavia might still be alive."

If only they knew where the dead girls had been held and the pho-tos taken. The cement wall made Jude suspect the holding and killing room was elsewhere entirely, with the property maybe used for burial, but a sweep of the grounds had to be made. "You need to get a search team out here. Immediately." The full implications of what had just happened continued to sink in. If they didn't find Octavia, if she wasn't anywhere nearby, that meant the only person who might know of her whereabouts was dead.

Knot undone, Uriah pulled the tie free of his collar. "Let's see your arm."

"I don't think I want to look."

He pushed the sleeve of her T-shirt over her shoulder. Rather than looking at her arm, she watched his face. He winced a little, and his brow furrowed in concentration, but he didn't make his expression go blank. That would have told her it was bad.

"This is gonna hurt. The bullet's still in there." He wrapped his tie around her arm, knotting it off while she sucked in a series of shallow breaths.

When he was finished, she let her head fall to the ground while she waited for the searing-hot pain to subside. It didn't. She'd always wondered what a gunshot felt like. Now she knew. Like having a red-hot poker twisted inside you.

Uriah called in the situation and location, relating the immediate need for a search team, then pocketed his phone. "Let's get you to a doctor."

She turned her head to the side. There was Adam staring at the same blue sky she'd just admired. "What about him?"

"He's not going anywhere. Think you can walk? I suppose I could carry you, but I don't really want to."

That was funny.

"Did you just laugh?"

Had she?

He held out his hand, and she grabbed it with her good one. With his other hand at her back, he carefully coaxed her to her feet. Upright, she stood there a few ticks while waiting for the ground to quit moving.

"Okay?" he asked.

She nodded.

Keeping one arm around her, they started to leave the area.

"Wait. The evidence."

Uriah swept up the backpack by one strap and slung it over his shoulder.

"How did you know to come here?" Jude asked, her words slightly slurred.

"Ava Germaine."

"I really thought she could keep a secret."

"I can be pretty persuasive."

They made it to his car. Jude might have mumbled something about getting blood on the seats, and he might have told her it didn't matter, that he'd send her the cleaning bill.

And even though his words were teasing, once they were in the car and moving down the road, his driving reflected the urgency of the situation. And when she nodded off, he talked to her, sometimes calmly, sometimes with obvious panic. "We'll be there soon," he said more than once. And she wondered where "there" was but was too ambivalent to ask. Not Minneapolis, she decided. That would take too long.

She blinked, trying to keep her eyes open, focusing on his blood-caked hands gripping the steering wheel.

She wanted to talk about the dead girls, the missing girls, Octavia, the necklaces and the photos and her mother and her theories, but she was too tired.

And then the car squealed to a stop and her door flew open and a gurney and nurses appeared with their peach-colored scrubs and black stethoscopes. The blue sky turned into a ceiling with bright fluorescent lights and green walls.

She knew she shouldn't care about such things, not now, but she felt a seed of satisfaction growing deep inside. She wasn't crazy.

CHAPTER 58

You have tissue and muscle damage, but you should heal with time and rest," the young doctor told Jude. "I doubt that arm will ever be a hundred percent again, but hey, you're alive, right?" He beamed at her.

It was the morning after Uriah had driven her to the ER. Turned out he'd taken her to Little Falls. It had a good hospital, it seemed, with good doctors. Really young doctors.

"I read about you," the young doctor told her. If she wasn't mistaken, he seemed a bit enamored. She supposed they didn't see many women this far into the frozen tundra. Oh, she'd made a joke. Interesting. Because of course Little Falls had women. Beautiful women, like the one standing near the door, tablet in hand, ready to sign Jude out.

She'd been told a cop was waiting to drive her back to Minneapolis. And just minutes ago, she'd watched a live feed captured in front of the governor's cabin, where Phillip Schilling had promised to do everything he could to help law enforcement with their investigation.

"I'm a father first and foremost, and I'd be lying if I said I wasn't deeply saddened by the loss of my son despite his unconscionable actions and his obvious involvement in the deaths of innocents," he'd said. "But I'm relieved that our streets are once again safe."

Jude figured public sympathy might win him the Senate. News anchors were already noting how well he'd handled all that had happened, including the drama with his daughter. And there was much talk of his children being bad seeds. Both she and Adam. Uriah was getting credited with cracking the case, and her father had mentioned how Jude's partner, or ex-partner, had been an impressive player in not one, but two personal events. "And he saved the life of my daughter, whom I still love," the governor had said.

Should she feel bad? About suspecting him for so long?

Yes.

And maybe she would, once this was over, but right now she had plans to return to the family property, where the investigation was taking place. Last she'd heard, when Uriah called to check on her, a grid search was being established and volunteers were on their way to begin combing the area.

"There's been a change of plans," Jude said once the doctor had left and the nurse had signed her out. "I'm going to the crime site."

The friendly female officer rested her hands on her belt as she contemplated Jude's announcement. From the crisp flatness of the woman's shirt, it was obvious she wore a bulletproof vest. Some officers did on a daily basis, some didn't. Could be she thought it might be dangerous spending a couple of hours with Jude. Could be she wanted to make it home to her kids, if she had any.

"If you don't take me, I'm going to hitchhike there," Jude told her. "Which I can tell you won't be much fun since I'm recovering from a bullet wound." She glanced down at the gray-blue sling. She was probably lying about the hitchhiking, but if her follow-up plan—renting a car—fell through, she'd resort to it.

The officer knew when to give up.

After reporting the change in plans, she drove Jude to the site, letting her out where the governor's property began—an area cordoned off with yellow crime-scene tape.

Jude got out of the car, thanked the woman behind the wheel, and walked toward the uniformed officers at the roadblock. Jude introduced herself even though their expressions told her they knew who she was, but that wasn't enough to get a hall pass.

"Nobody allowed in," one of them said.

"Call Detective Ashby," Jude told him. "He'll okay it."

Once the call was made, it didn't take Uriah long to get there. He pulled to a dusty stop, cut the engine, and dove from his car to stride toward her, arms swinging, looking like an angry parent. His hair was curlier and wilder than usual, the way curly hair got when exposed to the elements for too long. He needed to shave, and he was still wearing a white shirt with her blood on it.

"You're supposed to be on your way to Minneapolis. And"—he leaned close so the officers wouldn't hear—"you don't work for the department."

"What about you? This isn't your jurisdiction."

"The head of state police field operations requested my help. And somebody had to lead them to Adam Schilling's body."

"Even though it's been years since I spent time here, I probably know this land better than anybody walking the grid." Her voice dropped. "I might be able to help."

He looked at her sling. "How's the arm?"

"It hurts. A lot. But the pain meds from last night have worn off. My head is clear."

A black Cadillac appeared, coming from the direction of the cabin, heading toward the highway.

"My father," Jude noted as the man of the hour stopped at the checkpoint, lowered his window, and said something to the guard, who smiled and moved the wooden roadblock out of the way to allow the car to pass.

The governor gave the detectives a grim nod but thankfully didn't stop.

"I'm impressed," Uriah said, watching the taillights and trail of dust. "He drives his own car." His focus shifted, and he reached into a pocket to pull out his phone. He hit the screen and barked, "Hello." As he listened to the caller, his face changed to something Jude, for once, couldn't identify. Like a combination of disbelief and fear.

"Octavia?" she asked hopefully when Uriah tucked his phone back in his pocket.

He glanced in the direction of the officers. To Jude, he said, "Let's get out of here."

Side by side, they walked to his car. Uriah helped her in and slammed the door. Taking a seat behind the wheel, he cranked the engine, made a three-point turn, and headed back down the dirt road in the direction of the Schilling property.

"What is it?" Jude asked.

"They think they might have found something. A root cellar about a half mile from the cabin."

She straightened in her seat. "Has anybody gone inside?"

"No, they were told to stand down. They're discussing how to handle it." He glanced at her, saw her intensity. "It could be nothing. It could be more of his memorabilia. It could be a killing room. We don't know."

Or it could be the place where he'd photographed the girls and maybe kept them.

CHAPTER 59

They left the car on the dirt road that led to the cabin and followed Major Mark Shultz, head of field operations, through a dense area of birch and pine. A few minutes in, the tangle of overgrown woods opened to reveal a previously hidden clearing of knee-deep grass.

"I remember those apple trees," Jude said. "There was a house back here at one time. Not anything livable. Rotten, the roof collapsed. My mother had it bulldozed. She was afraid somebody would get hurt."

Along one side of the clearing were several officers huddled in a circle.

"We found what looks like a cellar or bunker." Shultz pointed. "Just beyond that rise. Behind it, there's a faint grass lane that shows signs of vehicular traffic."

"Recent?" Uriah asked.

"Yes, but unfortunately some overzealous searchers drove over it before the area was contained."

They followed the major to a mound of earth that often indicated a root cellar commonly used years ago to store fruits and vegetables underground. At the bottom of a short set of stone steps cut deep into the soil, an officer worked at a door with a pair of bolt cutters.

With Uriah and Jude watching, the bolt cutters did their job and were tossed aside, the padlock removed. Officers drew weapons while the man who'd cut the lock pushed open the door. He immediately recoiled, hand to his face, stumbling backward.

From where they stood, Jude caught a whiff—and remembered that smell. Of a body that had gone unwashed for too long. Of feces and urine and rotten food.

Uriah behind her, she pushed past the cluster of men and women who stood horrified at the entrance. The officer who'd failed to enter put out an arm, blocking the way.

"It's okay," Major Shultz said from above the earthen stairwell.

The arm dropped.

Without taking her eyes from the dark hole, Jude said, "I need light."

Someone passed her a flashlight.

With one hand, she thumbed it on and shot the beam around the small space, quickly assessing the situation. "Nobody here." She ducked inside, noting the cement-block walls, dirt floor, low wooden ceiling. And more. The mattress on the floor, the lantern, the open bucket used for a toilet. Junk-food wrappers that rustled under her feet.

She focused the beam along one wall. It was floor-to-ceiling books, all the same size, stacked spines out.

Beside her, Uriah snapped on black evidence gloves, handed her another pair. He slipped the flashlight from her, and while she gloved up—awkward due to her arm—he carefully removed a book from the top of a stack. He opened it and said in surprise, "A journal."

Jude looked around the room. "I think they're all journals."

"Here's a signature." Uriah grew very still. "Octavia."

She spotted another book on the bed. With a gloved hand, she picked it up and opened it to the last entry.

Uriah directed the beam at the page, and they both read Octavia's words: *Yesterday I heard something that sounded like fireworks. I wonder if it was Fourth of July.*

"She heard the gunshots yesterday." Jude looked up at Uriah. "Which means she was still alive today."

CHAPTER 60

Uriah went silent, probably trying to make sense of it all.

"Adam didn't relocate her," Jude said, slowly putting the pieces together. "Octavia was here when Adam was shot."

He looked up from the journal he held in his hand, puzzlement on his face.

"When we met my father driving down the lane, he might not have been alone." Maybe he knew Adam had been kidnapping and killing young women all along. "That might be why he chose to make his statement at the cabin." She was speaking rapidly now. "It wasn't about the best location for the press conference; it was about covering his own ass."

Uriah finally caught up. "Son of a bitch. He needed to get back here."

"Right. He wanted to get her out before we found her."

Uriah was already moving, pounding up the steps. Outside, he passed the journal to one of the crime-scene team as he filled in Major Shultz.

"You're talking about the governor." Shultz cast a doubtful and suspicious eye at Jude.

There it was: that look she was so familiar with. He knew her history, probably knew she'd recently been kicked out of Homicide. That kind of thing didn't instill confidence.

"If you're wrong, I'll be fired," he said. "I've got a wife and kids to think about."

"You can risk your job or someone's life," Jude told him. "Seems an easy choice to me."

The crime-scene specialist broke into their conversation. "You need to see this." She held up the journal Uriah had given her, the book flat and open wide, her gloved finger pointing to a specific area of text.

Everyone leaned forward to read in silence.

OMG, he's old! He's so old! Older than my dad. And I don't even care! How sick is that? It doesn't even matter to me that my kidnapper, the guy who's been fucking me for so long, is the governor of Minnesota. How can that not be cool? I think I love him even more now.

Not Adam. Her father.

Jude thought back to her conversation with her brother yesterday. He'd bragged about the death of Lola Holt and Ian Caldwell, but he hadn't confessed to the other murders. It seemed she'd been right about her father all along. She wished she'd been wrong.

Learning of his guilt was an indescribable feeling. Everything she'd sensed for so long had finally been substantiated. For a few hours after Adam had confessed, she'd felt disappointment in herself and the years she'd wasted thinking her father was a bad man. That had been immediately followed by the realization that she could put the past aside and maybe they could have a relationship. She'd even imagined having dinner with him, talking, sharing stories, offering and receiving support. Like a real family.

Shultz barked orders into his shoulder mic. "We're going to need an APB issued," he said. "The APB? It's on the governor of Minnesota." A pause. "That's right. The governor."

More calls were made, and a message went out to patrol units across the state.

"Keep us updated," Uriah said as he and Jude ran for the car.

"You need a weapon." Uriah popped the trunk and opened a flat black case. Jude spotted a Glock 17 similar to her confiscated piece, pulled it out, grabbed a box of ammunition. Uriah slammed the trunk, and they dove into the unmarked vehicle. Inside, they buckled seat belts while the just-launched APB scrolled across the mobile-data computer screen.

"We'll never catch up," Jude said. "He's got a fifteen-minute lead on us."

The car bounced down the lane, hit the narrow paved road that ran parallel to the highway, while Jude kept her eye on the computer, watching for new developments.

Within minutes of the APB, a report came through. The black Cadillac had been spotted heading south on 10, toward Minneapolis.

They merged onto Highway 10 South. Jude flipped on the lights, no siren, and Uriah stepped on the gas. The vehicle shot to ninety.

"State police are in silent pursuit," she said, eyes on the screen. "Chopper in the air, dispatched from Saint Cloud."

Keeping his eyes on the road, Uriah pulled his phone from his pocket and handed it to Jude. "Call the major. Tell them to tail Schilling, but no hot pursuit. No lights, no sirens."

Jude made the call and passed on Uriah's instructions. "We can't jeopardize Octavia," she added. "She could be in the car, so hang back. Don't spook him. And, Major? I'd like to be there for the takedown. He might talk to me."

"We'll give you a chance to close in, but if he spots us, if he increases speed, that's it. We'll initiate the PIT maneuver. In the meantime, traffic is heavy with people heading back to the city after the weekend. We're putting patrol officers ahead of the governor to see if we can slow the flow."

They disconnected.

Thirty minutes later, the major called to say they were going to engage sirens. "Chopper has a visual lock, and we're preparing to close the highway." He gave her the marker number where the rendezvous and capture would take place.

Jude passed the information to Uriah, who hadn't let up since pulling onto 10. Five minutes later, they heard the faint sound of sirens. Traffic speed rapidly decreased.

The road was a two-lane with a wide gravel shoulder. A few drivers spotted them in rearview mirrors and moved aside, dust flying. Far ahead, lights flashed. Above them, helicopter blades whipped the air. Jude turned on their siren, and more vehicles responded, breaking wider, moving left and right out of their way.

Another five minutes and everything came to a halt, civilian and police cars alike. Nowhere left to go, Uriah and Jude bailed and ran for the lights.

Surrounded by police cars, a helicopter hovering overhead, was a black Cadillac. The driver's door flew open, and the governor stepped from the vehicle, no sign of Octavia.

Had he dumped her? Was she in the trunk? Was she dead?

Jude pulled her weapon and slipped her arm from the sling, ignored the pain, braced her gun hand, and strode straight for him, aiming at his chest, prepared to fire.

"Jude," Uriah warned, urging her to hold, following her when he should have been behind the protection of a vehicle.

"Get back," she told him.

"Don't shoot," Uriah said. "He might be the only one who knows where the girl is."

She heard his footfalls beside her, knew he had his weapon drawn too. She didn't take her eyes off the governor. "Hands up!" she shouted.

The governor ignored her command and circled to the back of his vehicle, opened the lid, and dragged a young woman from the trunk while pressing a gun to her temple.

They should have rushed him.

"It's her," Jude said. "Octavia."

She was naked except for a filthy white T-shirt, gag in her mouth, arms tied behind her back. No panties, no bra, no shoes. She wasn't emaciated, but her legs and arms were thin, her stomach round, like somebody who was malnourished. Her long hair was matted, and even from a distance Jude could smell the unwashed odor of her.

The governor pulled the girl to his chest, an arm under her throat. She squinted against the glare of the sun. "Call everybody off, or I'll kill her. Right here, right now."

"Stand down! Stand down!" someone shouted. Officers moved back. All but Jude. Schilling had nothing to lose one way or the other, and if they let him leave with the girl, Octavia would most likely be dead within an hour.

Jude felt blood from the bullet wound trickle to her armpit and slide down her stomach to the waistband of her jeans, but she didn't feel any pain. She made eye contact with Octavia. She could read those eyes. She'd lived in that mind-set. No fear. The fear was long gone.

Jude gave her head a miniscule nod to the right.

Octavia understood. She *understood*. They were reading each other.

The girl ducked; Jude pulled the trigger, catching Phillip Schilling between the eyes. He dropped like a stone, his gun clattering to the blacktop.

Jude didn't allow herself time to think about what she'd just done— a daughter killing her own father. She filed it away for later. Later she would mourn, not her father and her brother, but what had never been.

She tucked her weapon into her belt and walked toward the man on the ground and the young woman standing over him. An officer approached with a blanket. Jude held out her hand and he passed the cover to her.

Octavia seemed oblivious to her surroundings. Instead, she stood staring at the dead man at her feet. Jude spoke her name in a quiet voice. She removed the girl's gag and untied her wrists. Eyes tracked away from the body to latch on to Jude.

"Are you cold?" Jude asked, holding the blanket out and open.

The young woman seemed to put the question to herself, wondered if she was or wasn't. Jude gently placed the blanket around Octavia's shoulders, then pulled Uriah's phone from her pocket.

"You're bleeding," Octavia said dully.

Jude looked at the drops of blood hitting her boot. She felt light-headed, and she didn't know how much longer she'd be able to remain upright. She poked at the keypad of the phone. After a quick Internet search, she found the number she was looking for, entered it, and lifted the phone to her ear. When a voice answered, she said, "I have someone I think you'll want to talk to."

She passed the phone to Octavia. "It's your mother."

The blankness melted from the girl's face as she awkwardly lifted the device to her ear. "Mom?" She spoke with trembling hesitation.

How slow and fast life moved. Octavia had spent over three years in captivity. Today she'd written in her journal like always, expecting nothing, certainly not knowing that on this particular day everything would change.

Jude watched a helicopter from Hennepin County Medical Center land in the grassy median, and she felt a hand on her back. She looked up to see Uriah's mouth moving as he pointed toward the aircraft. A medic stood in the open door, motioning them to come. It took Jude a moment to realize the medic wanted both of them, Octavia and herself.

Two injured people.

Uriah guided her toward the craft while an officer took the phone from Octavia and spoke into it, most likely giving Ava information about where they were going.

They were both helped into the copter, both strapped onto a gurney while medics bent over them. At one point, Jude looked out the window to see the ground falling away. Uriah was down there, watching them lift off, his clothes molding to him and his hair whipping around his head.

While one of the medics inserted an IV needle in the back of her hand, Jude looked across the aisle to reassure herself that Octavia was okay. Then she let out a sigh and closed her eyes.

CHAPTER 61

I'm telling you, this'll work," Uriah said.

Jude shot him a skeptical look. "I don't think so."

"Have some faith."

They were on the roof of her apartment building, eyes on the cat watching them from the nearby tree. Jude sat with her back against the air-conditioning unit while Uriah lay on his stomach, holding one end of a long string. The other end was attached to a stick propping up a laundry basket. Under the laundry basket was an open can of cat food.

Will Sebastian was no longer the building manager. He'd admitted to entering Jude's apartment while she slept. The new manager was unassuming and hopefully harmless. Grant Vang confessed to covering up the trail to Jude's abduction, along with orchestrating that abduction and planting false evidence so investigators would conclude that her kidnapping was obsession driven and close the case. Vang's motive? Money, and possibly hope of a promotion to chief of police one day. But Jude suspected he'd also never forgiven her for rejecting his more serious advances. She even wondered if he'd chosen Salazar for his reputation of extreme cruelty. She hoped not.

"You saw this in a cartoon, right?" Jude asked.

"And I've done it. You have no idea how many cats I've caught this way."

"I still think the Havahart trap is the way to go. I can borrow one from the Humane Society."

"And miss out on all this fun?"

"It's hot up here. The tar paper is gummy."

"This is an adventure."

"When that falls on him, *if* it falls on him, he's going to freak out, push the laundry basket off, and run. And I'll never see him again."

"He won't push it off, because you'll jump on top of it and hold it down. It's all in being prepared. Being hypervigilant."

"If we do catch him, I'm going to feel bad."

"You said you feel bad because he's getting skinny."

"That too."

"We're doing the right thing. He's not old. He's probably got a bad tooth or maybe an abscess from a street fight. We'll get him checked out."

"And then?"

"The apartment building allows cats, right?"

"I'm not ready for anything like that."

Propped up on his elbows, wrist bent as he kept the line slack, Uriah looked over at her. "It'll be good for you."

A week had passed since they'd rescued Octavia Germaine. The young woman had given a statement from her hospital bed, revealing that she'd attended parties at the governor's mansion with other underage girls, the drug-laden events likely serving as a way of vetting potential victims for Phillip Schilling.

At the parties, attendees were coerced into signing official-looking confidentiality statements promising to never disclose what happened in the mansion. Most had felt honored to be a part of it. A secret club. It was so exciting and adult. But once the Schillings were exposed, girls came forward and the mystery of Delilah Masters was solved. On the night of her death, Delilah had panicked. Naked and screaming, she'd tried to run from the mansion. Adam Schilling had caught her and dragged her into the pool, holding her underwater, forever silencing her. Poor Lola Holt had been one of the witnesses. And Adam must have figured that because rocks in the pockets had worked once with Katherine Nelson, it would work again.

During a sweep of the governor's cabin property, the four bodies from the Polaroids were discovered, all in shallow graves, one of the girls the daughter of a member of Ava's missing children's group, another the body of thirteen-year-old Hope DeMars, who'd gone missing shortly before Natalie Schilling's death. Two of the bodies were still Jane Does. Not far from the root cellar, a human fetus had been unearthed. What horrors poor Octavia had endured.

Along with the search of the cabin and surrounding land, an investigation of the governor's office had been launched. Unfortunately, since Jude's father and brother were dead, she'd never know exactly what happened the day her mother died. How the necklace got inside the book was anybody's guess, but it seemed likely Natalie Schilling hid it there, maybe fearing for her own life after discovering Phillip Schilling's aberrant behavior. The theory was that he killed Jude's mother and convinced the underage Adam to confess to what they reported as an accident. Maybe Adam had even believed her death hadn't been intentional, at least at first. Whatever the story, the son had been killing for his father and covering up his deviant obsessions ever since. That day in the woods when he took the blame for his mother's death had set his dark life in motion.

"I've been contacted by someone in Hollywood," Jude told Uriah. "They want to make a movie about me."

"You gonna do it?"

Keeping her eyes trained on the cat, she shook her head slightly. "No. I don't want to relive it for the screenplay and relive it when the movie comes out."

"If you'd agreed, who would have played you?"

She laughed softly. "No idea."

"More importantly, who would have played me? It'd have to be somebody pretty damn good looking."

They did this now. Joked around. Her sense of humor seemed to be returning, nursed, maybe, by Uriah.

"I don't get why the governor didn't just kill Octavia in the cell. If he'd killed her and taken the last journal, we would have always thought it was Adam."

"I think he cared about her more than the other girls," Jude said. "Look how long he kept her." Octavia had done the best thing possible by making him the hero of her own story. He read the journals, and he fell in love with her in return. And now the poor girl missed him. Jude had seen it in her eyes.

A thud sounded as the cat dropped from the tree to the roof. "Here he comes," Jude whispered.

He was skinny, and one side of his face was swollen, his pale-yellow coat matted and dull. He slinked across the roof, belly low, stopped, froze; then, little by little, he moved again, inching closer to the trap. Hunger made wild animals bold.

This was not going to work.

This was not going to—

Uriah jerked the string, and the basket fell over the cat.

Arm immobilized by the sling, Jude bolted for the basket and placed her foot on the overturned plastic bottom, holding it firmly so the animal couldn't escape.

Uriah produced a soft-sided pet carrier, borrowed from the elderly woman who'd moved in downstairs, and donned leather gloves. He gave Jude a nod, and she lifted the basket while he grabbed the cat by the back of the neck. Legs thrashed and twisted; fur flew; the cat yowled. Uriah shoved him into the container, and Jude zipped the door.

Straightening, Uriah tossed off the gloves like a hockey player ready to fight, and brushed cat hair from his T-shirt with the backs of his hands. "You might have your work cut out for you."

"Maybe he's been feral too long."

Uriah eyed the carrier, which was rolling around on the roof. "It'll take a while, but I think he'll be okay."

He was talking as if she planned to stick around.

Most of her self-doubt was gone, especially since discovering she'd been right about her father all along. From now on, instead of ignoring her gut, she'd listen to it. She wanted to write her gut an apology letter. She was a decent detective. She knew that now.

Uriah crossed the roof and lifted the carrier to peer inside. Without turning around, he asked her the big question. "What do you think? Are you coming back?"

He meant back to Homicide. Her old position was available, the firing and arrest of Grant Vang leaving a second opening. Ortega was conducting interviews, but it might take some time to get the new hires on board.

Deep down, Jude knew it would be best to pack up and move somewhere else, get a fresh start in a place where every street corner didn't hold a dark memory. But she kept catching herself thinking about the future *here*. Yes, people stared at her and talked about her, but that wasn't always a bad thing. It meant they knew her history. It meant she didn't have to explain or hide. She'd had some bad times in Minneapolis.

Bad. That was putting it mildly. But Jude was beginning to feel like she'd made some trustworthy friends. Ava, Chief Ortega, Uriah. And Ava was hoping Jude would visit with Octavia a few times a month. They'd had similar experiences, and it would be good to share, if not stories of what had happened, time together. Just hang out.

Jude looked at Uriah. He was holding the carrier high by the handle, peering in, sweet-talking the cat, and the cat was responding. It meowed, and the meow had a lilt at the end.

Uriah looked ready to say something. Couldn't decide if he should, finally put down the carrier. "You aren't going to do anything bad, are you?" *Like hurt yourself? End your life?* He was so easy to read, and she suddenly understood his reason for wanting her to keep the cat.

She couldn't answer his question. Now that it was over, now that Humphrey Salazar and her brother and father were dead, her mother's murder solved, Octavia found, Jude's distraction and drive for justice and truth were gone. What did she have to live for? What did she have to obliterate the horror of her own memories?

"There are three things I've seen once in my life," Uriah said, squinting against the sunlight. "Thick fog that stopped at my knees and swirled in circles when I kicked it, a rainbow that ended in a street right in front of me, and a rabbit dance. You ever heard of a rabbit dance?"

"No."

"It happens in the middle of the night. Hundreds of rabbits rendezvous in a clearing, and they kind of dance in the moonlight. I can't describe it, but it's bizarre in a good way. With all of those events, I didn't realize I was seeing something amazing for the first and last time. And I'm saying that those things, those random, crazy surprises that have nothing to do with life decisions or your past or your future, might be worth sticking around for."

Car doors slammed, and the voices of new residents carried from the street below. Jude had probably made a subconscious decision days ago. "I'm coming back to Homicide." She would return, and instead of trying to ignore her body-reading skills, she'd work on enhancing them.

"And the cat?" Translation: *Do I need to worry about you?*

"We'll have to get litter and a litter box if he's going to be living with me."

Uriah smiled and picked a yellow hair off his tongue.

ABOUT THE AUTHOR

Anne Frasier is a *New York Times* and *USA Today* bestselling author. Her award-winning books span the genres of suspense, mystery, thriller, romantic suspense, paranormal, and memoir. She won a RITA for romantic suspense and the Daphne du Maurier Award for paranormal romance. Her thrillers have hit the *USA Today* list and have been featured by Mystery Guild, Literary Guild, and Book of the Month Club. Her memoir, *The Orchard*, was an *O, The Oprah Magazine* Fall Pick; a One Book, One Community read; a recipient of a B+ review in *Entertainment Weekly*; and a Librarians' Best Books of 2011 selection. She divides her time between the city of Saint Paul, Minnesota, and her writing studio in rural Wisconsin. Visit her website to sign up for book-release announcements at www.annefrasier.com.